THE RISE OF THE RESISTANCE: PHOENIX ONE

What Reviewers Say About Jackie D's Work

Infiltration

"Quick question, where has this author been my entire life?…If you are looking for a romantic book that has mystery and thriller qualities then this is your book."—*Fantastic Book Reviews*

Lands End

"This is a great summer holiday read—likeable characters, great chemistry between the leads, interesting and unusual premise, well written dialogue, an excellent romance without any unnecessary angst. I really connected with both leads, and enjoyed the secondary characters. The attraction between Amy and Lena was palpable and the romantic storyline was paced really well."—Melina Bickard, Librarian, Waterloo Library (London)

Lucy's Chance

"Add a bit of conflict, add a bit of angst, a deranged killer, and you have a really good read. What this book is is a great escape. You have a few hours to decompress from real-life's craziness, and enjoy a quality story with interesting characters. Well, minus the psychopath murderer, but you know what I mean."—*The Romantic Reader Blog*

Pursuit

"This book is a dynamic fast-moving adventure that keeps you on the edge of your seat the whole time…enough romance for you to swoon and enough action to keep you fully engaged. Great read, you don't want to miss this one."—*The Romantic Reader Blog*

Visit us at www.boldstrokesbooks.com

By the Author

Lands End

Lucy's Chance

The Rise of the Resistance: Phoenix One

After Dark Series

Infiltration

Pursuit

THE RISE OF THE RESISTANCE: PHOENIX ONE

by

Jackie D

2018

THE RISE OF THE RESISTANCE: PHOENIX ONE
© 2018 By Jackie D. All Rights Reserved.

ISBN 13: 978-1-63555-259-1

This Trade Paperback Original Is Published By
Bold Strokes Books, Inc.
P.O. Box 249
Valley Falls, NY 12185

First Edition: November 2018

CREDITS
EDITORS: VICTORIA VILLASENOR AND CINDY CRESAP
PRODUCTION DESIGN: SUSAN RAMUNDO
COVER DESIGN BY MELODY POND

Acknowledgments

Thank you, Vic Villasenor and Cindy Cresap. Your abilities are far beyond my own. Thank you for helping to create and properly punctuate my worlds. Thank you to Bold Strokes Books for always being supportive and for continuing to give me this fantastic opportunity. Thank you, Stacy and Stacey, for always being willing to talk politics with me (ad nauseam sometimes), this book wouldn't exist without the two of you. Last but not least, thank you to all the readers. Without all of you, these stories would only live in our minds.

Dedication

For my wife—thank you for always being a
beacon of light in a world so plagued with darkness.

PROLOGUE

Every person popped to attention when Daniel Trapp walked into a room. He'd been president now for almost three years, and this salutation should've stopped giving him pause a few years ago, but he still fought the urge to look over his shoulder. He waved off the people sitting around the large table in the War Room. As they took their seats, he took several deep breaths, an attempt to put his public face on, a facade for his people. He wanted to seem unwavering, strong, and decisive. In the past, this hadn't been a problem. That had been who he was, until the world started to shift under him. He'd never been faced with a decision of this magnitude before. No one had, as far as he knew.

Several massive climate catastrophes had left the world in shambles. There were millions of people with nowhere to go, struggling to stay alive. He'd made America a refuge, a place where the people of the world who'd been affected could make their new home. This was met with such severe backlash that there was a constant stream of protesters at the gates of the White House. At first, he thought it was growing pains, people adjusting to what would be their new normal. Despite their initial reactions, he believed the spirit of the American people would eventually find its way into the light to do their duty.

Then the protests started to become more violent and new leadership began to emerge. Frank MacLeod had managed to manipulate and lie his way into the hearts of the people. It didn't matter how many of his statements were proven as lies, or how horrible his remarks about women and minorities, people rallied around his pervasive ideas of nationalism and isolationism. He laid the issues of the world at the feet of innocent people, insinuating that they somehow deserved what was happening to them.

Frank MacLeod seemed to be the backlash of a world that had started to turn toward humanity and progress. He gave a voice to people who'd been pushed into the shadows to harbor their bigotry and hatred in isolation. Now they'd all found each other and wanted revenge for their humiliation. The recent insurgence of refugees and the financial assistance the government was providing was the perfect catalyst to help convince people to join their side. The whole situation was unnerving, problematic, and sickening. Lines were being drawn, and the idea of being on the right side of history seemed to no longer matter.

Their forces were gaining momentum and talks of convening a constitutional convention once they were in power no longer seemed like a fevered dream. For this reason and the possibility of threats that weren't currently perceivable, the Phoenix Project was created. There would be four Phoenix total, each with their prescribed area of expertise. Each had a skill set that could help to bring unity and peace to the country if the unthinkable happened. If America fell, and it seemed there was no question they were headed that direction, eventually, these four people would be the last hope, a glimmer of what America once stood for and what it could be again. They would work together to restore the country to what it was supposed to be, when whoever was in charge deemed the time was right. The idea was brilliant, but the fact that his thirty-four-year-old daughter, Kaelyn, had been selected as one of the Phoenix, took the shine out of the prospect for him.

He was fully aware of her capabilities. Kaelyn had a broad and incredible understanding of American history and strategy. In fact, she taught American history at Duke University. All of this didn't help to squelch the fear of putting his daughter through the process. She would be cryogenically frozen until a time where there was an opening for the people to take the country back, once again. She would emerge as an immediate leader and a target. What hurt his heart the most was that she'd wake up and not know her surroundings. There'd be no familiar faces, no one to recount her childhood, no one who would understand her experiences the way a family member could. She'd have no one.

"Mr. President?" the army general asked. "We'd like to proceed."

He nodded, uncertain he could keep his voice steady if he answered aloud.

The Four Phoenix were brought into the room, each taking a place around the table. Daniel saw the others, but he couldn't take his eyes off Kaelyn. It seemed like just yesterday he had twirled her in circles at the park, watched her kick her first goal, and attended her high school and college graduations. She looked so much like her mother—elegant, confident, and beautiful. But right now all he could see was the little girl who would curl up in his lap and fall asleep after begging to watch a movie. The child who had stayed up far past her bedtime to finish her favorite book, *Peter Pan*, even though she had read it a hundred times before. He saw the best decision he'd ever made by creating her and now the hardest decision he'd ever made by giving her up to a plan he wouldn't see come to fruition. His heart ached at the gravity of the situation and he fought back tears when she straightened her back when the admiral addressed her.

"Ms. Trapp, you do understand what we are asking you to do? That you're agreeing to leave this time and the life that you know?"

"Yes, sir." She laced her fingers on top of the table. "I understand the importance of this project and what my role will be in the future."

The secretary of defense stood and paced, as was his habit. "Could you please explain the roles you will each play, for the official record."

Kaelyn stood and moved to the woman a few seats down from her, placing her hands on her shoulders. "Phoenix Two is a research professor for the military profession and ethics at the Army War College."

The professor beamed with excitement. "I have a bachelor's degree in philosophy and economics from Washington and Lee University, where I graduated cum laude with honors in philosophy, a master's degree in philosophy from Stanford University, with a concentration in the history and philosophy of science. I also received a graduate fellowship at the Center for Conflict and Negotiation. I have a master's in national resource management from the Industrial College of the Armed Forces, where I was a distinguished graduate. I received a doctorate in philosophy from Georgetown University. My objective is to hold our future government to the highest of standards and to ensure the ends always justify the means."

Kaelyn moved on to the next woman. "Phoenix Three is the executive director of the leadership center at MIT."

Phoenix Three pushed her glasses up on her nose. "I'm a senior lecturer in leadership and innovation at the MIT Sloan School of Management where I've pursued my vocation of executive teaching, coaching, and research by exploring how leaders in business, government, and society discover provocative new ideas, develop the human and organizational capacity to realize those ideas, and ultimately deliver positive, powerful results. There'll be a lot to rebuild in the future, and we'll already be behind the curve. It will be my job to catch us up and to make sure we'll be deploying the most effective techniques."

Kaelyn motioned to the only male Phoenix amongst them, Four. "The head of psychology at Howard University."

"I was the first in my family to attend college and the son of immigrants. I have a Ph.D. in developmental psychology, and the focus of my research is the development of young children. Though most of my research has been devoted to the academic development of African American children, I fear that many will join this persecuted class in the future. Skin color won't play as prominent a role because too many will have been placed into the 'other' category. My job will be to help bridge the gap between us and them, in hopes that we finally create a 'we.'"

Kaelyn dipped her head to the people around the table, and her eyes were alive and excited. "And as you all know, I'm the First Daughter, but after today, simply Phoenix One. I have an MBA in strategy and leadership from George Washington University and a Ph.D. in American history with a concentration on constitutional law from Duke University, where I now teach. Prior to that, I was a researcher at the RAND Corporation, where I focused on national security, strategic planning, risk management, force planning, and workforce development issues. During my time with RAND, I contributed to several publications where we developed philosophies on improving government process, presidential appointments, and broadening public leadership in a globalized world. By all accounts, my life has been one of privilege and very little struggle. I've never fought in a war, nor am I the daughter of immigrants. But I've watched my parents spend every day of my life fighting for the people of this country and all around the world. It has become our family legacy, a legacy I happily take my place in today. My job will be to bring the soul of the American people into the future. To remind us what we stand for, what we sacrificed, and what we can achieve. I have all our history living in my head, without the distortion MacLeod is trying to create, the details he's trying to change. The good, the bad, and the ugly should and will be remembered so we can do better and avoid the mistakes of our past."

Daniel watched his daughter as she took her seat. She was full of hope and determination. He wanted to siphon some of that from her, put it in a bottle to drink later or dole out to people as necessary. But that was the point of having her here, wasn't it? Long after he was gone, the Phoenix Project would be gifted to the future generation. Until that time, they'd be kept in their locations, a symbol of hope, a driving force to keep people focused on an objective, a mission.

Daniel leaned forward on the table, took off his glasses, and pinched the bridge of his nose where the stress of the day had manifested into pain. "The country and the world are in debt to all of you. Please, go get your affairs in order and we will notify you when it's time. We're hoping to put it off as long as possible, but it is inevitable."

The four filed out of the room, and he turned his attention back to the table. "Have we decided on the final locations that we'll place them?"

An army general pulled a box from under the table. "Each of these sixteen folders holds a possible location. Depending how the next several months or years unfold will determine optimal placement. We have teams in place to secure each of them, depending on the location that's chosen. However, for security reasons, the teams will only be familiar with their target location and will not be privy to the others. They will, in a sense, be the guardians of their assigned Phoenix. Per your instructions, they won't be awakened until the three protocols have been met: the people need to be ready and willing to support the effort, there must be instability within the reigning government, and there must be a military force that can back up their efforts."

The throbbing in Daniel's head was spreading. He could feel it moving down his neck and into his shoulders. "How will we assure that MacLeod doesn't find out about them?"

The Joint Chiefs all looked at each other, seemingly confused by his question. "The same way we've always kept secrets: we have to trust our people."

Someone from the other side of the table started talking, and Daniel didn't bother to look up from his folded hands to see who it was. "Sir, please remember, this is just a precaution. We may never need the Phoenix Project."

This was the attitude that infuriated him the most. He stood, slamming his hands on the table. "Do not try to placate me. We just had a midterm election. They placed enough people in power to call for a constitutional convention, and they have the votes to throw me out of office. Their followers don't care if what they're saying is true. They've convinced the American people that their fear is righteous, virtuous, and that there's only one way to stop it. There are people dying in the streets, people of color being brutalized, the LGBTQ community are being fired from their jobs and beaten to death. I've activated the National Guard, but all our resistance will come to a crashing halt if they have their way. The pillars are crashing down around us, and you think this is all a precaution? No, it's our Hail Mary, our last apology to the future generations, and it's all we have left."

"When do you want to call them in to begin the cryo process?" the admiral asked.

Daniel shook his head at his own realization. He hadn't picked a date until this moment. "The day before they remove me from office."

The army general stood. "Sir, we don't know—"

Daniel cut him off, finding himself annoyed for having to explain to these people what seemed so obvious. "They'll call the convention. They'll change the Constitution so they'll be able to elect whomever they want, and then they'll impeach me. It won't be my vice president taking my spot. It will be Frank MacLeod."

He walked out of the room before anyone had a chance to argue with him or to try to change his mind. It didn't bother him that people wanted him thrown out of office; that was part of the job. What scared him was who they'd replace him with. He continued to walk down the hallway, then stopped in front of a portrait of Abraham Lincoln. He paused, staring at the ill-fated president. Daniel had written his dissertation on Lincoln, who he believed was the greatest president who had ever lived. Daniel had always felt sorry for Lincoln, not knowing what would happen to him. If he'd known he could've made a plethora of different decisions that day, including the decision to attend the play. But now, in this moment, Daniel envied him. Unlike Lincoln, Daniel could see what was happening. That same evil that had lived inside John Wilkes Booth was alive and well again in America. Booth, like MacLeod, had believed there were certain people more deserving than others. Booth didn't want the newly freed slaves to have a vote in the

THE RISE OF THE RESISTANCE: PHOENIX ONE

country, much like MacLeod didn't want to accept the refugees from around the world. Booth had believed in isolationism for the South, MacLeod for America. Neither could accept change was part of growth and that the America they each longed for was only great for white male Americans.

He hadn't realized how long he'd been staring until he felt a hand on his arm. "Honey?"

He turned to look at his wife, Dorothy. He'd loved her since the first day they'd met in college and had loved her every day since. She was strong, smart, articulate, and beautiful. These were the same traits he now saw in his daughter, and the idea of losing her washed over him again.

He shoved his hands in his pockets and tried to focus on not letting the tears welling up in his eyes fall. "I don't know how to stop it."

She wrapped her arm around his. "I don't think you can. Sometimes, things need to be completely broken to heal, just like our bones."

"I won't be able to protect her," he whispered.

Dorothy put her hand on his cheek. "Did you ever think it will be them who will need protection from her?"

He leaned into her hand, allowing himself this moment. There might not be many more in their future, and he wanted to remember the small bit of beauty left in the world.

CHAPTER ONE

A rrow Steele glanced up at the monitor, watching the line seesaw along the screen, marking her heart rate. "Decrease oxygen level to six."

The soothing and familiar voice of the Computer Analysis Monitoring System answered. "That is not advised. Your current running speed is seven. Lowering the oxygen level in the room could have adverse effects." The voice had been a constant in her life since the day she was born. It belonged to the artificial intelligence server that monitored the compound. It was affectionately known to everyone as CAM.

"Advisement noted. Please lower the level to six. I need to simulate the western territory air quality." She had been born for this mission. Arrogance hadn't placed that thought in her head, nor was it some misguided musing. No, it was something she'd been told since she was old enough to understand words and their implications. Every day of training since her childhood had led to this week. Phoenix One was her destiny. Or that's what she would call it, if she believed in things like destiny.

Arrow heard the overhead exhaust fans click on as CAM's voice filled the room. "Oxygen level at nine…eight…seven…six. I have also notified Captain Markinson of your current training session, as he asked me to disengage the track once you have been on it for ninety minutes."

Arrow shook her head, annoyed with Valor Markinson for once again trying to dictate her training regimen. "CAM, I still outrank Valor. Is your system glitched?" The words were more difficult to choke out than she'd hoped, a direct effect of the decrease in oxygen.

"There is no glitch, Major Steele. General Steele instructed me to notify the captain whenever you step outside safety protocol."

She opened her mouth to argue, but it was becoming more difficult to breathe by the second. Her hands were beginning to tingle, and her chest burned. She blinked hard and tried to refocus the discomfort she felt on the fact that this was precisely what it would feel like in the western territory, and she needed to be ready. If she couldn't push her body past its normal limits, what use would she be to Phoenix One? It didn't matter what her father or Valor thought; she knew what her body was capable of, and she wanted more from it.

An alarm from the sensor pinged, and she looked up. The oxygen level in her body had decreased from ninety-eight to eighty-seven percent. If it dropped to eighty-five, the training session would end automatically. She reached down to her wrist and pushed the glowing blue button, releasing the monitoring bracelet. The monitor stopped beeping at her, and she smiled at her small victory. She'd tossed the bracelet over to the corner of the room when she heard the door slide open, and CAM's voice announced the entrance of the man now standing in front of her.

"Good morning, General Steele."

Her father had his arms crossed across his chest, pushing his muscles forward. His jaw clenched, and he was squinting, a positive indication that he was less than thrilled with her.

"You're being reckless." His voice was even and controlled.

"I'm training." Arrow was surprised she managed to muster the ability to get the words out through the burning sensation.

"CAM, terminate the session."

"Yes, General."

The track began to slow, and although Arrow's immediate thought was to say she could do another five minutes, her quivering legs didn't agree. She tried not to gasp for the air that had started to be pumped back into the room, but her body couldn't help itself.

"I could've gone longer." She had her hands on her knees and was trying to focus her vision, which had become blotted with small dots.

"What were you thinking? Level six? That's not an altitude you'll encounter, much less at the speed you were running."

She was still bent over. Proper etiquette required her to stand at attention while addressing a general. But this wasn't just a general; this was her father. She kept her eyes focused on his perfectly shined boots. "I just want to be ready for anything."

"You're ready. You've been ready. I'm very proud of you." His voice cracked at the end. Showing emotion had never been a strong suit of her father's, and she was caught off guard.

She stood and made eye contact. "Thank you."

She thought for a moment that he was going to hug her. But even as she thought it, she knew it was foolish. She could count on one hand the number of times he had embraced her in all her twenty-eight years. He nodded at her once and walked past her. "You're due in the control center in forty-five minutes."

"I know. I'll be there."

"See you then." The door slid open, and he walked out.

Arrow grabbed a towel from the neatly folded pile in the corner of the room. She blotted her face and stared at herself in the mirror. There were still blotchy patches of red on her neck and cheeks.

"Please put your monitoring device back on, Major Steele," CAM said.

Arrow grabbed the small bracelet from the corner of the room and put it back on her wrist. "You didn't have to call the general. I would've stopped eventually."

"General Steele asked for your location. I gave it to him as well as an update on your activity."

Arrow was in the process of stripping the clothes from her body, but she paused, surprised by this information. "How often does he check on me?" She wasn't aware that her father was all that concerned with her day-to-day happenings.

"Two to three times a day."

She tapped the monitor on the shower, dictating the temperature she wanted the water to be, along with the combination of soap she wanted to be included. "I didn't realize he cared that much."

She didn't expect CAM to answer. She'd been speaking to herself. "You're one of two Guardians assigned to Phoenix One. Your whereabouts and happenings are of the utmost importance."

This clarification made much more sense than the idea her father was concerned about her. It was about the mission. It was always about the mission. She hadn't picked it for herself, but now she believed that had she been given a choice like others in the colony, she would have taken it. There had been two Guardians assigned to Phoenix One before her and Valor. They had retired from their positions ten years ago when she and Valor were old enough to relieve them. Arrow wasn't sure how they did it, since she couldn't imagine a life outside of this.

The shower was hot and relaxing, precisely the combination she was seeking. She ran a rag over her chest and arms. The soap and cloth momentarily hid the tattoos on her arms that signified her place in the world. Her upper left arm wore the insignia of the Guardian class, Level One. On the right, her barcode. They were used to identify her—the Guardian insignia to her people and the barcode to her enemy. The Hand of God had perfected the brutal art of stripping away a person's uniqueness, which was what the barcode intended to achieve, and was given to every person at birth. But her Guardian insignia was a beacon of hope and safety for the people who entrusted her with their lives. To the Hand of God, it meant she was tasked with keeping the peace. But to anyone else, Level One Guardians were the keepers of the Phoenix.

"Arrow?" The voice echoed through the shower area.

She wiped away the condensation on the glass. "Hey, Valor. You checking up on me too?"

He shoved his hands in his pockets and leaned against the wall. "Well, you do stupid things sometimes. But no, I wasn't checking on you. I figured we could head up to control center together."

She turned the shower off and grabbed the towel off the hook, then wrapped it around her body. She stepped out of the steaming cube and looked up at Valor. He towered over her five-foot-six frame by a full nine inches. He had smooth black skin and a dimple in his left cheek. His slow and easy smile was reassuring and welcome.

She turned her back to him and pulled her underwear up under her towel. "Did you get any sleep last night?"

She heard him move around and then sit down, the squeaking material giving away his position. "Not really. I feel like we've been waiting for this day our entire lives."

She tucked her shirt into her pants and sat down to tie her boots. "It feels that way because it's true."

He leaned forward in his chair, his hands in perfect steeples. "Do you ever wish we had been Twos or Threes, maybe even just villagers?"

She faced the mirror and put her hat on and straightened it. "No, never."

He walked over to her, his face behind her in the mirror. "I knew you'd say that."

She tucked away the tiny bit of hair that stuck out under her hat. "Then why'd you ask?"

"Because your confidence gives me confidence."

She turned to face him. She reached up and placed her hands on his broad, muscular shoulders. "There's no one better trained for this than us. We've been preparing for this since the day we could hold a weapon."

He shook his head. "You started even before that."

She smiled at him and shrugged. "True. Sometimes I think my parents had me just for this purpose."

"I'd like to argue with you, but I think you're right."

She put her forearm out, an indication for him to bump it with his own. They'd practiced this friendly and straightforward maneuver since they were children. It was something they shared only with each other. He bumped her arm with his. "We've got this."

❖

Arrow had never seen so many people in the control center. There were people buzzing around every piece of equipment. The main screen took up forty feet of the front wall and typically had the locations and happenings of the Hand of God and its soldiers. Today, it listed all the necessary characteristics of the Phoenix Project and its status. There was always at least one general in the room tasked with the watch for six hours at a time. Today, all twelve generals were in the room. Four from Guardian One, four from Guardian Two, and four from Guardian Three.

Arrow and Valor found seats next to each other in the gallery and awaited further instructions. The door beeped and slid open. "Attention on deck," said a voice from another corner of the room.

CAM's voice made the official declaration. "Good afternoon, Madam President."

Macy Steele was smart, compassionate, capable, and beautiful. She was the best person Arrow had ever met, and she would've told anyone that, even if she wasn't her mother. She was six years into her term as president of the Resistance and her people adored her, but none more than Arrow. She made eye contact with Arrow and winked as she made her way to the front of the room.

She stood at the podium placed there for today's announcement. Typically, there would be cameras hovering in the air to broadcast her remarks. But today, they couldn't risk the possibility of the transmission being intercepted. Over the years, their scrambling abilities had become almost impenetrable. But *almost* wasn't good enough for today.

Her mother put her hands on the podium, and Arrow knew they were folded together. This was her mom's normal speaking position. Her face was calm and comforting, the epitome of class and reliability. She saw her gaze travel over to her father, who was sitting in the front row to her left. He beamed at her, just as proud of her as Arrow.

"Thank you all for coming. Today, we gather for the realization of a promise. A promise that was made to all of us sixty-seven years ago. The Resistance was created out of necessity. A necessity for a free people, a fair and just government, and a country that sought to heal, to help, and to be a beacon of hope for the rest of the world. The government that calls itself the Hand of God is the antithesis of everything we hold dear and even of its very name. Our parents and grandparents saw the need to create a force that would stand up to this evil, with the conviction that only a free society can offer. Today, we take a step toward bringing that promise to fruition. The success of the Phoenix Project will be the bridge to bring us together once again. It will no longer be us versus them. We'll be one people once more. We'll be met with confusion and disbelief, but we can't let that deter us from our goals. Our people will no longer stand on the outside. We'll no longer be kept from our relatives within the Hand of God, and we'll no longer remain in the shadows. Today will mark the beginning of a reckoning and the starting point of a prophecy spoken by the last real president the United States ever had, Daniel Trapp. It is all of you in this room who make this possible. You're the heart and soul of the Resistance, and I'm going to let you get to work. I just wanted to personally thank you for what you're doing. A grateful colony thanks you, and eventually, a grateful nation."

Her mother's remarks were met with a burst of applause. The typically stoic people in the room were smiling and smacking each other on the back. It was the first time in Arrow's life where she could taste the excitement in the air. It was heavy and sweet. It sat in her mouth like something that could be chewed on and enjoyed. She knew the road ahead of them was long and undoubtedly dangerous, but it did nothing to sour the excitement of the right now. The world was about to change.

CHAPTER TWO

Kaelyn Trapp knew she was awake, but she couldn't move a single muscle in her body. Voices were coming in and out of the room, and the light shifted behind her eyelids. The blanket draped over her was heavy and hot. It wasn't like any heat she'd ever felt. She understood that it was warm enough to create sweat, but there was none. She wanted to understand why, but her brain wasn't allowing her to put the pieces together. The soft lull of the beeping monitors was pushing her back to sleep, but she was desperately fighting the sensation.

Sleep was on the verge of claiming her. She knew she was losing the fight when she heard *her*. It was a voice she recognized, but she didn't know from where. The voice was moving closer. The person attached to the voice knew her name; the person even seemed to know her. Kaelyn wanted desperately to open her eyes to this familiarity. She willed her body to work.

"Kaelyn, whenever you're ready, we're here waiting," said the familiar voice.

Kaelyn sifted through her memory. It wasn't her mother, and it wasn't any of her female friends. She needed to know. She pushed and willed her eyes to open. Then slowly, more light started to slip in. The light hurt. It was bright, harsh, and unwelcoming. She must have worn the pain on her face because the voice spoke again.

"Turn down the lights," she said.

Then, Kaelyn felt her eyes blink. She couldn't make them focus yet, but they were blinking. Then a thirst she'd never felt before consumed her. She felt as if she'd been in a desert for a hundred years. Her throat, chest, and even her tongue hurt. She wanted to ask for water, but she couldn't make her mouth move to form words. The stickiness clung to her cheeks and tongue, making it impossible to vocalize her need.

She heard movement next to her, and then a straw was in her mouth. Her body responded with muscle memory, sucking down all the cool liquid the straw would offer. When the slurping sound started, the straw was removed from her mouth, only to be back a few moments later with more marvelous water. The blurry images of the room were starting to take shape, her focus becoming sharper. She saw the person holding the cup and straw to her mouth.

"That's all I can give you for now."

Kaelyn didn't know how she did it, but she felt her head nod her understanding. Her vision was becoming clearer now, and she could see the woman in front of her. She wore a uniform that Kaelyn didn't recognize. It was all black with unfamiliar insignias sewn on the collar and sleeves. Kaelyn decided to focus on the face, hoping there'd be something familiar there instead. The woman had short black hair, cut the way a man would wear it. Her eyes looked like a storm, gray and full of energy. Her lips started to turn up in a smile clearly intended for Kaelyn.

Kaelyn looked down at the woman's nametag and managed to repeat the word she read. "Steele."

Steele's smile widened, and her slightly tanned skin showed bits of red at her cheeks. "Yes, that's right. I'm Major Arrow Steele, and I'm the Guardian assigned to you."

Guardian? Am I dead?

Kaelyn's eyes must have shown her confusion and fear because Arrow followed up her initial introduction.

"Don't worry. You're okay. I know this is all going to be a lot for you to take in, but you're okay. I'm here to protect you."

Kaelyn wanted to ask her what she needed protection from. She wanted to know where her parents were. She wanted to know where she was and what had happened. She needed answers to a million different questions. But she didn't get the chance to ask them. A woman in a lab coat, whom she assumed was a doctor, came in and asked Major Steele to wait outside. The major looked like she was going to object but backed away from the bed anyway. Then, there were lights being flashed in her eyes and questions being lobbed at her in rapid succession. She tried to sit up; she wanted to see Arrow. She wanted to feel that familiarity again, but she was already gone.

❖

Arrow stood in front of the interactive map in the control center. She traced the magnetic pen over another route, and the possible issues they could encounter appeared on a list on the side of the screen. She made a wiping motion with her hand, and the information disappeared, and she started over again.

"We've gone over these routes a hundred times. We have the best one mapped out," Valor said from behind her.

She ran the pen over a different area. "I know. I'm looking for an alternative route, just in case."

"We have one of those too."

"We need a third, fourth, and fifth plan," Arrow said to herself as much as Valor.

She thought for a moment he might argue, but a retort didn't come. Instead, he appeared beside her. "You should get some sleep. We have a long few days ahead of us, and we're going to need our rest."

She didn't bother looking over at him. She put her fingers to a point and drew them outward, causing the map to zoom in further. "I'm fine. I'm going to wait for the doctor to say it's okay to talk to Phoenix One."

"Maybe we should start calling her Kaelyn. According to her psychological workup, we'll make more progress that way."

"Yes, of course, Kaelyn. I knew that."

He touched her arm. "Of course you did. You're tired. You've been at this for hours. Let's get some rest."

CAM's voice filled the room. "Kaelyn Trapp won't be available until tomorrow morning. According to your stats, Major Steele, you need at least five hours of sleep to be at your optimal efficiency. I can notify you in the morning when she's ready."

Valor wiggled his eyebrows. "See."

She put the pen down. "Fine, you win. I'm sure a little sleep would be good for me."

It wasn't far to their assigned dwellings, and once they arrived at Arrow's, Valor said good night and retreated into his, directly across the hall.

She changed her clothes, brushed her teeth, and made sure her uniform for the next day was pressed and ready for wear. Then, she sat back on her bed and pulled out her computer station. She'd looked through the photos and information on Kaelyn Trapp thousands of times before, but this time was different. She'd met her now, had made eye contact with her, knew what her voice sounded like in person.

She swiped through the photos. They began when Kaelyn was a child and went all the way through to a few weeks before her cryogenic state. She understood Kaelyn would be overwhelmed by the world now. It was vastly different from the last time she was conscious, nearly seven decades ago. When Kaelyn had entered her cryo state, the air was still breathable without the protective barrier that had to be created, governments around the world were still intact, and her parents were still alive. She didn't yet realize that science no longer held a place in the regular world and that she technically was no longer in the United States.

Arrow couldn't imagine what it would be like to wake up one day and have everything she'd ever known be nonexistent or completely different. There'd be no way to center herself because the center of everything she knew would be gone.

What she needed Kaelyn to understand was that this would be her purpose. Phoenix One was the key to restoring a sense of normal for herself and the rest of the world. The world needed her. The people under the Hand of God needed her, even if they didn't realize it. The Resistance needed her. Arrow was going to make sure that was entirely clear.

CHAPTER THREE

Kaelyn opened her eyes. The room was mostly dark except for the light that crept in through the cracked door. Her sleep had been fitful at best. There were so many images in her mind, memories that were coming to the surface of everything that had happened. Even with those images bubbling up, she still had questions that needed to be answered.

She looked around her room for a TV but didn't see one. "How can there be no TV?"

Then a voice that seemed to seep through the ceiling answered. "Good morning, Kaelyn. What can I help you with?"

Kaelyn wasn't sure what was happening, but the voice seemed to know her, which was odd. But it couldn't hurt to answer. "Who are you?"

"I'm an artificially intelligent computer analysis system, but people call me CAM."

Kaelyn looked down at her hands, straining her eyes in the light. No, this wasn't a dream. She could see, feel, and hear. "Nice to meet you, CAM."

"Introductions aren't necessary for my system. However, if it makes you comfortable, we can continue in this way," CAM said.

"Um, no. I guess that's okay. Is there a TV in here?" Kaelyn pushed herself up on her bed. Her arms shook from the minimal effort, but she was tired of lying down.

"I cannot make that available to you until you're caught up with all pertinent information. I have notified the doctors that you're awake. They'll be here momentarily."

Just as CAM finished, the door slid open, and a doctor walked in. "CAM, activate the lights but keep them at a lower level. I want her eyes to adjust."

The doctor walked over to her and grabbed her hands. "Can you squeeze for me, please?"

Kaelyn did as she was asked while studying the man in front of her.

"Very good." He reached into his pocket and pulled out a small metal bracelet with a glowing blue button. He unhooked it and slipped it on her wrist. "My name is Dr. Hyde. How are you feeling?"

"What is that?" She used her head to motion to her wrist.

He showed her his wrist where a matching bracelet glowed back at her. "It monitors all your internal functions. Everything from your hydration levels, to your heart rate, to your need for sleep, food, or assistance. They're standard issue. CAM keeps track of all of that information. You just need to ask, and she'll tell you or notify someone to help you."

Kaelyn focused on her other wrist, noticing something she hadn't before. Wrapped around like a watch was a red and blue flame tattoo. The flame took the shape of a bird at its apex, reaching up toward the back of her hand. Underneath the wrist were two characters. P1. She didn't remember wanting this tattoo, much less receiving it. Everything was still so blurry in her head. Too many memories overlapping, bumping up against each other, layering themselves like soft sand against sharp rocks.

The doctor mumbled something as he ran his finger over his tablet. He looked to be only about twenty-two years old, just a baby. "Where did you go to medical school?"

He smiled down at her while using a handheld device to scan her body. "That's not how things are done anymore. But don't worry. I was born into the healing class. I have been training for this job since I was old enough to walk."

Healing class? Glowing bracelets? Artificial intelligence oversight? The questions were mounting in her head, and she was finding it difficult to breathe. She'd never had a panic attack, but she'd read enough about them to assume that she might be having one.

He put his hand on her shoulder. "I know you have a lot of questions and you're going to get answers to all of them. Can you tell me what you remember?"

She took deep breaths in and out. She tried to focus on the things she could see and touch, things she knew were real. She knew the doctor was asking her the right questions, but she couldn't bring herself to answer.

He must have seen her hesitation because his voice became even calmer than it had been moments before. "On second thought, let's wait. I'm going to get you with people that will be able to answer your questions much better than I can. Do you feel up for a walk?"

A walk sounded wonderful. Kaelyn wanted to move around; her body felt as if it had been stationary for years. That would help clear her head, and if it brought her to people that could help her remember what happened, that would be even better.

"Yes, I would like that," she said.

❖

Arrow hurriedly put her uniform on and rushed to the Guardian lounge. CAM had woken her and told her that Kaelyn was awake and available. The doctor was bringing her to the lounge to make her more comfortable. She didn't bother to knock on Valor's door; CAM would let him know too.

The door slid open, and she heard CAM announce her arrival, but it was muffled by the buzz of excitement. Her parents were sitting in the lounge, along with a general from Level Two and Kaelyn. Kaelyn's face was pale, and she looked overwhelmed. Arrow looked at the tablet she was swiping through and wanted to take it from her. No one should be catching up on so much history and destruction like that.

Kaelyn looked at her from her seat and seemed relieved to see her. Arrow's need to protect Kaelyn had been ingrained in her training, and it showed itself now. Her hand twitched with the urge to go to her, to block her from the thoughts and feelings she must be experiencing. Arrow took a seat next to her mother instead.

Her mom put a hand on top of Kaelyn's. "Kaelyn, I'm sure you have many questions, and we want to answer them. I just want to make sure we start in the right place. So, why don't you go ahead and start."

Kaelyn leaned forward on the table, hands flat. "Who are you and where am I?"

Her mom nodded, probably trying to figure out where to start. "We are part of a government that is known as the Resistance. It was your father that gave us the name. The part that is going to take you a minute to process is that he gave us the name sixty-seven years ago."

Her mom turned. "CAM, please show us the footage from President Trapp and Kaelyn on her cryo date."

A few moments later, the screen fluttered with a few grainy images, and then Kaelyn and President Trapp appeared. They were sitting at a table with the cryo system in the background. Arrow had watched this video a hundred times; she knew it word for word. She'd always found herself transfixed by Kaelyn, and today was no different. Except now it was Kaelyn in front of her, not on the screen. She watched as Kaelyn's face changed, the emotions she felt making her jaw clench and causing her eyes to water.

"To whoever is watching this, I'm President Daniel Trapp, and this is my daughter, Kaelyn. If this recording is being viewed, then we've fallen further behind than we ever imagined. In fact, if you see this, I'm on the verge of no longer being the president, and our very way of life is in grave danger. An undeniable force has infected our nation and may bring all of us to our knees. A pervasive cancer has poisoned the minds of our country. I'm confident that although we have lost several of the battles, we will undoubtedly win the war." He faltered and looked at Kaelyn.

Kaelyn put her hand on his back and continued for him. "We are enacting something called the Phoenix Project. There are four of us in all, four Phoenix fail-safes. The details have been outlined in the files given to a few chosen individuals. We'll all be entering a cryogenically frozen state, until the time we can best be utilized to help us take back our country. Each of us holds a special significance to our value system, our history, and the soul of what our forefathers intended."

The image cut out, and a black screen appeared for a few moments before the picture reappeared. President Trapp was standing next to Kaelyn, who was lying in a clear tube. Doctors were pushing buttons on the screen as the glass casing became crystallized.

President Trapp looked back at the camera, and there were tears in his eyes. "The Phoenix Project will undoubtedly be our last hope. If you've chosen to activate the project, please make sure you can use it as it is intended. The timing must be perfect. I don't want to give my daughter up in vain. All three of the outlined protocols *must* have been met prior to you enacting the Phoenix project: the people need to be ready and willing to support the effort, there must be instability within the reigning government, and there must be a military force that can back up their efforts. And, Kaelyn, if you're finally watching this, I love you. Remember who you are and who raised you. You can do this. You all can."

THE RISE OF THE RESISTANCE: PHOENIX ONE

CHAPTER FOUR

The memories were coming back. The images of natural disasters, dead children, and mass homicides rushed back to the forefront of her mind. She remembered the year of planning the Phoenix Project took as the world crumbled around her. She remembered the Hand of God, a political organization that had decided on its new name after the collapse of the Republican Party. She remembered the way they'd used fear and manipulation to scare people into handing over their rights, their thoughts, and their conscience. She remembered everything. Then, she realized, if she was sitting here now, so many years later, things must have become much worse.

Her body reacted to the flood of memories and new information by forcing itself to vomit. She bent over a trashcan, her knees shaking, and the world spun around her. She heard a voice call for a doctor, but that wasn't what she wanted. She wasn't here for that. She turned, looking for the voice that had seemed so familiar when she'd first woken up. Arrow, she wanted Arrow.

As if her mind called to her, Arrow was beside her instantly. She grabbed Arrow's arm to steady herself. Arrow was strong, solid, an anchor she could use to ground herself. She looked up at her. There was so much concern in her gray eyes, so much desire to help, but it seemed impossible for a person she didn't know.

"I need you to tell me everything," Kaelyn managed between desperate breaths.

Macy Steele interrupted. "We don't need to do that yet. We can give you a chance to get your bearings."

Kaelyn sat back down at her seat at the table and wiped her mouth with a cloth someone handed her. "With all due respect, President Steele, I know what I'm capable of, and I'm capable of this now."

Arrow sat beside her. "Why don't we start with where you are. There'll be time for everything else."

Kaelyn wanted to know as much as she could as quickly as possible, but she resigned herself to the idea that Arrow might be right. She'd been asleep for a long time, and she didn't trust all her limbs quite yet. She should take a little bit of time to acclimate to her surroundings.

"Okay, Major. I'd like a tour." Kaelyn pushed herself out of her chair, her stomach a little queasy.

Arrow was beside her instantly, steadying her. "Why don't we start with some food?"

Kaelyn nodded and followed her to the door. It slid open, showing an advanced version of what Kaelyn knew in her time as an elevator. Arrow explained that they were now called lifts, but it worked in the same manner. The lift moved down and then seemed to move forward until it came to a very subtle and smooth stop.

"This is the canteen. There are three of them inside the facility, but this is where the officers eat." Arrow stepped up to the counter.

There was no line, and the room was empty except for the people who were serving the food and one man sitting in the corner, eating at a table by himself. The counter was shiny and black, reflecting the soft overhead lights. The daily menu hung behind the counter, a digital display with numbers next to each food item.

"What are the numbers for?" Kaelyn pointed.

"All the food is tied to a point system. Depending on your activity level for the day, you need to take in a certain amount of points." Arrow looked at the glowing band on her wrist. "As of right now, I need seventeen points worth of food to keep my caloric intake balanced."

Kaelyn looked at her band, and her activity level read four. "What does that mean?"

"Just double it and that's how many points you need." Arrow smiled. "So, you get eight."

"What does eight points get me?"

Arrow shrugged and looked up at the menu. "You can either have a vegetable salad with an apple or three pieces of fruit."

"A vegetable salad seems redundant. What kind of salad dressing can I have?"

"There's only one kind, oil and vinegar."

"There's no ranch?"

Arrow's eyebrows furrowed. "What's ranch?"

Kaelyn put her tray on the counter. "I can't believe you woke me up and put me in a society where there's no ranch dressing." She looked at the woman behind the counter. "Vegetable salad with an apple please."

Arrow slid her tray next to Kaelyn and ordered. "We're what you'd call vegan. So, whatever this ranch stuff is, it must have had animal byproducts in it."

Kaelyn sat at the table and put the first tomato in her mouth. "It would be better with ranch."

Arrow laughed. "Well, when you're put in charge, put that at the top of your list."

Kaelyn tapped the side of her head and winked at Arrow. "It's already at the top of the list." She looked around the table. "No salt or pepper, either?"

Arrow went to the counter and came back with a small container and handed it to Kaelyn. "Pepper, no salt."

Kaelyn rolled her eyes. "Let me guess, because it's bad for you?"

"That and because salt has to be mined. You can find it in Eden but not here. There are substitutes, as you know, but we don't have access to that here. Pepper is a plant, so we can make it ourselves."

Kaelyn put a carrot into her mouth and really tasted the food for the first time. She wasn't sure if her memory was playing tricks on her, but these vegetables tasted different than she remembered. The carrots seemed crisper and the tomatoes juicier.

"I have to admit, it's better than I remember. But why vegan? Are there no longer animals?" Kaelyn dashed a bit of pepper onto her cucumber.

"We aren't entirely sure if there are animals outside the weather bubbles. I'm not sure how many of them would survive the harsh environment, but we haven't been able to do that much research on the subject. Inside the weather bubbles, we don't raise livestock. The impact it would have on the weather bubble is too severe. We wouldn't be able to process the air quality fast enough, so we simply don't do it. There are still cats and dogs. People managed to keep them when they fled to the Resistance camps, but that's it."

Kaelyn hadn't considered the loss of animals before now. It hurt to think of them suffering and perishing for no fault of their own. Some surely would have survived. Animals, after all, had endured through some of the most extensive transformations the earth had ever undergone. Something would still be out there. She needed to believe that.

"Tell me more about the weather bubbles." She sipped her water and saw her bracelet brighten slightly, highlighting her hydration level.

"They're pretty much exactly what they sound like. It's sort of a dome, and it regulates the climate inside it. You can't see it necessarily, but you'll know once you leave it. We're responsible for their maintenance, but the Hand of God has a kill switch. They could, if they were so inclined, turn it off."

"And then what?" Kaelyn asked, although, she was pretty sure she already knew the answer.

"We'd be exposed to the elements it's protecting us from. Everyone would die pretty quickly." Arrow wiped her face with her napkin and picked up her tray. "You done?"

Kaelyn looked down at her tray, not realizing she'd finished everything. She grabbed the apple and put it in her pocket. "Yeah, thanks."

She followed Arrow out of the canteen, wanting to know and understand everything in her new world. She wasn't sure where they were heading, but she didn't really care. She liked listening to Arrow talk. Yes, a lot of the information was frightening, if not shocking, but the way Arrow explained things and her slow and easy speech made her feel secure somehow.

"What do you do for water?" Kaelyn asked when they made a right at the end of a long hallway.

"There are a few different ways we conserve. The weather bubbles are limited when it comes to creating a rainstorm because the technology just isn't there yet. But we create our own water from the air and sun. Our water panels draw air in with fans, and the water vapor in the air passes through a condenser, creating water. The water is collected and mineralized for optimal health and taste. When we shower, the water that goes down the drain is collected, treated, and reused for more showers or for crops. Toilets, on the other hand, are a little different than they were from your time. They're all compost machines."

"That's incredible," Kaelyn said.

Arrow looked at her, surprised by her answer. "The technology was there during your time. People were just too greedy to do the right thing with it."

"Unfortunately, that doesn't surprise me in the slightest."

Kaelyn wanted to know more, but she had a feeling their tour was ending for the day. "I haven't asked you the most obvious question of all. What exactly is a Guardian? I mean, I've put together that you're a combination of a soldier and a police officer, but what is it exactly?"

Arrow shoved her hands in her pockets and leaned against the wall. "There are classes and levels. I'm Guardian class. The military force has been divided into three levels of Guardians. I'm Level One. This means I'm assigned to the overall safety of the people within the Resistance colonies. Except for Valor and me, we've been assigned to the Phoenix Project our entire lives. The other two levels may also serve as teachers or trainers in various professions. But this is all we do, and it's all we know. We're placed into these levels at birth. The other classes can pick their professions or pursue their interests, but we don't have that option. If you're born Guardian class, you stay Guardian class."

Kaelyn looked surprised. "How do you feel about that?"

"Feel? Feeling anything about it isn't an option. This is how it's done," Arrow said.

Kaelyn leaned against the other wall, taking in the information. "That's not really what America represents. This is supposed to be the Resistance, the enduring will of the country. I don't understand."

Arrow shrugged. "Things are different now, and we do what we have to do to survive."

"Why were you chosen for Level One?"

"My grandfather on my dad's side was one of the top military advisors to your father. My grandmother and grandfather on my mom's side flew combat missions during the same time. Both my parents were about ten when the Hand of God dealt the final blow to the Republic. They helped form the colony where the Resistance now resides. My dad and mom both ended up becoming generals in the Guardian class, and then Mom became president."

"Are you assigned to me by choice?" Kaelyn asked.

Arrow stood up a little straighter. "No, Valor and I were chosen for you at birth."

Kaelyn had more questions. It was a tremendous amount of pressure to realize that people had been chosen specifically for her, the day they were born. The expectations for her success in this project were far greater than she had ever imagined. It felt like a weight being placed on her shoulders of an even greater magnitude than what was already there.

Arrow turned them down another hallway, and for the first time since they started walking, Kaelyn recognized where they were. "I don't want to go back to the hospital."

CAM's voice came through the speakers. "Kaelyn, you have an appointment with the physical therapist, and then you will require nine hours of sleep to be at your optimal level."

Kaelyn looked up at the ceiling. "Does she listen to everything?"

Arrow and CAM answered at the same time. "Yes."

Kaelyn didn't know why, but it made her uneasy to realize she'd be separated from Arrow. She wasn't a needy person, or she'd never been before, but she found that she trusted Arrow. And that was a feeling she needed amid so much unfamiliarity.

Arrow must have noticed because she put her hand on her shoulder and slightly squeezed. "I'll be back for you first thing in the morning, and as soon as the doctor gives the go-ahead, we'll get you set up in your own room. Then I can keep answering any questions you still have, okay?"

This made Kaelyn feel better, but only slightly. "Okay."

Arrow smiled at her, not just any smile, one that came from her eyes, the best kind. She watched as Arrow moved down the hallway and made a left, leaving Kaelyn to herself. She was thankful for Arrow, glad she had someone who felt trustworthy and reliable. It made this crazy experience a little more bearable.

CHAPTER FIVE

Arrow walked through the treatment center doors just as she'd done the last four mornings. The only aspect that had changed since the initial visit was the excitement she felt knowing she'd see Kaelyn again. She waved to the nurses and headed toward the rehabilitation center. Kaelyn would be finishing her morning workout, and Arrow wanted to be there when she was done.

She stopped in front of the large glass wall. Kaelyn was on the treadmill, moving faster than she had been the day before. She glanced up and saw Arrow waiting and smiled. Arrow felt a flush of excitement work its way through her limbs. She put her hand on the palm reader, and the door slid open.

"Good morning, Major," Kaelyn said between breaths. "I only have about a mile left."

"You're doing great, Kaelyn," Arrow said as she walked over to the doctor.

"Her speed and stamina have increased very well. It's impressive." The doctor tapped a few keys on his tablet.

"She's very impressive," Arrow said.

"She'll be ready to go in no time."

"You don't have to talk about me like I'm not here," Kaelyn said. "But I like the praise, so please continue." She smiled and dabbed her face with a towel.

Kaelyn pulled the water bottle from the holster next to her and took a few sips. "CAM, increase my speed to six."

"That is not advised, Kaelyn. Your heart rate is in the optimal training zone. An increase at this time may cause injury. You'll need an override."

Kaelyn stared at Arrow, who felt herself stiffen . "CAM usually knows best. I'm not going to give you an override."

Kaelyn's eyes grew larger. "CAM, how often does Major Steele ignore your advice to increase her training routine?"

"Major Steele has ignored my recommendation one thousand four hundred and seventy-three times."

Kaelyn laughed. "Oh, is that all?"

Arrow looked at the doctor, hoping he would back her up.

He shrugged. "CAM, increase speed to five and a half."

"Thank you, Doctor." Kaelyn smiled.

Arrow glared at him, and he shook his head. "I don't want the Phoenix mad at me."

Arrow understood his logic and didn't have a reasonable rebuttal, so she changed the subject. "How much longer does she need to be under supervised sleep?"

The doctor scrolled through his tablet. "As far as I'm concerned, she's okay as of today. If anything major changes, CAM will alert me and I'll have her come back in."

The treadmill started to slow and then came to a complete stop. Kaelyn hopped off and clapped her hands together. "Check me out! I did three miles today. I haven't run three miles in like seventy years!" She laughed at her own joke.

Arrow, try as she might, couldn't help finding this aspect of Kaelyn adorable. She often laughed at her own jokes, which always fell somewhere between terribly obvious and not all that funny. But Kaelyn's enjoyment made Arrow laugh just as well.

"So far, you've showed me where you eat, your control center, the photo archives, and where you work out. When are you finally going to show me what's outside these walls?" Kaelyn ran the towel over her arms and then tossed it across her shoulder.

"We'll show you today as soon as you shower."

"Who's we?"

"You finally get to meet my better half," Arrow said as she walked toward the door. "I'll meet you right outside the rehabilitation center when you're done."

❖

Kaelyn showered quickly. She'd fallen asleep the last several nights wondering what it was like beyond the walls she'd been confined to since she'd awakened. She was both curious and terrified to see for herself. She'd asked Arrow hundreds of questions about what it was like and what to expect but had received very little information. Arrow told her to take her time to acclimate and to rest before trying to fully understand. Kaelyn wasn't sure if that was because things were so bad she couldn't put them into words or if she was truly that concerned with her well-being.

In the four days since she'd been awake, almost all her contact had been with Arrow and her doctor. Not that she minded. She thoroughly enjoyed Arrow's company. Arrow was patient with her questions and had a rare ability to focus on her like she was the only one in the world. Kaelyn assumed Arrow had a million things going on, but she'd taken the time, all her time, to be with Kaelyn, to make sure she was acclimating and adjusting. Arrow laughed at her jokes and walked her to the rehabilitation unit every night, even when Kaelyn had insisted she knew the way by now. She'd explained the intricacies of her bracelet, of CAM, and of her training regime. She made Kaelyn comfortable and, well, happy. She'd avoided discussing several subjects, explaining that Kaelyn would come to understand with time and that too much information at once could be overwhelming.

Now, she'd be meeting her partner. Arrow spoke of him frequently and with great fondness. Today, her real training and understanding would begin. She felt like she was getting her training wheels off and that she could be trusted. It felt good to think Arrow could trust her and saw her progress. Arrow believed in her. For some reason, this seemed to mean everything. She wanted Arrow to feel that way about her. She wanted to impress her.

Arrow had eased the transition, but just the same, it hadn't been easy. Everything was new and different, from the food to the walls inside the complex. They looked like cement but felt warmer when you touched them. Arrow had explained that they were made of an energy conserving material that kept the facility at a certain temperature, eliminating the need for tools like air conditioning and heating.

All access was either granted through CAM or by a palm recognition system. The floors, while sounding and looking like metal, had a much softer feel under her feet. People who passed her in the hallways nodded at her in recognition, but no one ever spoke to her. It would've been tremendously isolating had it not been for Arrow.

Now, she was ready to take the next step, to move forward. She pulled on her clothes and headed out to the area where Arrow told her she would be.

Arrow stood there waiting and smiling. "The transport is ready."

❖

The transport was waiting in front of the lift when the doors slid open. Arrow put her hand on the fingerprint pad on the back door, and it rose.

Once she got in the front seat, she said, "We still use ground vehicles. They make it easier to evade and hide. We can put them in places the government drones can't reach. Inside Eden, the main city, they have hover vehicles. We'll get around to that."

Valor turned around from the driver's side of the transport and put his hand out to shake Kaelyn's. "Hi, Kaelyn, I'm Captain Valor Markinson. I'll be your other tour guide today."

"Nice to finally meet you, Captain. I've heard a lot about you."

Valor pulled up to the protective barrier. "Please, call me Valor. CAM, clear the barrier."

A few moments later, the wall in front of them dissolved from sight. This was an everyday occurrence for Arrow and Valor, but she heard Kaelyn gasp from the back seat. "Holy shit."

"I'm sure you're going to see some things you aren't expecting, and we'll do our best to explain, but if there is something you don't understand, please ask," Arrow said.

Kaelyn moved over to the middle of the bench in the back seat. "My father was painfully vague about what this project would look like in the end. The people that planned Phoenix were meticulous about how to get here, and they were clear about not wanting to give too many instructions for the future since it was impossible to predict how things would unfold. So I want to start with the basics. Where are you taking me, exactly?"

Arrow pointed out the window. "This is NV2, a Resistance colony. Each colony is overseen by one of the headquarter units, where we just came from, where you've been staying. Our headquarters, Station One, oversees eight colonies in total. NV2 is the closest to Station One."

Arrow turned in her seat to see what Kaelyn was seeing. She tried to imagine looking at it for the first time. The world Kaelyn was from only existed to Arrow as pictures from history lessons. The tall buildings that once existed here with their bright lights and flashing signs were now diminished to identical dwellings and small gardens.

"This would be what you once knew as Las Vegas." Arrow couldn't imagine the gaudy place she'd seen in photos.

Kaelyn gasped from the back seat and Arrow turned to look at her. She had her hand over her mouth, and tears welled up in her eyes. "What happened?" She reached for a door handle and then looked around when she didn't find one.

"You can't get out. No one outside headquarters can know Phoenix has been initiated. Not yet, anyway," Valor said.

Arrow hopped over the middle and got into the back seat. "After you were put into the cryogenic state, you were moved to a secure underground location, which is now our base. About a year later, a massive drought swept through California, Arizona, and Nevada. It wasn't like anything anyone had ever seen. Temperatures reached one hundred and forty degrees for two full years. Even when the temperatures tapered off to one hundred and thirty, it was still too hot to grow food. The water supply dried up, farmers couldn't produce anything, and people began to starve."

Arrow watched as the horror crossed Kaelyn's face. She didn't want to tell her everything yet, but she needed to know, and somehow, she knew Kaelyn would appreciate the truth as opposed to sugarcoating anything. "It wasn't just here. There was a mass migration all over the world. People were coming here from Mexico, Africa, South America. The whole world had heated, and people who had almost nothing to begin with were left with even less. They flooded the borders of surviving countries all over the globe, hoping someone would take them."

Kaelyn looked down at her hands. She was rubbing her thumb up and down her palm. "This had already started when I went into my cryo state, but it clearly escalated. I think I know what happened, but I'd like you to tell me anyway."

Arrow nodded. "The Hand of God and their followers took to the streets. Your father, well, he tried to restore order. He let as many refugees into America as possible, setting up camps everywhere until they could figure out what to do next. It was mayhem. Then, the Hand of God overthrew our democracy. They declared martial law and restored what they called order. The new president, if you could call him that, had a force field of sorts erected around the United States. They burned the refugee camps and killed anyone who wouldn't swear their loyalty to the president and his family. The hotels and casinos that used to be here were demolished during something the Hand of God called a purge. They'd been shut down because of the drought and were being used by refugees for shelter. MacLeod destroyed them, hoping it would force the people out of the country. He dropped bombs, used tanks, and when all else failed, he'd simply set them on fire. This dried up area to your right, where you see the crates of food ready for transport, is what you'd know as the Bellagio fountain." Arrow pointed to the empty expanse.

Kaelyn wiped away the tears from her eyes and took several deep breaths. "So, everyone now lives like this?" She nodded toward the small colony. People were moving about, carrying baskets of vegetables back to their dwellings and talking amongst themselves in the community square.

"No," Valor said. "We live like this. These people here are the descendants of the Americans who refused to swear their loyalty to the new president. At first, he attempted to kill everyone as an example. It was starting to become humiliating for him, though, because too many people were escaping and there was civil war in the streets. So, instead, thirty million of us were banished. It didn't matter to him where we went, just that we stayed outside of the areas he designated. He erected an archaic wall around his kingdom to ensure we couldn't slip back in and poison the minds of his people. As part of his wall, he used the force field that separates us from Canada and the sea wall in the Atlantic Ocean, which was initially erected to combat climate change, as three-quarters of the wall. The last quarter is four hundred and twenty-one miles of stone, fencing, and barbed wire. There are only four access points to get inside: Buffalo, New York; Erie, Pennsylvania; Morgantown, West Virginia; and Fredericksburg, Virginia. All those access points are guarded, but not with significant force. There really isn't anyone trying to get in or out of the area. We fend for ourselves, and we've created systems to obtain food and water, but we aren't allowed in what remains of the United States, or God's country, as it's called now. Eden is now the capital, but it's what you knew as Washington, DC. We're self-divided into four locations. Each location was chosen because it is where a Phoenix was housed, unbeknownst to the Hand of God. It was too dangerous to move any of you at that point, so we built colonies around you."

"Eden? Like in the Bible?" Kaelyn looked dumbstruck.

"Yes. But if you ask me, it's not very biblical." Her attempt at a little humor to lighten the moment clearly fell flat.

"The Hand of God just lets you live out here now?" Kaelyn's face was flushed. It was either anger or sadness; it was hard to tell which.

"The government leaves us be because they're unaware that we're a threat. They've banned socializing and even basic communication between them and us. I'd venture to say that some of the children there now aren't even aware we exist. The government pumps a mild sedative through their water system. It keeps them complacent and agreeable. That doesn't stop them from forcing us to provide their main source of food. It was an agreement that was struck between our leaders; they'd allow us an acceptable climate inside weather bubbles to grow and maintain a food source as long as we provided them with eighty-five percent of our yield."

Valor's expression was neutral, but his hands were tight on the steering wheel. "If the colony falls short of the required eighty-five percent, it's added on to the next week's requirement. If they fall short for a second time, a drone randomly eliminates one citizen."

Kaelyn looked queasy. Her face had turned chalk white. "What you're describing is slavery. I thought you said they leave you alone, for the most part?"

"They do. There used to be armed soldiers here, but we finally negotiated this agreement about thirty-five years ago. They still patrol the areas on occasion, harass and threaten people for no reason, but it isn't anything like it used to be. I know it doesn't seem like it, but this is an improvement."

Kaelyn rubbed her eyes. "How do you know about the sedative?"

Arrow waited a moment before answering. She wasn't used to giving away their intelligence. But this was Phoenix One, and she had to be informed appropriately to be effective. "We have a few moles. Families that for the last two generations have risked their lives to provide us with information. The issues with the water supply are just the beginning."

Kaelyn's eyes were full of pain and anger. She looked as if she felt betrayed. Her words were barely above a whisper. "I can't believe it came to this." She looked at Arrow, determination replacing the horror in her expression. "I want to get out to talk to these people."

"You can't." Arrow winced at the look of disbelief in Kaelyn's eyes.

Arrow was going to explain her point as to why this was a bad idea. It wasn't authorized, there wasn't enough protection, but she couldn't seem to form the words. She thought back to everything she'd read about Kaelyn. Her work with the underprivileged classes from her world, her devotion to children, and her speeches about protecting the high-risk population. She understood the importance of Kaelyn getting to interact with people; she needed to understand what they were feeling and experiencing. Kaelyn needed the world to not just be tangible by sight, she needed to feel it as well. But this wasn't something Arrow could give her right now.

"Bringing you here now, without the proper preparation, puts these people in danger. If word were to get out before we intend it to, these people would be seized and possibly tortured for information. The government sends out drones to keep an eye on everything that happens out here. They don't directly interfere, but they're aware of our fundamental comings and goings. If they managed to catch a glimpse of Phoenix One or hear mutterings about it, it could risk everything. Right now, we have the upper hand, but if you show up, the Hand of God is going to have questions that we aren't ready to answer."

"How would anyone know it was me?"

Arrow pointed to Kaelyn's wrist where the blue and red tattoo stretched out around her wrist and hand. "Our people would know it's you because you have the insignia of the Phoenix, something that's become a kind of legend in our world. If the government heard the excited whisperings of a stranger, they'd come looking for you. Thinking you were either a defector, or worse, a secret."

Kaelyn traced her fingers over her wrist and stared out the window. "I understand. I'd like to know as much as possible, whatever you can show me, without putting anyone at risk. I know you kept me inside to let my body acclimate. I understand why you did it, but I feel behind now. I need to catch up."

Seeing the pain on Kaelyn's face burned in the bottom of Arrow's stomach. She'd spent her whole life with the sole intention of protecting her and eventually placing her in power. She'd never considered the thing that could hurt her wouldn't be a physical threat. "Drive slowly through the colony. Head over to the training facility."

Valor, to his credit, didn't question her decision. He kept the transport on manual drive and moved toward the center of the dwellings.

CHAPTER SIX

Kaelyn was trying to take everything in as quickly as possible. After the recording of her father, she remembered everything that had brought her to that point. But nothing could prepare her for what she saw now. A world ravaged by climate change, people pushed out of their country, and a society built out of necessity and fear.

Arrow had moved closer to her in the seat. Kaelyn knew it was so she could point to things through the window and explain their existence, but it still felt nice to have her near. Kaelyn understood intellectually that Arrow was there to protect her and her nearness was out of necessity, but the close contact felt good all the same.

The empty, crumbling shells of long-forgotten casinos and hotels in the distance were an eerie reminder of what once was. Dozens of small houses, which Arrow called dwellings, lined the street. They appeared to be made from concrete, but Kaelyn assumed it was the same material that was used inside headquarters. There were doors and windows, but everything looked identical. There was no individuality, no décor, no way to identify one home from another.

"Is there a monetary system in place?" Kaelyn asked

"The government deals with electronic funds, but there's a hefty tax associated with each transaction. We have access to it, but most of our people barter, not wanting to give the Hand of God any more than they already take. The salaries for their jobs are essentially nonexistent. The community works together to produce enough goods to share amongst themselves. But the majority is picked up at the end of each week and taken to Eden." Arrow's voice grew angry as she explained; bits of vengeance seemed to cling to her words.

The transport was starting to head out of the colony and toward a much more massive building. They passed four young girls with shield insignias on their left arms.

"What does that insignia mean?"

Arrow leaned over her to get a closer look. "They're healers; they'll grow up to be the colony's version of nurses and doctors."

One of the young women waved at the transport, and even though Kaelyn knew they couldn't see into the window, she waved back. "They seem happy. How can that be?"

"This is all they know. Their jobs are chosen for them through aptitude tests early on in their lives. They can decide to persue something different, but it isn't usually done. They're loyal to the cause, and the cause requires them to perform certain functions. It might be hard to believe, but these girls have it better than the women of Eden. The women under the eye of the government can't work outside the home. They're seen as little more than property of their husbands, fathers, and MacLeod. Our girls consider themselves lucky."

Her words, as accurate as they might be, stung. Just a few years before she'd entered her cryogenic state, the Women's Rights Movement had a rebirth in the United States. Feminism was starting to be seen as an admirable attribute instead of the way it had been viewed just a few dozen years before. Kaelyn had imagined a future where women were free the way men were free during her time. They'd be making the same money and choosing birth control methods that were suited for them, and not selected by the government. She had imagined women being titans of industry and making up a significant portion of all levels of government. They'd be inventors, scientists, and whatever else they damn well pleased. But sixty-seven years later, and a large section of the female population had been forced back into the service of the patriarchy.

"Why don't they fight back? There have to be women there that still remember a time when things were different." Kaelyn wasn't sure she wanted to hear the answer.

"They don't have a choice. It's one of the reasons we need to reunite the country and toss MacLeod out of office. Fighting back would mean death or public beatings. Plus, they lead comfortable lives there. They want and need for nothing. They have unlimited entertainment, beautiful homes, and are never hungry. The only time there is any strife is when someone steps out of line."

Kaelyn sat back, her mind whirling. "And then what? Let's say we overthrow MacLeod and take back the government. You think the minds of the people inside Eden will be easily swayed? You're going to undo generations of thinking with a single act? Not to mention, from your own account, they aren't suffering."

Arrow looked both hurt and surprised by her questions. "What other choice do we have? We must remind them there's another way. Despite what they may think of us, they're still our brothers and sisters. Complacency isn't freedom. Keeping people's minds soft and entertained isn't the same things as living. At the very least, they should be making that choice for themselves. If MacLeod was confident in the lives he'd given them, he wouldn't keep them drugged. He seizes their businesses and property in the name of God, makes them keep working and then sells their goods to other countries, keeping the profit for himself. Other countries that he offers no refuge for, no protection. He takes the women he wants for himself, regardless of their relationship status. So, yes, everything might be fine on the surface, but the evil that festers underneath cannot be allowed to stand."

Kaelyn knew that it wouldn't be as easy as Arrow believed it would be. You couldn't and wouldn't change people's minds when they had nothing to gain from it, and if going against the current government could land them here, they wouldn't risk it. People weren't wired that way. Change wasn't something people typically gravitated toward if there wasn't any reason for them to need it. Sure, the idea of it was romantic, alluring, but it was difficult.

Kaelyn tried to tap down her annoyance, but she could hear it in her words. "And what makes you think they'll fall in line with the Resistance? What makes you think they want to give up their comfortable way of life?"

Arrow sat straight up, apparently surprised by the question. "The same reason their ancestors fought for their freedom from the King of England without the promise of success. The same reason their ancestors risked their lives for generations to protect what was once the United States. Because people desire freedom, it's as much a part of their genetic makeup as the color of their eyes. They all have a hole in them right now, and they don't know what it's from. They can't pinpoint it. You, Phoenix One, are going to point it out, and then they'll have no choice."

Kaelyn hadn't realized she'd crossed her arms over her chest until she looked down. Arrow made her feel vulnerable, questioning and testing her moral compass. "You've been reading too much poetry."

Arrow's brow furrowed. "Everything I just said was taken directly from one of the classes you taught at Duke."

Kaelyn felt her arms drop slightly. "You listened to my classes?"

Valor started turning the transport around. "She has them all memorized."

Arrow pulled herself forward into the front seat. "It's my job to know everything about you."

Kaelyn wasn't sure how she felt about that revelation. Really, it made sense that she'd been studied to the extent that Arrow had apparently taken. The Phoenix Project had been their hope and what they hung their dreams on, for almost seventy years. Plus, she was used to having every part of her life looked at under a microscope. Being the First Daughter had brought cameras, fans, and enemies into her life. And now she was about to take on an even bigger role. The enemies would increase exponentially. She was always in a significant amount of danger as the First Daughter, but it would be nothing like this.

"I need to talk to your president," Kaelyn said.

Valor gave her a thumbs-up from the front seat.

CHAPTER SEVEN

This is terrible, disgusting, and insulting." President Adon MacLeod pushed his dinner plates to the floor. "Bring me something else."

A thin, shaking girl hurried over to pick up the mess. "What would you like, Mr. President?"

He looked down at her frail frame. She wouldn't make eye contact with him, just the way he liked it. It was infuriating to have to explain to these idiots how to do their job, yet here he was again. "It doesn't really matter. Anything has to be better than this crap."

The girl bowed her head. "Yes, Mr. President. It's just that, I don't know what to tell the chef to prepare."

Annoyance crawled up his body, like a spider rushing to his mouth. He pulled his gun from his waistband, ready to take her out at the knees. A voice from the other side of the room stalled his movement.

"That would be the second one this month. Please don't." Nora MacLeod was beside him a moment later.

"Stop sending me incompetent idiots then."

"Dad, just tell her what you would like and there won't be any more issues," Nora said.

He slid the gun back into his waistband, fighting the urge to smack the servant over the head with it. "Soup. Bring me soup. And not that bullshit you tried last time. Just regular chicken noodle soup."

The young girl scurried out of the room, and he could hear her crying as soon as she was out of sight.

Nora sat on the couch. She ran her hands down her form-fitting red dress. She was perfect. Hell, if she hadn't been his daughter, he probably would've tried to sleep with her by now. She tucked a strand of her blond hair behind her ear and smiled at him, slowly swinging her crossed leg up and down.

"Those young women have to go through months of training to work here. It's not good for your public image when they keep turning up maimed or dead," Nora said.

He leaned back in his seat, putting his feet on the desk. "Like I give a shit. What's going on?"

She pushed a few buttons on her tablet and then brought the images up on the projector module in front of him. The translucent imaging allowed him to still see Nora while looking at the charts and reports. "The prime minister of England has petitioned us, again, to help with the global climate crisis. Their sea wall has started to fracture, and their weather bubble has been malfunctioning. England has been without the sun for almost two hundred days."

"No. What else?" He pulled a string from his shirt.

She sent the next image up. "The colonies have been producing their regular amount of fruits and vegetables. But our consumption has gone up almost seven percent, and we'll need to cut back to stay on track."

He rolled his eyes. "No. Tell them we need more. Hungry people are angry people, and we don't need to deal with that right now."

"We already take eight-five percent of their total production. If we increase that to ninety-two, they won't survive," she said.

He walked over to the couch and put a hand on her knee. "Then they'll just need to produce more or reduce their population size."

Nora didn't look pleased with his answer, and he hated to disappoint Nora. "What do you suggest?"

Nora sat up in her seat a little straighter. She turned to him and looked him in the eye. "I think it's time to consider bringing them back into the fold."

"The Resistance? They're traitors; they turned their back on this country decades ago."

"Dad, the division between the lower and upper class here is intensifying by the day. The lower class is growing tired and angry from working twelve to fourteen hours a day without seeing any significant gains. Their children are being born into the lower class without any opportunity to move forward."

"Are you suggesting we offer them more opportunity?" He was barely able to speak the words, unsure where Nora was heading with this line of thinking.

"No, of course not. Grandfather was right to eliminate college for anyone who couldn't pay in cash and to create the standard that only people with college degrees could make over eighty thousand a year. I don't want to undo that. I want to give them a tangible enemy. People they can point to as worse off, to ensure our prosperity for the next generation."

"How would allowing them back in do that?"

She smiled at him. Her eyes matched her mother's, blue with flecks of green around the edges. "Bring in an even poorer group of people. We 'forgive them' and let the so-called Resistance become the labor force and move the others up to mid management. This would make our people even more well-off, make them happy, and the people from the Resistance would have actual money for the first time. They'll be so grateful for the opportunity, they'll look at you like a hero. Plus, beefing up the workforce will allow us to increase production. England wanted our help with the climate control devices? We can sell it to them. We'll sell them to everyone. Countries all over the world will be lining up to hand over their treasures to save their people. We'll be the greatest force the world has ever seen. Things are different now than when Grandfather took control. We wouldn't be pushing for globalism; it's supply and demand. We don't offer free trade. We set the prices, we set the expectations, we'll set everything. People are desperate to survive right now, and they're out of options. People have been born into the Resistance; they weren't part of the uprising, and they'll be glad to have a chance at what they think will be a better life."

"And it will all belong to me." He couldn't stop the warm bubbling feeling in his chest. The prospect was exhilarating. The whole world could be his, and they'd hand it to him. It would be the most exquisite conquering in human history. "Who else have you told about this?"

She put her hand on his knee. "No one. Only you, Daddy."

He took her hand and kissed the knuckles. "Let's keep it that way. See if you can get in touch with whoever is in charge over in the Resistance these days."

She practically jumped from the couch. "Right away."

CHAPTER EIGHT

Kaelyn watched Arrow's face as her mother, the president, walked into the room. She and Valor jumped to attention when the door slid open, but she'd waved them off when she moved past them. She didn't know Arrow very well, but the pride on her face whenever her mom was near was apparent.

Macy Steele sat at the table and patted the empty seat next to her. "I can't imagine how overwhelmed you're feeling at the moment. It's a lot to take in. That's why we held so much back from you for the first few days."

Kaelyn wasn't sure what she'd been expecting from this woman, but a mothering aura wasn't on her list. It put her more at ease. Macy seemed approachable, easy to talk to, and well respected. "Why did it take so long for the Resistance to elect a female president?"

Macy smiled knowingly, as if she'd been expecting the question. "What you really want to know is if we've really made any progress after all these years. It is, after all, what you had fought so hard for during your time."

"Yes, that's exactly what I'm wondering," Kaelyn said.

Macy stood and waved her hand in front of a wall, and a pixilated screen appeared. "CAM, please pull up the Guardian class, Level One photographic archives."

Dozens of pictures appeared on the screen, and she put her fingertips on top of one and seemed to pull it forward, letting it fill the screen.

Kaelyn leaned forward, wanting a closer look. Macy noticed and sent the image to the table, where it hovered a few inches from

Kaelyn. It was a picture of Boston almost completely under water. The next was one of Miami, completely submerged, then New York, San Francisco, and Seattle. Kaelyn felt horrified and ill. She had understood, intellectually, that this would eventually happen, but seeing it front of her was something entirely different.

Macy's voice was calm and even. "It all happened very fast. Once climate catastrophe became a way of life, there wasn't a lot of time to react. Your father did everything he could to help the people of the world, but it didn't matter. By that time, people were terrified and unwilling to give up any extra they had to people they didn't know. MacLeod came into power by calling for the camps to be burned, and he created a civil war."

Kaelyn braced herself as she asked the question she'd been waiting to pose since she'd woken up. "What happened to my parents?" She wanted Macy to tell her the truth, no matter how gruesome or painful it was.

Macy stared at her for a long moment and then nodded once. "After your father was removed from office, MacLeod eliminated his Secret Service detail. He was killed by a pipe bomb at a demonstration for the refugees. Your mother lived for another twenty-three years. CAM, pull up all the images for Dorothy Trapp starting from the building of this facility. She passed peacefully in her sleep when she was eighty-six years old."

Kaelyn hadn't realized she started crying until she tasted the salt on her lips. There were hundreds, if not thousands of images of her mother in the exact facility she was sitting in now. She was sitting in front of computer screens in various stages of their advancement, digging in the ground with a shovel. There were dozens of her with a twenty-something version of Macy Steele and even younger. "You knew my mother?"

Macy smiled at the images. She looked thoughtful and happy, like she was recalling memories that Kaelyn wasn't privy to. "Technically, I'm only the first female president of the Resistance in name. Your mother was in charge for several decades. She didn't want a title; we only came up with it later as we came closer to deciding it was time to enact the Phoenix Project. We needed a specific leader the whole Resistance force could look to, a definitive decision maker. We had an election and I was chosen, though any one of my colleagues would've done a good job." She looked at her and smiled genuinely. "I was only twenty-five years old when your mother passed, but I had worked for her since I was seventeen. She had been very close to my mother, and when my mom passed, Dorothy took me under her wing. She was the greatest woman I've ever known. That's why I know this will be successful. She's inside you; she lives in you still. Your father might have been the one in the spotlight for all those years, but she was his source of strength and drive."

Kaelyn was trying to take all her words in, but she couldn't really put everything together. And what about Arrow? She'd said being a Guardian was all she knew. If everything Macy was saying were true, how did Arrow not know anything else? How did she not get a choice in what she became? She glanced over at her. Arrow was still beaming with pride as she listened to her mother talk. Kaelyn needed to spend more time with her now that she had more information. She needed to find out if this was really the utopia Macy described, or an excellent brainwashing exhibition. If the Phoenix Project was going to be successful in restoring the country, it had to more than just lip service.

"What exactly is the plan? I assume the others have been brought out of their cryo-states, and you must have something in mind." It didn't matter to Kaelyn who answered. She looked at Macy and Arrow, waiting for someone to respond.

Macy nodded. "Yes, the last time we met with each leader of the colonies, we decided on a date to wake all of you. You haven't been in communication with them in order to eliminate the risk of discovery. We were only to contact each other if there was an issue. However, as of this morning, the generals were permitted to start telling their people the Phoenix Project had been initiated and to start preparing for the next phase."

Macy motioned for Arrow to continue. "The mission is to get Phoenixes Two through Four to one of the entry points of Eden undetected. For this reason, the Guardian forces won't be accompanying them, only their security details, which will help avoid detection. In your instance, that will be Valor and me. Our objective will be to get inside Eden and disable the water supply that feeds the sedatives to Eden's population. The Guardian forces will move to each of the described entry points once we've accomplished this. When they're in position, we will begin the second phase, which revolves around you.

We'll start broadcasting you, describing to the people of Eden what has happened to them, that there is an alternative, that we're there to help. This, in theory, should start a modest uprising, if not set the stage for a tremendous amount of confusion. At that point, we'll ask that MacLeod release his people, allow them to start making decisions for themselves, and demand he step down. He won't do this of course. He'll fight back. Stage Three is to remove him from office and place you in charge until we can establish a voting system."

Kaelyn hadn't realized her hand was over her mouth until she tried to speak. "You do realize that this will be far more complicated than what you've just described."

Arrow nodded. "Well, this plan has taken years to develop. I gave you a very brief version. I also understand that the success of this mission rests on the idea of the people of Eden *wanting* us to help them."

Kaelyn watched Arrow's facial expressions, looking for a sign that she truly understood the gravity of what she was hoping to accomplish. "And what if we don't succeed?"

Arrow leaned back in her chair and steepled her fingers against her chin. "Then, I assume we'll be taken into custody and presumably put to death. But I believe this is the perfect time. Our moles on the inside have indicated that there are rumblings inside Eden. People are growing weary of MacLeod and his need for absolute power. They feel forgotten and manipulated, and even the water sedation can't stop that. Right now is the best option we've ever had." Her voice was even and clear.

"Can the Guardian forces defeat their soldiers?" Kaelyn asked.

"Yes," Arrow answered without hesitation.

Kaelyn chewed on the information for a moment. There seemed to be no question in Arrow's voice, and the faces around her mimicked her certainty. "When do we leave for Eden?"

A half smile tugged at Arrow's lips. "Three weeks. In the meantime, we'll get you completely up to speed with all this new information."

Kaelyn wasn't sure of anything in this strange world, but as she felt Arrow's eyes on her, things seemed calmer. Maybe it was because she was there to protect her. It could've been because Arrow knew so much about her, but even while she was thinking it, she knew it was something else. Arrow had a quality about her that Kaelyn couldn't quite pin down. She was strong, sure, and gave off a sense of subtle power. Had she met Arrow in her world, she would've asked her out to dinner. She would've dreamed of the seemingly untapped passion behind those gray eyes. But this wasn't her world. This was a time and place where the future was uncertain. The nation had been split apart, and the fate of all the above rested squarely on her shoulders. Nevertheless, she was grateful to have a person she felt she could trust.

"Could we please get something to eat?" Kaelyn hadn't realized how hungry she was until the question slipped from her mouth.

Arrow and Valor were out of their seats and next to the door in an instant, waiting to escort her. She stood and looked at Macy. "Thank you, I appreciate you talking to me. I'm sure you're very busy."

"I'm never too busy to speak with you. Please find me if there is anything else I can help you with."

CHAPTER NINE

They moved through the hallways, working their way toward the canteen. Every person they passed nodded in recognition toward Kaelyn. Arrow had done a decent job of keeping Kaelyn isolated the last few days. They'd seen people on their brief tours of selected locations, but Arrow made sure to keep interaction to a minimum. Every general had been briefed about the reawakening of Kaelyn. It was up to them to disseminate the information to their people as they saw fit, until today. Even if people had never seen a photograph of Kaelyn, which was unlikely, they would recognize the insignia of the Phoenix on her wrist. Now they weren't worried about exposing Kaelyn to too many people in a short period of time. She was out in the open as of today.

At first, Arrow thought this would make her uneasy, but Kaelyn took it in stride. Which made sense considering she'd spent her entire life with people recognizing her. Kaelyn seemed right at home with the recognition, and Arrow felt the prospect of the Phoenix Project being successful tingle throughout her body.

Kaelyn had started her normal routine of making faces about her kale and longing for ranch dressing. Valor had the same look of confusion about the kale that Arrow had at first.

Arrow was about to explain to Valor what this ranch dressing concoction was when a loud pinging sound began through the speakers, followed by CAM's voice. "All Guardians, Level One, report to the control center, immediately. Level two security protocol has been enacted."

Valor and Arrow stood at the same time. She grabbed his arm and motioned to Kaelyn. "Take her to lockdown. I'll meet you there."

"Roger that, Major." He picked up Kaelyn's tray. "We have to go, but I'll bring your food so you can finish eating."

"What's going on?" Kaelyn's voice gave away her fear, but her expression was calm.

Arrow was already walking toward the door. "They're here."

❖

Kaelyn sat with Valor in a large room, which was clearly intended to protect the inhabitants from anything and everything. The walls were heavy steel, from the looks of it, unlike the rest of the building. The bolts protruding toward them were the size of fists. It seemed as if this was one part of the facility that hadn't undergone a technology upgrade over the years. There was even a flat screen television attached to the wall.

Valor looked worried, which unnerved her. She knew that he didn't know any more than she did, but it didn't stop her from asking. "What's going on? Who's here?"

He pointed to her food tray. "You should finish eating."

"Okay, but can you tell me while I eat?" To show she'd keep up her end of the deal, she shoved a carrot into her mouth.

"Level two security means that people from the government are here."

There was no hint of worry in his voice, but she didn't expect there to be one. That didn't mean she missed the tight lines around his eyes. Her nerves stood on end with that information. "Is that normal?"

He looked like he wasn't going to answer for a minute. He shoved his hands in his pockets and leaned against the wall. "No, not really."

"Do you think they know about me?"

"I don't know how that'd be possible. Unless someone from here relayed the information without us knowing. I can't think of anyone who would've done that." His eyes said he believed his words. "They're probably doing a random inspection. We haven't had one in years. Their current president is lazy. You're safe in here. Don't worry. I'd never let anything happen to you."

"I know you wouldn't. You and Arrow, do you have any other jobs but me?"

He smiled at her. "Do you mean have we just been waiting for you this whole time?"

She looked down at her tray and grabbed a slice of cucumber. "Yeah, I guess that's what I mean. I've asked Arrow about it a few times, and she just kept telling me that I'd find out everything as I needed to know. But it seems we have some time to kill now."

He took a seat next to her and helped himself to a few of the granola pieces. "Kaelyn, the whole world has been waiting for you and the other three. But no, you weren't our sole purpose up until now. We've always studied you, prepared for you, but that hasn't been the only thing to take up our daily activities. Arrow and I oversee all patrol watches and outposts. We need to stay on top of the happenings within the colonies to better protect them. It's also to serve as a security blanket of sorts for our people when the government comes around to inspect their dwellings. They're allowed to inspect and investigate whatever they want, and we're there to make sure nothing gets out of hand and that our people aren't seized or hurt. We are also charged with the training regime of all Level Ones. So, don't worry. We stay busy."

She felt her face flush. "Of course you stay busy. God, I didn't mean to sound so arrogant."

He was still smiling at her. He was an incredibly handsome man. His eyes were warm, like melted chocolate. His skin was smooth and dark, and he seemed to have a perfect jawline, which bunched with each chomp of the granola.

"Do the Guardians date?" she blurted out.

His eyes got wide with amusement. "We have to procreate." He paused for a moment, allowing her to feel the full burn of her embarrassment. "I don't date. I'm married."

Kaelyn realized as the conversation continued that she'd been thinking so much about the state of the world as a whole and her own rehabilitation, she'd barely considered what the current social construct had developed into. "Oh? Is she or he a Guardian? I don't want to assume anything."

"Her name is Eleanor, and no, she isn't a Guardian. She's a teacher down at the facility we went to earlier. I hope you can meet her."

"Me too. I'd like that." She paused for a moment before continuing. "During my time, marriage equality was still relatively new and the LGBTQ community was still struggling for acceptance."

"You want to know if the struggle remains."

"I'm a little scared to know, but yes." She took a deep breath and sat up straighter.

He grabbed her last carrot from the tray and popped it into his mouth. "People here, in the Resistance, are free to be whoever they want to be. There's too much going on and life can be too hard for that to matter. I never really understood why it did in your world. But that's here. In Eden, it's different. People with different sexual orientations have two options there—be banished beyond the wall or death."

She almost choked. "That's insane. Why do they put up with that?"

"Because they don't have any other choice."

She could feel her blood burning. Anger surged through her veins for people she'd never met and for those who were perishing as she spoke. "What about race relations?" She waited for the next wash of anger, already anticipating the answer.

He rubbed his hand across his face, as if he could wipe the injustice away. "The first plan was to rid Eden of anyone who wasn't white. They tried and there aren't many people of color remaining there. They discovered it would never completely work because so many ethnicities had been mixed together over the years, and they needed numbers. So, instead, wealth was redistributed. Families with the purest Caucasian ancestry were given the largest portions, and it was divided up from there. Now, anyone who isn't white works in the servant class."

She stood, needing to move, and she knew the anger coursing through her was palpable. These people were tyrants. They'd taken the country back hundreds of years to a time where their comfort and well-being was paramount to anyone and anything else. She didn't just want this regime removed from power; she wanted them tossed out on their asses.

CHAPTER TEN

A rrow listened to her parents talk back and forth about the options that were now available. She'd already asked CAM to notify Valor that the threat was over and to report to the control center. The plans were changing, and Arrow wasn't comfortable with any of it. They needed time to make sure Kaelyn was adjusted, that she understood the gravity of the world she'd just woken up in and could understand everything that was at stake.

The door slid open and CAM announced Kaelyn and Valor. Kaelyn took a seat next to Arrow, a look of concern and a bit of anger etched around her mouth, causing a frown. Her eyes read of questions, but before she had a chance to see what they were, her mother spoke.

"The situation has changed. We no longer have three weeks to initiate the Phoenix Project. President MacLeod wants the Resistance to rejoin the people of Eden. It wasn't so much a request as it was an ultimatum. Either we come to Eden or he will destroy all of the colonies." Her mother paused, waiting for Kaelyn to respond.

Kaelyn took a deep breath and leaned back in her seat. "What's the plan?"

Her father took a step forward and spoke. "We told him we would have to convene the council. Obviously, we don't intend to comply, but it bought us a few weeks. That should be enough time to get the four Phoenixes to Eden. The rest of the plan stays as it is; the timeline is just being moved up. You'll have to make some changes along the way, depending on how long we can keep the government in the dark. The president will accompany the three of you on your trip."

This was the first Arrow had heard this part of the plan. "What? No! You need to be here! The people need you to lead them."

Her mother took a seat next to her and put a hand on her back. "No, I need to go with you. The fourth entry point was supposed to be covered by the Phoenix Four headquarters, but that general is a man, and if he's missing, they'll know. I'm the only other person with all the information. It has to be me."

"There has to be someone else." Arrow rubbed the back of her neck.

Arrow didn't like the idea of her mother being out of the protective barriers of the compound. It would be hard enough to protect Kaelyn, but security for her mother too would be stretching them thin. Someone would be left vulnerable.

Her mom put her hand on her cheek. "Honey, you forget that before I was president, I was a general. I'll be fine. Plus, it's better to let the two soldiers they sent believe that your father is in charge. We have a lot to accomplish, but none of it matters if we don't get to Eden with the final plan intact. We need to contact the other Phoenix locations and make sure everyone is on the same page. We'll have to be clear about our approach, spread out. We have to make it impossible for the Hand of God to fight us on several fronts. They're looking at us now, so time is of the essence."

Arrow thought of several arguments against her mother's proposal, but none of them would've mattered. The decision had been made. The information was squeezing her lungs. Breathing became more difficult, and her ears burned hot. "Yes, ma'am."

"Where are the soldiers, now?" Kaelyn asked.

"They never stay inside the compound. They're in their transport pod right outside the main barrier. They'll be watching," her father said.

Arrow stood and turned to Valor. This trip would be the hardest on him. Having to leave his wife for an undisclosed amount of time wouldn't be easy. "Go home. Spend some time with Eleanor. We'll leave at zero-six hundred. Leave your bag in my compartment and I'll take it to the transport."

He only looked like he was going to disagree for a moment. Then he stood, saluted, and headed out to do exactly as she'd asked. She made a silent promise to Eleanor, a woman she'd known her whole life, to bring Valor back home safely.

She looked at her parents next. "I'll get everything ready. I'll have CAM check one of the transports out, and the destination will be listed for a meeting with the other colonies. Even if they check, they'll think nothing of Valor and me escorting Mom to the meeting."

"Yes, that's a good plan." Her father looked at her mother and gave her a small smile.

"I'll help you get ready," Kaelyn said.

She could have protested because there wasn't anything she needed to do that would require Kaelyn's assistance. But the thought of having her nearby brought an unexpected jolt of pleasure.

"Okay, thanks." Arrow tried not to sound too excited about the prospect.

Arrow looked at her parents. She thought briefly of hugging her father, but he made no motion forward. So she saluted him instead. "Mom, I'll see you in the morning."

Her father spoke when she and Kaelyn were almost out the door. "Don't forget your training, Major."

She knew what he meant. He wanted her to remember him and what he would do in any given situation. And she would; she was counting on it. Their training would be the only thing to protect them and help them complete the mission. They'd be the only thing standing in the way of her people being forced into servitude inside Eden. It didn't matter the cost; she would see this mission through.

The door opened directly into the lift. Arrow pushed the number on the screen that would take them down to the gear lockers. She glanced over and noticed that Kaelyn's posture had slumped. "Everything is going to be okay."

"It has to be." She chewed on the cuticle of her pointer finger, a trait that Arrow had never read about.

"You're going to have to trust us." She was still watching her mouth, amazed that there was more to discover about Kaelyn. Even something as simple as a nervous habit, and she'd believed she knew everything.

Kaelyn put her hand down. "I don't know why, but I do."

Arrow smiled. "I just have one of those faces."

Kaelyn's eyes were moving back and forth, searching Arrow's expression. Her face was damp with perspiration, and a few strands of hair clung to her cheek.

Arrow almost reached to push them away and then remembered her place when Kaelyn spoke. "You do."

"I do what?" Arrow's last few moments blurred together, and she couldn't recall the last words that had left their lips.

"Have a trustworthy face." Her smile was tired but genuine.

Luckily, the lift slowed and the door slid open before Arrow had to come up with a response. "CAM, please check out Transport Vehicle One, length of time to be determined."

"Would you like me to plot your course for your trip, Major Steele?"

"No, CAM. In fact, I want you to disable the tracking protocol on the vehicle."

"Major, that isn't advised. If there's an issue, we'll need to locate you."

There was no question it was a risk. But being tracked by the bad guys would be worse. "I understand the risks. Please disable it."

"Yes, Major."

"CAM, open the weapons vault."

The wall in front of them dissolved, and all the weapons the Resistance had managed to hoard, build, and smuggle over the years appeared.

"Do you know how to use any of these?" she asked over her shoulder.

Kaelyn stepped up beside her. "I can use a handgun and a rifle, but I don't know what the rest of these are." She ran her hand over the tops of stun weaponry.

"They're designed to stun instead of kill. We won't be needing those."

Kaelyn looked as if she were going to argue with her and then changed her mind.

"Take what you know how to use. There are a few holsters over on the back rack."

Arrow loaded several different weapons into the vehicle. She also brought a few special grade weapons, just in case. The small bombs she brought would do maximum damage, and she had no intention of using them unless there were no other options.

She was taking a few of the high-power binoculars off the rack when she heard a voice from behind her. "Is there anything I can help you with, Major?"

Arrow turned around to find Max Westcott, the armory attendant, standing in the doorway. "No, Corporal. Thank you."

"That's a lot of firepower," Max said.

Kaelyn came around the corner, presumably to see who had joined them. When he saw her, he looked shocked.

"Phoenix One. I wasn't sure I'd have the opportunity to meet you." Max's faced flushed with excitement.

Kaelyn stuck her hand out. "Hi, I'm Kaelyn Trapp."

He didn't take her hand, but instead saluted her. "Corporal Max Westcott, Guardian Class, Level One."

She crossed her arms and smiled at him. It wasn't condescending; it was genuine. "That's not necessary. It's nice to meet you."

The color in his face started to come back, and he looked back and forth between Arrow and Kaelyn. "What can I do to help?"

Arrow didn't want any more people to know about this than necessary. She'd come down here now because she didn't think anyone would be here. The normal shift should have ended thirty minutes ago.

"Corporal, this is going to sound strange, but I need you to forget seeing us here, entirely. You know the soldiers are here, and General Steele will be briefing all of you tomorrow about why."

"Yes, ma'am. I know the protocol. We don't speak about the Phoenix Project with anyone outside the Resistance." He recited familiar orders that were spoon-fed to them from birth.

"I wasn't going to check any of these weapons out. I trust that's okay with you."

"Of course, Major. It'll be as if you were never here. But at least I won't have to run around figuring out who stole weapons, either."

It's what she wanted to hear, but the words rang strangely in her ears. *As if you were never here.*

She spoke again before she had the chance to dwell on why that made her uncomfortable. "Thank you, Corporal."

He looked like he wanted to ask something else, and Arrow nodded to him.

"May I ask you something, ma'am?" He was looking at Kaelyn.

"Yes, of course," Kaelyn said and took a step closer.

"When you're put into your rightful place as president, may I serve on your guard?"

Kaelyn looked at him thoughtfully. "How old are you?"

"Sixteen, ma'am." He stood up a little straighter.

"Sixteen? Don't you want something else? Wouldn't you like to go to school?"

He looked almost offended by the question. "This is who I am, ma'am. It's what I was born to do. There's nothing else."

Kaelyn's eyes looked sad. "Let's talk when all this is over."

His smile was contagious. "Thank you, ma'am." He saluted Arrow and left.

Arrow was still smiling at his retreating figure when Kaelyn put a hand on her arm. The touch stopped any other thought she was having. Her fingers on her sleeve seemed to burn through her shirt. She wanted to look down, to see if Kaelyn was holding something in her hand to make this possible, but she didn't. She knew there was nothing to see. Kaelyn was the heat.

"He's so young," Kaelyn said.

Arrow didn't say anything. The grip had now turned to a light touch, but it was still there, tempting her. She knew Kaelyn was waiting for an answer; she wanted Arrow to explain to her why a man that young would want to devote his life to a person he hadn't met until just now. She was looking for a glimpse into their world, a world that she was being thrust into. One they were all looking at her to lead. Arrow had all the right answers; she knew them by heart because she felt them too. Loyalty, devotion, honor—these traits weren't just taglines for the Guardian class; they tried to emulate these ideals by how they lived their lives, every day.

"We should get you out of here. Enough people have already seen you. I know no one will say anything to the soldiers, but it will be safer, all the same." Arrow put the last of the weapons inside the vehicle. "CAM, program Transport Vehicle One to leave tomorrow morning at zero-seven hundred hours to go to the Northern Colony. Set speed to take four days. Once it arrives, send a message back to the control center stating its arrival. It should return three days later, same travel time." It would serve as a decoy, one that would only take a week to uncover, but it would buy them a bit of time.

"Will there be any passengers, Major?"

"No, this will be an unattended vehicle, but I want the passenger list to read Major Steele, General Steele, and Captain Markinson."

"It's in the system, Major."

Kaelyn had a slight smile on her face. Her hands were in her pockets and her auburn hair fell into her eyes. "You're pretty sneaky."

"Just covering all our bases." They walked back over to the lift, and Arrow pushed the level of her compartment. "You can stay in my room tonight, if you want. We had one ready for you, but you shouldn't be walking around unattended."

Arrow couldn't be sure, but she thought she saw a light blush cover Kaelyn's cheek. "Okay, if you think that's best."

CHAPTER ELEVEN

Kaelyn followed Arrow down the hallway, past dozens of doors with the names of different military personnel on each side. She was doing her best not to allow this silly crush she seemed to have formed on Arrow get the best of her. She'd told herself a hundred times that it was because Arrow was there when she'd woken up, because she'd spent the most time with her, and because she was really the only woman in her relative age group she'd encountered.

Of course, she was intentionally keeping off the list the fact that Arrow was strong, kind, determined, and androgynously beautiful. When Kaelyn spoke to her, she had her full attention. Her eyes held compassion and warmth, along with passion and fury. None of this changed the fact that Arrow was with her because she had to be; Kaelyn was her assignment.

She was caught up in thought and hadn't realized the door to her home for the night slid open. She stepped inside. The room had no decoration, no way to indicate that anyone lived here, much less Arrow. There were no pictures on the walls; it was the same drab gray the hallway had been. There were several books on a desk in the corner and a closet with a full-length mirror. A set of bunk beds sat against the opposite wall.

Arrow took off her jacket and hung it up in the closet. Then she turned, putting her hands in her back pockets and shrugged. "Not what you were expecting?"

Kaelyn got the impression that her face might have given away her feelings about the room. "Do you live here full-time? I can't believe I never asked you that before."

"Sure do, since I was sixteen and moved from my parents' compartment."

"Don't you have any personal items?"

She pulled open the closet door and pointed. "My clothes are in here. What else would I need?"

Kaelyn sat on the bottom bunk. "I don't know, pictures, novels, maybe some art."

Arrow's face lit up and she pulled one of the books from her desk. "Here, this belongs to you. I have a whole box of your things. I've looked at them over the years, trying to understand your world."

Kaelyn took it from her and turned it over. It was a book that detailed some special pieces of art that hung in the Louvre from its inception. A flood of memories from her old life came to the front of her mind. Beautiful glimpses of a world that no longer existed, only kept alive now in her memories and in books like this one. "Did you look through it?"

"Several times. I think I could memorize every word in there."

"What did you think?" She wasn't sure why, but this answer would be an important one.

Arrow was untying her boots when Kaelyn asked the question. She paused, seeming to give her answer a great amount of consideration. Kaelyn smiled at Arrow's meticulous behavior.

"I hope at least a fraction of all that art has been preserved. I'm not sure what the current state of the world is beyond the North American wall, but it would be an absolute travesty if these pieces were only ever seen in books."

Kaelyn skimmed the pages, briefly remembering the summer she'd spent overseas during college. "Yes, it would be. What else do you have?" The idea there might be more links to her past made her heart speed up, the possibility creating a warm bubble in her chest.

Arrow pulled a container out of her closet and slid it in front of Kaelyn. "These are all things your father asked us to keep for you. I'm sorry if it's weird that we've all looked through them. I didn't even consider until right now that it would be a violation of your privacy."

Kaelyn hadn't really considered that either. Had this been seventy years ago, she would've. People fingering her belongings, searching for meanings, learning intimate details. But now, in this moment, it didn't bother her in the least, though it was strange to feel like an archeology project. "That's okay. I understand." She unclasped the sides of the metal container and opened the top.

She fell into a tunnel that led to her past. There were pictures of her with friends, graduations, her parents, even her dog. Dozens of memories that had been sealed away, waiting for her to awaken and briefly transport her back to a time she could never see again and people she couldn't touch. Before she'd agreed to participate in the Phoenix Project, she'd considered the loss of all these integral parts of her life. At the time, they seemed to be a part of the abstract, something that would happen but not something she could touch or feel. Now, here, with the proof in her hands, the reality of it all stuck in her throat, causing tears to well.

She pulled out her old laptop and wiped away the film of age and wear covering the old case. She traced the Duke sticker that still clung to the top. The colors were fading and the edges were peeling up, a representation of a life that she'd never recapture. She pulled open the screen and pushed the power button. Unsurprisingly, the screen did nothing, not even a flicker. "I don't suppose you have a plug in here?"

Arrow's brows came together. "A plug?"

Kaelyn picked up the charger and held it in front of her. "You know, a power source. So I can turn my computer on."

Arrow smiled and was obviously trying to suppress a laugh. "I know what a plug is. Remember, we've had years to look at this stuff. We even came up with an adapter for you." Now she was laughing. "You should have seen the look on your face."

She walked over to her desk and pulled a small box out of the drawer. She handed it to her. "Here, this will work."

"Has anyone ever told you that you're hilarious?"

"All the time." She beamed.

"Yeah, well, they were lying."

"Honestly though, I'm not sure if it will work. We never opened your computer. There were explicit instructions from your father that this was the one thing that was to remain private." She sat in the chair, leaning forward on her knees.

Kaelyn allowed herself a moment to watch the muscles in her forearms twitch with the movements. It might have been a moment too long, since when she looked back up at Arrow's face, there was a small smile.

She pulled her focus away and plugged the adapter into the AC jack unit. "What powers the unit?" The computer gave a low humming sound, indicating that it was turning on. She felt a flare of hope.

Arrow was taking off her shoes. "That source should last days, but if it runs out, it just needs to be in the sun for about an hour or so to recharge."

Kaelyn waited as the familiar sounds came from the speakers. "Solar power has come a long way."

"It would've happened in your lifetime too, if it hadn't been for big oil." She pulled her black shirt from her pants and started walking toward the bathroom.

Kaelyn forced herself not to think about Arrow taking the rest of her clothes off. She thought of baseball. *Do they still play baseball?* She started listing the presidents in her head and realized she didn't know exactly who came after her father. The distraction worked because she didn't realize Arrow had said anything until her voice grew louder.

"I'm going to take a shower."

"Okay."

"Okay." Arrow leaned in the doorway, looking at her speculatively. "Everything okay?"

"Mmm-hmm." She nodded.

Arrow disappeared into the bathroom and Kaelyn heard the shower. *Jesus Christ, get it together.* She looked down at her computer screen. A picture of a dog with a blinking cursor asked for her password. She closed her eyes trying to remember her password. *Should have written this down somewhere.* She closed her eyes and tried to transport herself back in time, wanting to remember the last time her fingers had touched the keys. She tried her dog's name first, *Leo.* The computer bounced back a message saying it was wrong. She tried her best friend's name, still wrong. She slid her hand over one of the books in the container, typed in "Suffragette" and waited. Her desktop came into focus a few moments later. Photos, books, music, letters to herself, were all listed on the desktop. Her entire digital life was back in front of her. The instant jolt of familiarity and comfort ran through her and it felt like reconnecting with an old friend. She rummaged through the box for her headphones and quickly hooked them up.

Music. In relative terms, it wasn't all that long ago she had listened to music; the suspended state saw to that. But as she listened to the voices come through her headphones, it felt like it had been forever. Next, she opened her favorite book of poems written by Margaret Atwood, *The Circle Game*. She clicked through the pages, skimming each of the works.

She was almost through the book when the foot of the bed shifted. She lowered the screen of the computer and saw Arrow on the edge. She was now in black sweatpants and a black tank top, and her dark short hair was wet. She was beautiful. It could've been the music, possibly the poems, or the way the light captured half her face, but she couldn't keep from touching her. She put her fingertips to the tattoo on Arrow's arm. Arrow didn't move. Kaelyn felt her eyes on her, watching her face as Kaelyn ran her fingertips over the eagle holding an olive branch in one talon and arrows in the other, the seal of the president. The Latin words along the bottom weren't anything she recognized, *Tutor Fidem.* She looked at Arrow.

"It means guardian of the promise. It's the emblem for the Guardian class." Her voice was quiet, almost a whisper.

She leaned closer, wanting to see it better and drawn to Arrow's momentary vulnerability. "That's a lot to take on, a promise for everyone. Even those you don't know."

"They need it the most."

Her face had gotten closer to hers now. She could feel her breath on her cheek, and it was intoxicating. She watched as her jaw tightened and loosened, signaling that she was feeling something as well. Kaelyn brought her mouth closer to Arrow's chin. She could smell her skin; it was clean from the shower, hints of lavender and vanilla. There were still droplets of water sliding down her neck and onto her chest. "You can't protect everyone."

Arrow turned her face, bringing her lips even closer to Kaelyn's. She was sure she was going to kiss her. She could feel the moment in the air. She could sense Arrow's hesitation, but her resolve was slipping. The heat from her skin prickled against Kaelyn's cheek.

"Captain Markinson is here, Major." CAM's voice seemed to grab Arrow by the back of the shirt and pull her straight up off the bed. Arrow was standing, face flushed, and looking around the room as if she could find a place to hide the moment that had just passed between them.

❖

Arrow had a brief moment of not knowing whether to thank or hit Valor for coming into her compartment. She moved away from Kaelyn automatically, feeling as if she'd just been caught doing something illicit. Valor, for his part, didn't seem to notice he had interrupted anything.

He took his hat off and ran his hand over his bare head. "I just wanted to make sure you two were ready."

Kaelyn leaned back against the wall. Her face was still flushed, and she seemed perturbed. "Don't you guys have phones?"

Arrow smiled, keeping her gaze on her feet.

Valor cocked his head, looking confused. "I'm sorry. Were you two ready for bed?"

Arrow decided to change the subject and waved her hand in front of the back section of the wall so a screen appeared. She typed a few words into the translucent keyboard, and all the itineraries for the next day appeared. She pointed to the two that were of importance. "Everything is covered. We're heading out and so is another transport just in case the soldiers request to see any records."

Valor shook his head. "That won't hold up for more than a couple of days, a week at the most. It will only take them a few calls to figure out something is happening. I'm sure they sent more soldiers to the other colonies."

Arrow waved her hand in front of the screen and it disappeared. "I know. But it will buy us some time. I'm actually banking on them figuring out what's happening. We just need a head start."

Valor scratched his chin. "You want them to sound the alarm. That way, everyone will know the Phoenix Project is really happening."

Arrow smiled. "Exactly. It's time to make some noise. It wasn't part of the original plan, but they're forcing our hands now. If we can start to stir up the people of Eden a little early, that might be in our favor."

"You two would've made great spies in my time," Kaelyn said.

"Thanks," they said in unison, and then smiled at each other.

Valor grabbed Arrow by the arms and stared at her for a long moment. "We've got this."

She returned the motion. "Without a doubt."

Valor gave Kaelyn a quick smile before he walked out of the room and the door slid shut behind him. Arrow looked over at Kaelyn, who was smiling at her. "What?"

Kaelyn pulled her knees up to her chest and leaned forward, resting her chin on her knees. "Do you really think everything is going to work out?"

Arrow sat on the bed next to her. "Yeah, I do. It has to. There's no other outcome that's acceptable for these people."

"What will happen if it doesn't? I know what will happen to us, but what will happen to them?"

Arrow looked at Kaelyn's eyes. They were sincere and concerned. Her heart hitched at the vulnerability that was shining in the flecks of green. "If we fail, they'll become indentured servants, and getting out from under enforced servitude…I don't need to tell you how hard that would be. The colonies will be burned to the ground and millions will die."

Kaelyn took a deep breath. "You don't sugarcoat anything, do you?"

"There's no point. You're Phoenix One, and the truth is what I'm sworn to give you."

"No matter what?" She had her cheek resting on her knee now.

Arrow wasn't sure where this was going, but she was compelled to find out. "No matter what."

"Before Valor came in, did something happen between us?"

The easy answer was denial. But her forwardness caught Arrow off guard. She'd only had two romantic encounters with women, and neither happened with straightforward questions. Both had ended the way they had started, without much fanfare or emotion. But neither of those women had looked at Arrow the way Kaelyn was now.

"Yes, it did." The truth jumped from her somewhere inside her.

Kaelyn smiled and moved her hand like she was going to touch Arrow's face.

"But that doesn't mean anything can happen," Arrow said.

Kaelyn put her hand back down. She looked disappointed and hurt. "Because I'm the Phoenix?"

"That, and we can never be together. It'd be nothing but a distraction for us both. You're going to be president, and I'm, well, I'm just a Guardian."

"Your mother is the president and your father is a Guardian."

Arrow grabbed the sides of the top bunk and pushed herself up onto it. "Yes, but my mother was just holding your place, as the Project outline states. Our people have read about your family their whole lives. Your name is easy to rally behind. Relative to the Kennedys of your time. This is your destiny and mine is to get you there. Once I've done that, I'll come back here and I'll be assigned a new mission, I assume, from Phoenix Two, although that hasn't really been discussed yet."

Kaelyn walked toward the bathroom. "Don't you think I deserve a say in my own destiny?"

Arrow wanted to tell her that she should have a say-so, but that wasn't true. "Choice isn't an option in this world. We do what we must. You're too important."

"And you're too scared." Kaelyn went into the bathroom.

Arrow wanted to disagree. She'd been called several things in her life, but scared was never one of them. She heard the shower turn on and decided that it was probably better if she let the conversation end there. She'd only make things worse, and she wasn't wrong. Kaelyn was meant for greater things than her. She would see that the more time they spent together and the more she found out about the world she was now living in. Arrow would just be a blip on her radar, the way it should be. Even thinking it made her uneasy. She barely knew Kaelyn; she shouldn't be having any of these feelings. But even as she thought it, she knew it wasn't true. She'd spent her whole life reading about and studying Kaelyn Trapp. The fact that she also happened to be charming and funny was icing on the cake she didn't need. For the first time in her life, she closed her eyes and wished she could be someone else.

Chapter Twelve

Arrow watched as the minutes ticked off the clock on her wall. She had fallen in and out of sleep all night. Each time she woke, she was keenly aware of Kaelyn only a few feet away. Her breathing was slow, methodic, and comforting in a way Arrow hadn't expected. Now, with only a few minutes from needing to wake, her heart started to beat faster.

She got up and carefully put away her blanket and pillow, doing her best not to make a sound. Her eyes had adjusted to the lack of light hours ago, and she was able to make do with the glow from the lighted numbers of the clock on her wall. She pulled her uniform on quietly and was lacing up her boots when she heard Kaelyn begin to stir.

"How do you turn on the lights?" Kaelyn's voice was gravelly with sleep.

A moment later, the lights turned on in the compartment. "Good morning, Kaelyn," CAM said.

Kaelyn sat up and rubbed her face. "I don't know if I'll ever get used to that."

Arrow pulled on her hat and looked at herself in the mirror. "It's a rather handy mechanism, actually."

Kaelyn's feet hit the floor and she stretched. Her shirt came up just enough to show her stomach, and Arrow forced herself to look away.

"What time did you get up?"

She put her pack on the bed and checked it one last time for any provisions she might need if they were forced to leave the transport. "Just a few minutes ago. We have ten minutes to get down there. I put several uniforms together for you. They're in the pack over there. You'll need to look like one of us until we can get to Eden."

Kaelyn stood next to her and put a hand on her arm.

Arrow felt that tingling sensation she was beginning to associate with Kaelyn wash over her body.

"I'm sorry about last night. You're right about what you said. We both have enormous tasks in front of us, and a distraction, even a good one, isn't what we need."

Arrow felt her body tense at the statement. As true as it was, it still made her sad. But Phoenix was bigger than the two of them, and it deserved their undivided attention. She figured with time, the burning desire she felt in her stomach would dissipate. She wanted to say something meaningful, thoughtful, a way to express her feelings without the promise of a tomorrow. But all she was able to do was nod her agreement.

Kaelyn went into the bathroom and Arrow busied herself with straightening up her room. She wasn't sure when she would be back, but she needed to know that things would be in order upon her return. Her return without Kaelyn.

After a few minutes, Kaelyn emerged from the bathroom and put a few of the items from her storage box into her pack. "Will you send me the rest later?"

"Of course." Arrow already knew she'd use any reason to see Kaelyn after they had parted ways. She'd bring the items in person if she could.

Kaelyn pulled the pack onto her back, and Arrow took a minute to look her over. She could pass for a Guardian now. Her uniform made her indistinguishable from her colleagues, and no one would think twice about her being in the transport with the rest of them, which was the important part. No one outside of the Resistance would know what the tattoo on her wrist meant, and if asked, they'd deal with it then.

"You ready?" Arrow intended it to be more of a statement rather than a question.

"As I'll ever be," Kaelyn said.

Kaelyn's body language betrayed her words. She looked nervous as she shifted her weight back and forth and played with the straps on her pack. Arrow wanted to ease the uncertainty that seemed to be coursing through her. She put her hands on her shoulders. Kaelyn's cheeks flushed pink, and she took a deep breath.

"I'm going to get you there, I promise." Arrow rubbed the sides of Kaelyn's arms.

"Have you ever felt completely out of place? Like you're living someone else's life?"

Arrow's stomach turned. Kaelyn had been thrust into this world, she hadn't had enough time to adjust, and now she was feeling the weight of it all, crushing down on her. "I can't imagine how difficult this must be for you. You're in a new place, new people, there isn't anything you recognize, and now you have to take on a seemingly insurmountable task."

"This might be the nerves talking, but I feel like I recognize you. I know that sounds bananas, but I just can't shake the feeling. I feel better with you around." She looked straight into her eyes.

Arrow swallowed and fought the growing urge to be as physically close to her as possible. She had to tamp it down before it spiraled out of control. She allowed herself to pull Kaelyn close to her. She hugged her for a few moments, allowing her body the warm sensation Kaelyn provided with her mere proximity. "I know. It doesn't make any sense. I've talked to you for as long as I can remember. I'd sit beside your tube for hours, trying to keep you up to date on everything that was happening. I knew you couldn't hear me, but it made me feel better."

Kaelyn's grip around her back tightened. She could feel her breathing into her shirt, and the soft, slow movement was making Arrow's head spin. She forced herself to pull away from Kaelyn's embrace.

"Thank you," Kaelyn whispered.

❖

Several minutes later, in what seemed like a blur, Kaelyn found herself in the back seat of a transport next to Macy Steele. Valor was in the driver's seat and Arrow sat next to him. Everyone was busy typing things into a variety of devices. She gave herself a moment to pretend Arrow's arms were still around her. She knew as it was happening that she was etching those seconds into her mind. A piece she'd hold on to as long as her memory would allow. The strength in Arrow's arms, the way she seemed to wrap her in a barrier of protection from everything they were about to face. The unknowns, the questions, the unwritten future, seemed to fade away in the circle of calm Arrow provided. Kaelyn would remain thankful to her for those few precious moments.

The vehicle hummed to life and started to move forward. Macy handed her a flat metal plate. She pushed a blue button, and a holographic screen appeared. Kaelyn wasn't sure what to make of all the technological advancements, but she was still awestruck when they were put in front of her. The Guardian emblem hovered above the plate, slowly spinning clockwise. She put her fingers through it, needing to see if it was as solid as it looked. When she did, she felt the smallest buzz on her fingertips as they went through the emblem and out the other side.

Macy gave her a set of headphones and smiled. "CAM put together some information for you. You'll still have questions, but it will help get you up to speed."

"Up to speed with what?" asked Kaelyn.

"Everything."

Everything. The prospect was overwhelming but necessary. She placed the buds in her ears, and Macy pushed a different button. Images appeared in front of her. The narrator was CAM, and she couldn't help but marvel at the calmness her voice inspired. It was rather soothing as the history she'd missed started to unfold in front of her.

Kaelyn was horrified and angry at what she was seeing. MacLeod had plainly and openly convinced an entire portion of the population that he was their only source of protection, that he alone could save them from what would be their inevitable demise. He took all the beautiful things about the country and painted them with an evil brush. Immigration was a threat, the press was a threat, fellow citizens were considered threats. He tossed out phrases like liberal cancer and railed against long respected policies and ethics. Even the worst-case scenarios she'd once envisioned had never included the atrocity of seeing democracy so clearly being torn down, while so many citizens stood by and watched it happen.

She felt the tears begin to roll down her cheeks as she watched people from the LGBTQ community marched into internment camps, and trans people stoned in their neighborhoods. Black churches were burned to the ground and protestors shot in the streets. Images of people of color starving and forced out of their makeshift shelters at gunpoint were nauseating.

"Pull over." Kaelyn managed between deep breaths. She was reaching for a handle, but there wasn't one. "Seriously, pull over, now."

The vehicle came to a halt, and the door started to lift open. Kaelyn unclasped her seat belt and fell from the car. As soon as the dirt hit her knees, she began to vomit. She could feel the sweat drip from her neck, and her vision blurred. There were so many emotions demanding to be let out of her all at once, she couldn't contain them.

Footsteps approached as she felt her body force out more liquid, trying to purge itself of all the injustice and pain she'd just witnessed. She was crying and coughing at the same time, her body incapable of dealing with the truth of the world.

"Kaelyn?"

She felt Arrow's hand on her back. It moved in a deliberate pattern, an attempt to console her. She grabbed as much dirt as her hands would allow, balling her fists and squeezing the earth as hard as she could. She wanted to scream, to cry. She wanted to go back in time and stop this evil with a bullet to MacLeod's head.

"It's just so horrible." Kaelyn sobbed, letting out the devastation of what she'd seen.

Arrow knelt next to her. She had an arm around her and was still rubbing her arm. "We can set things right."

Kaelyn turned her head into Arrow's shoulder. "I should've stayed. I could've done more."

Arrow spoke against the side of her head. "You couldn't have stopped any of what happened. The country caught a disease. A disease that almost wiped it out completely. But we're still here and we're still fighting."

"Fighting? You've been hiding for an entire generation!" She wasn't angry at Arrow, but she couldn't stop herself from taking it out on her, either.

"I know it must seem like that to you. But an illness like that, there was no easy solution. It's almost like the country needed to be completely broken in order to heal," Arrow said.

"What if it never heals?" She knew Arrow couldn't answer the question with any kind of certainty, but she wanted her reassurance all the same.

"Breaks never heal completely. You'll always feel them a little. They're always there. But the reminder serves a purpose too. It makes you a little more cautious, a little more delicate. It reminds you what caused the wound, and not to do that thing again." Her voice was so calm and confident. "As a historian, you know exactly what I mean."

Kaelyn wanted to crawl into her arms and just stay there until this feeling passed. But there was no time for that now.

Kaelyn stood, her arm still on Arrow's shoulder. "Okay."

Arrow led her back to the transport and watched as she got back in her seat. She looked at Macy when she was situated. "I'm sorry."

Macy patted her knee. "If you'd had any other reaction, I'd wonder if you were the right person for the job."

She wanted to smile at her comment, but she didn't have it in her. Instead, she put the buds back in her ears and continued to watch the nightmare she'd slept through play out in front of her in a series of images.

CHAPTER THIRTEEN

W hat do you mean a small group of them left?" Adon could feel his blood pressure rising with each word.

"Just what we said, sir. A few of the Guardians went to discuss the premise of coming back to Eden with one of the other colonies." Commander whatever-his-name-was fidgeted. His eyes were darting back and forth, and he looked nervous.

Adon leaned forward on the desk. He wanted to reach into the hologram projection and squeeze the moron's neck. He should have never sent these incompetent idiots to the colonies. He should've sent his daughter, like he'd originally wanted.

Nora put her hand on his arm, and he relaxed slightly. "We have another soldier en route to the other colony. He'll cut them off there. Have you spoken with their leader?"

The commander nodded. "Yes, and we ran a check on the Computer Analysis Monitoring System. Everything seems to be on the up-and-up."

Adon ended the call without saying another word. He didn't want to hear any more of his incompetent drivel. "Doesn't make any sense."

Nora sat back in her chair and crossed her legs. "I agree. They could've easily made a transmission call. But maybe we're giving them too much credit. They've been playing soldier for decades with those Guardians, with no real enemy to fight. Maybe they feel more important if they have this kind of meeting face-to-face."

Adon appreciated the sentiment, but he didn't share her optimism. "They might not be well educated, but don't underestimate the Resistance. They've been fed the same lies for years. They have an enemy, and it's us."

"We've always left them alone, for the most part. We haven't given them a reason to be plotting our demise. You've been more than benevolent to let them continue to exist. I don't think they'll risk that."

Adon scratched at his beard, trying to allow her words to calm his suspicions. "You weren't around when your grandfather first came into power. Dorothy Trapp, Daniel Trapp's wife, was a manipulative and vengeful woman. She hated your grandfather for asking her to take her place in society. She fought him at every turn with her vile words and accusations. She went out of her way to embarrass him, to shame him, and dig up all the dirt she could after the pipe bomb exploded that killed her husband. She was a nasty woman. She spent years in those colonies, filling their heads with poison. I can only assume they hold her up as some kind of saint now, wanting to follow in her footsteps."

"You've told me, but she died years ago. Plus, women no longer hold any political power in the Resistance. And what man would dare to challenge or question you?"

He rubbed the small coin in his pocket. His father had given it to him when he pushed the Resistance out to the far ends of the country. He had eliminated their current monetary system and put a new one in its place. Each coin had a bust of his father's face on one side and a cross on the other.

"All the same, put a statement together telling Eden of our plans to bring in another working population. Everyone will be moving up the ladder, placing the Resistance at the bottom. That way, even if they're up to something, it will fall on deaf ears. People won't see them as anything but a stepping stone, a group of people to take over their daily responsibilities."

Nora was jotting down notes. She stopped when he was done speaking. She tapped the stylus against the tablet. "Should we ready the fighting force?"

"Not yet. That gives the impression that we have something to be afraid of, and they're just a bunch of misfits without a home." He paused and looked at the large map that was on the back wall of the room. "But I think we should triple the drone patrols out over the lost lands. Keep an eye on things."

She stood, pulling the tablet to her chest. "Yes, Daddy."

CHAPTER FOURTEEN

Arrow checked the time and was surprised it had only been eight hours. It felt like a lifetime. She'd only take her eyes off the specter monitor for fleeting moments when it was absolutely necessary. The specter was able to evaluate objects within a half-mile of their transport. It was capable of a much longer range, but dialing in to that intensity would send out a larger magnetic frequency, making them easier to locate.

The transport turned into a small village that at one time served as a suburb of Albuquerque, New Mexico. Valor changed the transport into manual drive and maneuvered along the back streets until they came to a small building. Arrow jumped out and pulled the old door open, allowing the transport to enter.

Kaelyn got out of the car and looked around. "What is this, an old mechanic's shop?"

Arrow slid the old locking mechanism into place and pulled on the door, making sure it was secure. "Yeah, we'll be safe here."

"So, you know these people?" Kaelyn asked, her brow furrowed as she looked around.

Arrow knew she'd just spent eight long hours watching some of the most horrific footage she'd ever been exposed to. It wasn't bloody, but it did show how the soul of her beloved nation had been stolen and crushed. Now, only pieces remained. Pieces they were trying to put back together.

A door opened, and a beautiful and familiar smile radiated from the doorway. She shuffled down the stairs and threw her arms around Arrow.

Arrow welcomed the embrace and kissed her cheek. "Hi, Ms. Darcy. How are you?"

She smacked Arrow's arm. "Stop calling me that. You make me feel about a hundred years old." She walked over to Valor next and pulled him down by the neck. "Nephew, I swear you get bigger every time I see you."

Valor beamed in her embrace. "You look great, Aunt Lily. I've missed you and I've been worried about you. How's your health?"

She put her hands on his cheeks, inspecting him. "You have far more important things to do than to worry about me."

She let him go and moved on to the next in line. "Madam President."

Her mother shook her head and stretched out her arms. "Don't you dare call *me* that, Lily. Thank you so much for having us. I hope we didn't put you in unnecessary danger."

She laughed. "At my age, I'm always looking for a little excitement."

Kaelyn stretched out her hand when Lily made it to her. "Nice to meet you Ms. Darcy, I'm—"

Lily cut her off. "Kaelyn Trapp, or Phoenix One. I know who you are, sweetheart." She looked at her thoughtfully. "You don't remember me, do you?"

Kaelyn studied her face. She looked like she was right at the tipping point of remembering, scouring her brain for a piece of information she knew was there, hiding.

"Oh, my God!" Kaelyn smiled and grabbed Lily, hugging her tightly. "You worked in the executive residence at the White House, for my parents."

"One of the greatest honors of my life, working for them. I was just a kid when you knew me, twenty-two years old and thinking I could change the world." She sighed. "Now, I'm old enough to be your great-grandmother. But you, you're still as beautiful as ever. Come on inside. You all must be starving."

Arrow was transfixed on Kaelyn as the anguish of the day slid from her expression as she talked to Lily. It'd been the right call to come here. Giving Kaelyn even the smallest piece of familiarity was the least she could do for her. She knew the risk had been worth it when Kaelyn walked by and squeezed her hand, smiling from ear to ear.

Arrow didn't know how many of those smiles would be left the closer they got to Eden, but she'd do anything to see them as often as possible.

❖

Kaelyn stepped into the small house that was attached to the old mechanic's shop. The walls were bare, which wasn't what she expected. There was a simple brown couch in the living room and a small kitchen table sitting next to it. She didn't understand how Lily, who was clearly full of life, didn't allow that to be reflected in her home. It was one thing for it to be that way in the military area, but here that seemed so…sad.

Lily must have seen her looking because she spoke to her from the kitchen. "We can't keep any personal effects in plain view. The colonies get randomly inspected by the soldiers, and it's just not worth the hassle."

"I can't believe they do that." Kaelyn grew angry every time she was reminded of these intrusions.

Lily washed some lettuce, put it on a cutting board, and began to chop. "We suffer much less here than in some of the other colonies. We aren't close to any of the headquarters, so we go through random inspections and occasional harassment, but it isn't as frequent as the colonies close to headquarters. Hand of God soldiers sometimes come out here and make threats or try to push people around, but it's nothing we can't handle. I'm grateful for what I have."

Macy took the carrots from the bowl and started to chop as well. Lily tried to stop her. "Madam President, you don't have to do that."

"Lily, please call me Macy. And I prefer to help." She smiled at her and continued to chop.

Kaelyn was grateful to be in Lily's presence, a reminder of her old life and of her parents. She trusted her because of these ties. "Do you think we can pull this off?"

Lily stopped chopping and stared at her. "Kaelyn, the knowledge that you'd eventually be here is what has kept me going. Your family, they embodied the very ideals that we've held on to all these years."

Kaelyn felt every muscle in her body tighten. She felt the weight of all these people, their hopes, aspirations, their dreams, resting solely on her shoulders. Her parents were no longer here to help carry the burden, which meant it would now be up to her. She felt the walls start to close in on her.

"What if people don't want to listen?" Kaelyn asked as much to herself as to Lily.

Lily put the lettuce into bowls and looked at Macy, who nodded at her. She came around to the end of the couch, where Kaelyn was perched. "I know it's hard to see it now, but there was a time when I was actually younger than you. Sure, I watched you on television talking to reporters, giving speeches. I even saw you manage the fans that waited outside for you to sign whatever they had. But you know what I remember the most?" She put her finger under Kaelyn's chin and brought her eyes up to match hers. "I remember you packing up all the leftover food from the kitchen and taking it to the shelter. I remember your op-ed pieces demanding social justice for women and children. But most of all, I remember how you'd take the time to talk to anyone who felt they had a worthy cause. It didn't matter what the staff told you, or how trivial they believed it would be. You made sure people felt heard, appreciated, and important. Those traits aren't taught, easily faked, or easy to come by. You're going to save us because it's not just what you were born to do, it's who you are."

Every word seeped into Kaelyn. She was grateful not just for Lily's words but the reminder of who she was and who she'd wanted to be. She hugged her, fighting back the tears of appreciation. "Thank you for that."

Arrow and Valor came through the door. She caught Arrow's eyes, who immediately came to her side.

"Is everything okay?"

"Better than okay," Lily said as she walked back into the kitchen.

Valor put a monitor on the kitchen table and sat in front of it. "We put up some surveillance around the outside of the house. We'll take it down before we go, Aunt Lily."

"Do what you need to do to protect these two." Macy and Lily brought the bowls over to the table. "I'm sorry I don't have more to offer you."

Macy shook her head. "Nonsense, it looks wonderful."

Kaelyn could hear the talking behind her, and it was all registering. But that's not where her focus was at the moment. She was watching Arrow pull her tactical vest off. Arrow was sweating from whatever task she and Valor had completed outside, and her shirt clung to her torso. She didn't fully understand how Arrow had this kind of magnetism. A moment before, Kaelyn had been overwhelmed with emotion, trying desperately to regulate so many conflicting feelings. Then, Arrow walked into the room and completed a simple and understandable task like taking off a rather heavy looking vest, and Kaelyn slipped into a small fantasy land comprised of taut muscles and sweaty bodies.

She heard her name being called but didn't understand how Arrow was managing this feat. She was looking right at her perfect lips, which were just asking to be kissed, but they weren't moving. *How is she calling my name?*

Then a hand on her back snapped her back into reality. Arrow hadn't been speaking to her at all. It was Macy calling her to dinner. Her embarrassment thumped in her chest as she turned to sit at the table. A moment later, Arrow sat next to her and she was both grateful and resentful for the effect she had on her. She really needed to stop whatever this was. It couldn't happen, and someone was going to get hurt if she kept stumbling down this path.

She glanced around the table, unable to believe that anyone could have their wits about them with Arrow in the room. It couldn't just be her. It had to be an airborne illness of some kind. Her look around the table finally landed on Macy, who had a half smile and was watching her and Arrow closely. *Perfect.* That is just what she needed, the president to catch her lusting after her daughter when she should obviously be focused on a million other pressing issues.

Thankfully, Lily managed to take the attention off her with stories about the colony. The table fell into easy conversation about the state of the world, how to move forward, and the travel schedule of the soldiers. Lily took detailed notes and had found their pattern of travel, making it much easier to anticipate their next visit.

Kaelyn took the time to watch Arrow. The adoration she felt for the three other people sitting at the table was apparent in her softened expression and easy smile. There were the earliest indicators of age etched into the edges of her eyes. Her cheeks blushed easily whenever her mother heaped praise on her, which seemed to be more frequently sitting at the table than out in public. And Kaelyn thought she could almost see the remnants of the little girl Arrow had been before. Upon first impression, Arrow appeared to be confident, intelligent, articulate, and devoted. She was still all these things, but Kaelyn also saw the other more vulnerable side. Arrow was also shy when discussing anything besides military maneuvers. But the thing she'd noticed most was that Arrow was also kind and compassionate. She was concerned about the well-being of all the colonies' citizens, not just as a concept, but how they were doing as people as well.

Kaelyn was caught up in her analysis of Arrow when she realized all eyes were now focused on her. She focused her attention on Lily, who had apparently been speaking directly to her. "I'm sorry." She felt herself blush. "Did you ask me something?"

"Would you like to go to the town center? There are many people who'd like to meet you." Lily's expression was hopeful.

Kaelyn looked over at Arrow, unsure if that would be okay. There seemed to be no opposition. "I'd really like that, thank you."

"We'll just need to place jammers down so the drones can't find the transport, and we'll need to stay isolated to one area," Arrow said.

"What exactly is a jammer?" Kaelyn asked, feeling out of place again.

Arrow pulled a device the size of a lip gloss from her pocket. She pushed a button on the side and it started to glow purple. "It masks any electronic pulses in a twenty-foot radius. It will keep the transport hidden from any passing drones."

Lily stood, collected the bowls, and headed back into the kitchen. "Go ahead and put your jammers in, but we're going somewhere the drones can't see. We'll be safe there."

CHAPTER FIFTEEN

Arrow trusted Lily, but she couldn't in good conscience take Kaelyn out without being prepared. She and Valor both put back on their tactical vests and secured their weapons in place. She needed to be prepared for anything.

Lily brought them back into the garage and asked Valor to push the large workbench to the side. Under it was a steel hatch that Valor pulled open upon Lily's direction. Lights started coming on as they walked through the mysterious tunnel. In all the years she and Valor had been coming to visit Lily, she'd never mentioned this tunnel, and she wasn't sure if she was impressed or insulted by the secret.

Kaelyn walked a few feet in front of her, next to her mother, and Valor and Lily were in the front of the group. She watched as Kaelyn and her mom fell into easy conversation, and she marveled at Kaelyn's ability to adjust to her new surroundings. Most people would be overwhelmed by everything that was happening around them, but Kaelyn seemed to fall into place, like she'd been there all along. Her mom must have said something funny because Kaelyn reached out and touched her arm, laughing. And as was becoming her normal response to Kaelyn, Arrow's chest slightly burned.

After about four minutes of walking, the tunnel opened into a large, underground communal space. There were people gathered in different areas talking, laughing, and there was one group gathered in front of someone who played the guitar. Arrow couldn't believe her eyes. How did she never know about any of this? Apparently, people kept secrets from the Guardians, too.

Silence fell among the thirty or so people who were gathered, all attention falling onto them. Arrow instinctively put her hand on top of her weapon. She didn't like walking into areas that were so unpredictable. Anything could happen, and she didn't deal well with those scenarios. She hadn't realized that she'd come to stand next to Kaelyn until she felt her hand on her arm.

"Lily wouldn't have brought us here if these people were dangerous. But I think you're scaring them," she said quietly.

Arrow looked at the widened eyes focused on them and even noticed a small child duck behind her father's leg. Arrow forced herself to take her hand off her weapon. She had never been in the village with her weapon drawn, on the alert. She was causing unnecessary unease.

Lily motioned to the benches near the center of the room, and they followed her direction, moving toward the seating area. A rather tall man walked over to them as everyone watched.

He hugged Lily first and then turned his attention to her mom. "Madam President, it's an honor to have you here."

Her mom smiled and took his hand. "Thank you for having us."

He looked past her, his eyes fixated on Kaelyn's wrist. She felt Kaelyn tense beside her for a moment but then relax, apparently falling into old habits honed from being the First Daughter.

He came closer, and Arrow suppressed her desire to step in front of Kaelyn. He looked awestruck. "Phoenix One. I can't believe it. It's really you. My name is Samuel."

Kaelyn extended her hand to him, keeping part of her body pressed against Arrow's side. "It's nice to meet you, Samuel."

He turned and waved over a small girl. The girl came as she was asked and stood in front of them, chewing on one of her thumbs. Kaelyn knelt on both knees and touched the little girl's arm. "Hi, I'm Kaelyn."

The little girl stared at her for a moment, seemingly trying to decide if she recognized her. The man leaned his head down. "Dorothy, this is Phoenix One."

The little girl's eyes lit up with recognition, and she removed herself from her father's leg and threw her arms around Kaelyn. Kaelyn seemed caught off guard for a moment and then returned the embrace. "Dorothy, that's a very pretty name."

"She's named after your mother. My father used to tell me stories about her every night as I fell asleep, and now I do the same for my daughter," Samuel said.

Dorothy pulled out of her arms and looked at Kaelyn. "Stories about your mom are my favorite."

Kaelyn smiled at her. "She was a very impressive woman, and I'm sure she would've liked you very much."

The little girl's face lit up and she hugged Kaelyn one more time. Then she released herself and took off running for the group of children she'd been playing with, undoubtedly to tell them about her triumph.

Several other people came over now, wanting to see and talk to Kaelyn. Kaelyn took it in stride. She sat as people came over to her, tossing questions like little flowers at her feet.

A short woman pushed her way to the front. "We've heard whispers of you and the Phoenix Project for years. Some people were convinced it was real, that you'd come back. I must be honest, I was never one of those people. I thought it was a myth we used to give ourselves hope, to help us keep pressing forward. But now that you're here, sitting in front of us, it all seems surreal." She wiped her hand across her face, seeming to bring herself to the realization. "Do you think it will really work?"

Kaelyn paused before answering, assumedly giving the question consideration. "That's certainly our intention. I don't know what the future looks like, but I'm going to do everything I can to help all of you."

A woman came and sat beside her. "How long will you be traveling for?"

Kaelyn glanced over at Arrow and then looked back down at the woman. "I'm not entirely sure. The major says it should take about a week, but that's assuming everything goes as planned."

Arrow noticed that Kaelyn touched each of the people she was speaking with, helping them to feel connected, heard, and so they knew they had her full attention. She was impressive with her ability to reach people, and Arrow thought, not for the first time, everything was going to be okay.

Arrow was watching Kaelyn carefully when her mom appeared next to her.

"She's everything we knew she would be, isn't she?"

Arrow continued to watch Kaelyn. "She's more."

She could feel her mom's eyes on her, and she shifted under the scrutiny, unsure what her mom would think. In true Macy Steele form, it didn't take long.

Her mom spoke quietly but firmly. "Arrow, you need to be careful."

"It's never going to happen, Mom. We know our places in the world." Saying the words, as true as they might be, still hurt a little.

"I'm not talking about that. I'm talking about you being careful with your heart. Just because something can't happen doesn't always register with someone's heart. I don't want to see you hurt."

She would've loved to promise her mom that she'd come out of this without any scars, but she knew it would be a lie. As if she knew she was being talked about, Kaelyn looked over and smiled at Arrow before going back to her conversation. Her smile was warm and kind. Arrow felt her stomach flip, and her palms began to sweat. "I won't let anything interfere with the mission, Mom. You have my word."

❖

Kaelyn leaned back in one of the chairs, listening to a group of colonists play a guitar and sing a variety of songs she'd never heard. The environment was welcoming and happy, despite their current set of circumstances. People were laughing, dancing, and joking. The human spirit was alive and well in this makeshift underground meeting space, and it was exactly where she wanted and needed to be. She'd felt so emotionally depleted after the day, she was grateful for the reprieve.

Arrow was in the corner of the room talking to Valor and a man she'd met earlier. It was a weird feeling, knowing where Arrow was without intention. She wanted to walk across the room and take her by the hand, pull her into the group of people who were dancing. She wanted to be near her, wanted to press up against her, feel her breath on her neck. She pushed down the feeling, willing her body to ignore its impulsive thoughts.

Lily sat next to her, drinking a form of moonshine they had created. Lily was much older than the woman she'd once known. There were deep lines etched around her eyes and mouth. Her skin seemed paper thin, like it would tear if you touched it with too much force. Her eyes had lost a bit of their shine, the product of decades of change and survival. But her laugh was the same. Kaelyn was comforted by the fact that there were certain things you could count on, even when time and wear bumped up against you.

Lily handed her the glass. "You can't leave here without trying this."

Kaelyn's first instinct was to decline. She wanted to have a clear head for what was to come, but another part or her told her to indulge. She didn't know when serenity like this would be obtainable again, and she wanted to enjoy every minute. "Thank you."

Lily laughed as she coughed out her first sip. "It grows on you."

Kaelyn took another sip and recoiled as the liquid burned her throat and warmed her body. "That's terrible."

"It gets the job done." Lily laughed.

"I believe you." After only two sips, she could feel the repercussions flowing through her body. Her limbs felt heavier, and her brain became slightly fuzzy. "What will you do after?"

Lily took the glass back and took a sip. "You mean if Phoenix works out?"

"Yeah. You won't need to host any underground parties. Where will you go?"

Lily handed the glass back to her and chuckled when Kaelyn choked on her third sip. "I'm ninety-one years old. I won't be going anywhere. I'm perfectly happy to stay here for the rest of my days, however many that may be. I'll just be happy to see that family finally removed from your father's old place." She sighed. "But what about you?"

"What do you mean?" Kaelyn asked.

"Well, once everything is as it should be, what do you intend to do about that?"

Kaelyn followed her line of sight to Arrow. She was still laughing with Valor, and Kaelyn realized Arrow was never fully relaxed. Even through her enjoyment, she kept scanning the room, intermittently placing her hand on her weapon.

"Arrow has made it clear she intends to return to her colony. Her people need her, and we may be able to take back the government, but that doesn't mean it won't be met with opposition. We'll have to continue to strengthen our forces and prepare for a long battle, if not war. This won't end quietly."

Lily sat back in her seat and took a deep breath. "Doesn't seem fair."

"Some things are bigger than two people. This is one of them."

"You sound like Valor and Arrow." Lily tilted the glass toward the two.

"I'll take that as a compliment." Kaelyn watched Arrow laugh, and she shivered at the way it made her pulse race.

"You want some advice from a very old woman?"

Kaelyn put her hand on Lily's leg. "I would like some advice from an old friend."

Before Lily had a chance to answer, the whole room shook with a strength Kaelyn had never experienced. Dust shook loose from the ceiling and walls, lights flickered like candle flames struggling to stay lit, and a second shockwave sent parts of the roof crashing to the floor. She heard children cry while adults hurried to quiet and console them. Cries from areas she couldn't make out in the dark echoed with people in pain. People started running toward different tunnels, disappearing into the dark.

Kaelyn quickly got behind Lily and picked her up from where she lay on the ground. "Are you okay?"

Lily nodded. "We need to find out what's happening."

Valor rushed over. "Are you two okay?"

"Yes. Where's Arrow?" Kaelyn couldn't see her, and fear started to grab at the inside of her throat, wanting to drag her down.

"She's helping one of the guys who was hit by a falling rock." He pulled a small device out of his pocket and pushed a few of the buttons. A view of the street in front of the garage came into view.

Macy was next to them a moment later. "We have several injured people. They need medical attention."

"Can we get them to my house?" Lily asked.

Valor was staring at the screen. "I see one vehicle. It looks like they just bombed a few buildings. I don't know if they were picked randomly or purposefully. I don't know if your house is safe."

"What the hell is going on?" Kaelyn asked. "I thought they left you alone for the most part?"

Lily ran her hand over her hair. "It's hard to say. They've harassed us in the past, just for the fun of it. It could be just one of their games, or it could be more."

Macy grabbed his arm. "If they find the transport, they'll know we're here and all these people will be in danger."

Valor looked as if he was ticking off possibilities in his head when Arrow ran up beside him. She had blood coming from a cut in her head that was threatening to run into her eyes. She swiped it away, leaving a smear of it behind. "Report."

"Unknown bombing for unknown reasons. If they find the transport they'll know we're here. If we move it and they catch us, they'll know we're here. Some of these people need medical attention, but we can't put them in more danger."

Arrow looked around. Her eyes were calm, and Kaelyn noticed her hands weren't shaking, unlike her own.

"Mom, I need you and Kaelyn to get all these people into one area. There are a few first aid supplies in my vest. Do what you can." She looked at Valor. "Let's go see what we're up against."

Kaelyn wanted to protest. She didn't want Arrow taking off into a tunnel where she had no idea what was waiting for her at the end, but the decision wasn't hers to make. Instead, she did what she was asked. She held out her hands as Arrow began to hand her several first aid items. She felt her heart speed up, not with fear for her own safety but for Arrow's. She wanted to tell her to be safe, but that seemed ridiculous in this situation.

Arrow gave the items to Kaelyn and Macy. "You can do this. We'll be back before you know it."

There was that confidence Kaelyn found so mesmerizing. "You better come back. I can't do this without you." If she'd said it to someone else, Kaelyn would've been worried about sounding dependent. But in this instance, it was the truth. She didn't think she could survive this without Arrow.

Arrow handed her a weapon and a transmission device. "Valor's frequency is the first number in there. If things get bad, let us know." She grabbed her hand and held her gaze. "And, Kaelyn, I'll come back for you. I promise."

CHAPTER SIXTEEN

The tunnels were much darker now that the lights had gone out because of whatever was happening above them. Arrow flipped on her light on the front of her vest, and Valor did the same. They moved through at almost full speed, each with a gun in their hand. She slowed at each tunnel intersection, clearing the corners on the left while Valor took the right.

They reached the stairwell to Lily's garage and stopped. Valor looked at his transmitter again and shook his head, indicating that the soldiers had yet to make it to the house.

"What's the plan, Major? There's only one vehicle showing up on the transmitter, so there shouldn't be more than two guys." Valor checked the additional gun in his holster.

"We only have two choices. We can either find out what they're doing here or let them press on and hope they don't find anything."

"I'd like to know what we're dealing with."

"Agreed. We need to get to our transport and grab some more weapons."

Valor crept up the stairs, checking his transmitter as he moved. He unlatched the door and pushed it open. Arrow took note of the silence when the door swung open. He walked out and Arrow followed closely behind. The garage was empty, just as they had left it. Valor put his palm on the trunk of the vehicle. The light blinked green, accepting his credentials, and the trunk opened.

Arrow quickly grabbed several grenades from the back and two helmets, both equipped with night vision lenses. She handed one to

Valor, and they put on the helmets and turned off their lights. "I'll take the south side of the street; you take the north. When we reach them, I'll toss the grenade. They should evacuate their vehicle on your side. Use the Night-Blind and grab them."

"Roger that, Major." He put the small Night-Blind canister in his front left pocket.

The streets were dark and quiet. It was easy to see the dwelling they'd destroyed. Half a wall was exposed, and mangled pieces of rebar stuck up from the heap. The kitchen table that had sat inside the dwelling was now in smoldering pieces behind it. Arrow moved down the north side of the street, ducking behind buildings and making sure she stayed close to the wall. She could hear the soldiers' vehicle, so they were heading in the right direction. Arrow listened to her footsteps on the ground. It was an eerie kind of quiet, the kind that only happens when you fall asleep, wake up, or when you're about to be either hunter or prey.

The vehicle turned down the street. Its wheels were as tall as her, with ground-grabbing tread designed to climb over the destruction it was capable of causing. Its only weakness was its height off the ground. If she was able to get the grenade where she wanted it, the explosion would knock it on its side. It was moving slowly, she assumed to do surveillance. It stopped ten feet from her, and she watched as the large gun on top started rotating in her direction. *Click, click, click.* It was only a few seconds, but it felt like years. She watched as the indicator light started to flash more rapidly. Her time had run out. This was it.

She came out from behind the corner and tossed the grenade alongside the vehicle. All she could do was hope it landed close enough to knock the vehicle over. She heard the grenade hit the ground at the same time that a bright light illuminated the street and shook the ground beneath her.

She hit the ground and rolled onto her side. Her shoulder throbbed and her ears drummed with pain and a piercing ringing. She pulled herself up onto her elbows and looked across the street. The vehicle had tipped over on its side, and Valor was in the process of pulling one of the people from the window.

She needed to help him. She willed her body to move the way she intended. She purposefully told her legs to pick the rest of her body up from the ground. She forced her arms to lift her body from the ground. She envisioned all of it happening, but her body collapsed to the side. There was copper in her mouth, coating her teeth and tongue. She focused on Valor again. He had one in restraints against the vehicle but was struggling with the other.

On shaky legs, she finally stood. She was dizzy and her hand and shoulder were throbbing. She pulled off her helmet. The lenses were shattered and making it difficult to see. One of the soldiers had managed to knock the gun out of Valor's hand, and they were now involved in a fist fight.

She pulled the gun from her back holster and aimed it at the man who had just hit Valor. "Put your hands up." She thought her voice would have cracked, the way her throat felt, but it didn't.

The man turned and looked at her, then spit in her direction. "Go fuck yourself, Guardian."

The distraction gave Valor enough time to land a solid left hook, knocking him against the vehicle and then onto the ground. This would've been the perfect opportunity to say something clever back, but her mind was still too frazzled to put anything together.

Valor put the restraints on the second guy. "You okay?" he asked her.

Arrow pulled the other soldier to his feet and spit out a mouthful of blood onto the ground. "Yeah, I'll be fine. Let's get these guys over to Lily's."

"You sure you don't want to take them somewhere more secluded?" Valor was undoubtedly worried for the safety of his aunt.

She was concerned too, but her focus had to be on the greater good. And she knew that was something Lily would understand. "I have a plan."

❖

Kaelyn put the bandage up to the young woman's head. "You need to keep pressure on this until it stops bleeding. When you get home tonight, make sure you clean it out."

Macy had just finished using a piece from one of the broken chairs as a splint for a man's arm. She put her hand on Kaelyn's shoulder. "Looks like that's everyone."

"Do you think they know we're here?" Kaelyn was scared of what the answer could be, but she needed to know.

Macy took a deep breath and leaned back against the wall. "It's hard to say. These guys can be real pricks sometimes. They go around demolishing buildings in colonies because they can, and although it doesn't happen too often, it does happen." She used the sleeve of her shirt to wipe away the sweat and dirt from her eyes. "Then again, yes, they might have been looking for us. The excuse we left under wasn't going to hold up forever, although I thought we'd have at least a couple of days. Everything would've gone much smoother without MacLeod's ultimatum."

Kaelyn leaned against the wall with her, mimicking her pose. "Do you think they're okay?"

Macy took the transmitter from Kaelyn's hand and turned it over a few times. She looked glum and contemplative. "There's nothing those two can't handle."

"Arrow's special." Kaelyn breathed the words out, unsure if they were meant to reassure herself or Macy.

Macy smiled and looked up toward the dirt ceiling. "You know, there was a time when some of the generals didn't think she'd make it through basic training."

Kaelyn was shocked. She couldn't imagine why anyone would think that, and looking at Macy, she knew she felt the same.

Macy laughed and shook her head. "They thought she was too compassionate, too attached to people and their emotions. They weren't wrong about that, mind you. We exhausted our favors to allow her to stay in, to prove herself. And over time, they finally saw what I knew instinctively."

Kaelyn snorted. "That she was a badass?"

"Well, that and that her compassion was her greatest asset. She's not just a Guardian because the title was bestowed upon her. She's a Guardian because she truly believes in protecting her people, in helping those that can't help themselves. She doesn't just want to take this country back because she's been told that's what's best. She wants it back because she sees MacLeod's evil and how it touches every living being's life in some way or another."

The transmitter lit up and Valor's voice came through the speaker. "Team one to team two."

Macy picked up the device and pushed the button. "We're here, team one."

"We have the soldiers in custody. The major would like you and the Phoenix to return."

"We're on our way." Macy stood and put her hand out to Kaelyn. "Let's go see what's happening."

Kaelyn held her breath while listening to the interaction. She was worried any shift in the air, any sudden movement would cause their transmission to be lost. Was it a crazy thought? Obviously. But Kaelyn rationalized that she couldn't risk it. The good news was that Valor didn't report back anything gut-wrenching. The bad news was there were now soldiers in custody that had to be dealt with. Kaelyn straightened her shoulders in the direction Macy was heading. Valor didn't say anyone, or more specifically Arrow, was hurt. As frightening as this situation had been, no one underground had lost their lives, and it sounded like no one above ground had either. Kaelyn decided to chalk this up in the win category, mostly because she didn't know how many of those they'd get and she wanted to gather all the hope she could in case she needed it later.

CHAPTER SEVENTEEN

Kaelyn pushed the hatch to the garage open and stepped into the space. There were two men in uniforms she didn't recognize sitting in chairs, restrained with metal bracelets that looked far more sophisticated than any handcuffs she'd ever seen.

Arrow was leaning against the vehicle with her arms crossed. She had dried blood on the side of her face and the inside of her ear. Kaelyn's impulse was to go to her and find out what happened. She wanted to wipe the blood away and see if there were any more injuries. But she stayed rooted to her spot across the room. The look on Arrow's face said that her sole focus was on the two men in front of them, and Kaelyn needed to have that kind of focus too.

"Why are you here?" Valor asked.

The man on the right spit on the ground and then looked straight ahead. "We don't talk to women or monkeys."

Kaelyn felt her ears and her neck run hot. Anger pulsed through her body at his comment. These men were disgusting. Her fists tightened into a ball and she dug her nails into her palms.

"Pretty brave words coming from two people who were just outsmarted and caught." Arrow's voice was steady. "We can call your commander; tell him you were captured after destroying colony property. If I remember correctly, being captured isn't tolerated. They won't send anyone for you. They'll leave you here to starve and die."

The men looked at each other. One looked like he was going to cry. It was bizarre to think they'd be abandoned so easily, but it was apparently true by the look on their faces.

"What are your names?" Valor asked.

The crying man sniffled. "I'm Corporal Clayton and he's Corporal Johnson."

"Shut the fuck up, Clayton." Johnson shook the chair and almost fell over trying to hit him with his shoulder.

Arrow looked at Valor. "Get Johnson out of here."

Valor grabbed him by the arm and pulled him out of his seat. He opened the vehicle door and pushed him inside.

Arrow pulled over the chair Johnson had just been sitting in and slid it in front of Clayton. "How old are you, Corporal?"

"Seventeen," he mumbled.

Arrow pushed his head to the side and pulled down the collar of his shirt. There was a numeric sequence tattooed on his neck. She pulled a small device from her pocket and ran it over the number.

Arrow read whatever message appeared on the screen. "I got this little device from your friend over there. Do you know what it does?"

He nodded. "Yeah."

She put it back in her pocket. "Good, so you understand that I now have all of your information. I have your military record, your address, your parents' names. I have everything. So I want you to think very carefully before you try to lie to me."

He nodded again.

"What are you doing here?" she asked, staring him down.

He shifted in his seat and looked around the room. He made eye contact with Kaelyn. He squinted , but there was no recognition. She wasn't sure why Arrow had wanted her here for all of this, but there had to be a reason. She made sure not to shift under his scrutiny. She wanted to project power and confidence. She wanted him to believe she was a Guardian.

He looked back at Arrow. "We were sent to patrol the colonies."

Arrow leaned back in her seat. "Obviously, but why?"

"We were told to double the patrols and to identify Guardians. We were to destroy buildings as we saw fit in order to draw out Guardians, to see if any of you were outside your colony perimeters. You're supposed to set up a beacon once you've left your designated area. There was no beacon in this village, so we decided to come and see for ourselves. I don't know any more than that. They don't tell us a lot." He looked again at Kaelyn, obviously trying to place her.

"Do you normally blow up the buildings in colonies without being provoked?" Arrow's voice held a bit of an edge to it now.

He smiled. "Sometimes. It's fun; people run around like scattering rats."

Arrow's back stiffened. "Do you know who that is?" She nodded in Kaelyn's direction.

His eyes bore into Kaelyn. "No, but she isn't one of you. She's too soft."

Kaelyn didn't appreciate that description, but she was curious as to what Arrow was planning. Macy apparently understood something she didn't because she stood next to Arrow now, placing a hand on her shoulder.

Macy rolled up her sleeve to reveal a symbol that resembled Arrow's, only slightly different. Her eagle was surrounded by a wreath of some kind, but Kaelyn couldn't make it out from her position.

Clayton's face went red, and his jaw clenched tightly. "I've seen that emblem before. That's the seal of the old president. That hasn't been allowed to be seen or shown for over sixty years. You can't have that! It's treason. He'll hang you."

Macy rolled her sleeve back down. "Oh, but I can. I'm President Steele of the Resistance. That woman over there is Phoenix One. But you probably will recognize her as Kaelyn Trapp."

"That doesn't make any sense. There's no way she can be alive. We read about her family and how they tried to destroy our country. If it wasn't for the MacLeod's, we'd all be in the grasp of the devil. Kaelyn Trapp would be an old lady now, if she was alive at all." He continued to stare at her.

Kaelyn didn't fully understand what was going on, but she trusted Arrow and Macy. "They're telling the truth. I'm Kaelyn Trapp, daughter of Daniel and Dorothy Trapp. I was the First Daughter of what once was the United States."

Clayton looked like he was going to pass out. "I don't understand."

Arrow stood and placed restraints on his ankles. "You don't need to understand. Here's what's going to happen. I'm going to let you go in the morning. I assume it'll probably take about twelve hours for one of Eden's drones to find you. Then you're going to report back everything that happened here tonight to your commander. Understand?"

"What about him?" He nodded toward the vehicle.

"He's coming with us. We may need him."

Clayton didn't answer; he just squirmed in his seat.

"Corporal, I want you to remember that I have all of your information now. If I don't see your report flash on this screen by nightfall tomorrow, I'm going to use this device to report you as a traitor. Can you remind me what happens to your family if President MacLeod suspects you've turned on him?"

"He'll banish my family to the lost lands," he mumbled.

"So, do we have an understanding?"

"Yes."

Arrow turned to Valor. "Sedate Johnson and bring him inside. Secure him in one of the rooms. We'll leave at sunrise."

Chapter Eighteen

Arrow turned toward her mom once they were back inside the house. "I hope we did the right thing."

Her mother paced back and forth in the small living room. "I wasn't sure at first, but I think it was a good call. They must be suspicious in Eden that we weren't being entirely forthcoming about where we're headed. Who knows how many other villages they're bombing looking for us."

Arrow leaned against the wall, a little dizzier than she'd been a few minutes before. "Yes, exactly. I couldn't bear the thought of our people being killed while they tried to put the pieces together. And he might not understand the significance of Kaelyn or the Phoenix Project, but as soon as the word gets back to MacLeod, the information will be everywhere, and he won't be able to help himself. He'll be screaming it from the rooftops. We wouldn't be able to get the information out faster if we tried. The people inside Eden will know, including the people who are friendly to our cause. Once everyone hears what's happening, even the fighting forces in the outskirt villages will start to assemble. They'll know it's started, and they'll be more willing to fight back if more soldiers come. We've trained people within the villages to defend themselves if the need arises. They usually don't because any amount of resistance is met with more trouble than what's necessary. Knowing things are in motion will signal their allowance toward defense. Hopefully, MacLeod will focus almost all his attention on finding us and give the villagers some reprieve, but they'll be ready if he doesn't."

Kaelyn was chewing on her thumb. "You wanted everyone to find out we were coming, to give them time to ready their defenses and start preparing for the war that's going to follow?"

"Yes. It's not how I wanted it to happen nor is it what we'd planned, but we needed to improvise. We wanted to get closer before we sounded the alarms, but he's just going to keep blowing up buildings until he finds something. At least this gives the people a fighting chance. Unfortunately, it's going to make our journey to Eden that much more difficult. They're going to be looking for us now, and we won't be able to hide in the villages."

Kaelyn ran a hand through her hair and let out a breath. "I'm okay with it being a little more difficult for us if it gives the villagers a fighting chance."

"I believe it will," Arrow said.

Arrow was thankful Kaelyn understood her methods. She wanted to discuss it further, but her shoulder was throbbing and she was getting more tired by the minute. "I'm going to take a shower."

Arrow stood in the bedroom and struggled with her shirt. Excruciating pain shot through her shoulder as she undid her buttons. She was about ready to give up for the night when Kaelyn came through the door.

"Hey." She crossed the room to her. "Let me help you."

Arrow was going to protest, but the pain was too much. "It will be okay. I'll put the reanimation unit on my shoulder as we drive tomorrow, and I'll be good as new in a few hours."

"Reanimation unit?" Kaelyn asked quietly as she undid Arrow's buttons.

Arrow watched Kaelyn's hands tremble as she worked her way down her shirt. "It's a device that stimulates rejuvenation."

Kaelyn carefully pulled the shirt off Arrow. "Your shoulder's in really bad shape." Kaelyn slid her hand over the bare skin. It was painful and wonderful at the same time. She put her fingertips on Arrow's face. "You took a beating out there."

Arrow remained as still as possible, afraid that any sudden movements would cause Kaelyn to remove her touch, and that was the last thing she wanted. "I dodged a bullet. I'll be okay."

"You probably have a concussion." She used her fingertips to gently push Arrow's head to the side. Kaelyn stepped closer to her under the pretense of examining her injuries. But her green eyes were showing another emotion besides concern.

Arrow allowed her mind to briefly flash an image of what it would be like to kiss Kaelyn. Her body hummed with excitement, and she moved closer. Kaelyn slid her hand down Arrow's arm, leaving shivers where her fingers touched.

It would be so easy to give in, to fall into Kaelyn. It would be easy to get lost in this moment. *A moment.* That's all it would be, and it would make their mission that much more difficult.

Arrow took a step back, moving away from Kaelyn. "I'm going to take a shower." She walked into the bathroom before the closeness of Kaelyn changed her mind.

The water was hot and seared her skin in the best possible way. Dirt and blood drifted down the shower drain. She watched the colors combine in perfect harmony and then disappear. It was rather beautiful. She could cleanse her body of the misfortune of the evening while remaining whole. But that thought made her realize she wasn't as complete as she'd always believed.

She could still feel Kaelyn's hands on her face, her arm, her back. The way her eyes had grown dark because of their simple proximity to each other. Arrow wasn't sure if this was normal, but she knew it was unlike anything she'd ever experienced. She let the water strike her face, hoping the water would extinguish the heat she felt burning in her body for Kaelyn Trapp.

❖

Kaelyn sat on the edge of the bed, waiting for Arrow to come out of the bathroom. Her heart still hammered from their closeness. She wanted Arrow, that much was apparent. But it wasn't just lust. She wanted to make sure she was okay; she was concerned about her health, and how hard she pushed herself. She didn't care how far technology had come; concussions weren't anything to mess around with, and she wasn't going to let Arrow out of her sight for the next twelve hours.

The bathroom door opened, and a cloud of steam escaped. Arrow appeared a moment later, using her good hand to dry her short black hair with a towel. She wore sweatpants and a sports bra. Her stomach muscles flexed with each swipe of her arm. Kaelyn gripped the side of the bed tighter as Arrow walked over to her.

"I'm sleeping with you tonight," Kaelyn blurted out.

Arrow's eyebrows shot up in surprise. "What?"

"No, I mean, you have a concussion and need to be woken up every hour or so, to make sure you're okay. That's what I meant by sleeping with you. Not whatever you were thinking. What were you thinking?"

Arrow laughed and sat on the bed. "I'm not really sure what I was thinking. But you don't have to do that. I can set the alert on my wristband to wake me up. It has a concussion protocol."

"Of course it does." Kaelyn wondered how anybody in this time managed to subtlety seduce anyone with all these damn advancements. *Not that I was going to seduce her. Obviously.*

Kaelyn was going to leave when Arrow lay back on the bed. "I meant, you can sleep in here if you'd like, but you don't have to worry about staying awake. Or you can always go sleep with my mom and Lily."

Kaelyn did her best casual walk toward the bathroom. "I guess I'll just stay here with you. I'm going to shower."

A dozen or so quick minutes later, Kaelyn came out of the bathroom to find Arrow asleep. She quietly crawled into the bed next to her. The warmth of Arrow's body against her back brought her into a space of calm she shouldn't have been experiencing in the middle of all the chaos. But it wasn't until Arrow's arm came around her waist and she pulled her closer that she was sure it was exactly where she was meant to be.

Throughout the night, Kaelyn felt the buzzer of Arrow's wrist. It was a subtle reminder of the pain Arrow must be experiencing. Arrow would sit up for a moment, take a few deep breaths, and lie back down. Kaelyn wanted to wake with her each time, wanted to check to see if her pupils were dilated, if she was okay. She was far from a medical expert, but she'd spent four summers as a lifeguard at her community pool in high school. Doing basic first aid and identifying injuries such as a concussion were part of the job. Instead, she remained as still as possible until Arrow fell back into a rhythmic sleep pattern, so she didn't keep her awake longer than necessary. Each time, Arrow would fall back asleep without touching her, and each time, her arm would inevitably find its place back around Kaelyn.

The morning came sooner and with more fury than Kaelyn was prepared to handle. She was awakened by a loud crash from somewhere in the house. Before she had time to figure out what was going on, Arrow was up and through the door, gun in hand.

Kaelyn followed but allowed several steps of distance between herself and Arrow. Arrow turned the corner and lowered her gun. Valor stood with his hand on the back of Johnson's neck, pushing him into the table.

"What happened?" Arrow asked.

"He said he needed to take a piss. I was moving his restraints to the front so he could use his hands and he tried to take off."

Arrow pulled out one of chairs at the table and sat down. She tapped him on top of the head a few times. "What were you thinking?"

His voice was muffled, undoubtedly from his mouth becoming one with the table. "I thought he'd kill me."

"Is that what you want?"

"It's better than being a prisoner."

Arrow leaned back in her seat. She seemed to be unaware and unashamed that she was still in a sports bra and sweats. "I'll make you a deal. You do what we asked. If you still feel like you want to die when we get to Eden, I'll kill you myself."

She motioned to Valor to let him up. Johnson's face was beet red. There was fury in his eyes and in the way his chest heaved. He struggled against Valor as he put the restraints back in place.

He looked like he might scream. "Fine."

Arrow stood and patted him on the arm. "Captain, we'll leave in fifteen minutes."

Valor nodded his understanding, and Arrow turned, heading back toward the bedroom. Kaelyn followed closely behind. She couldn't believe what she'd just witnessed. "Are you really going to kill him?"

Arrow carefully pulled on her uniform shirt and gingerly clasped the buttons. "I won't need to kill him."

Kaelyn was so caught off guard at the threat of violence that she didn't want to help Arrow, but she gave in at the sight of her wincing. "But that's not what you told him."

Arrow grimaced when she tried to shrug. "He wants to die because the consequences for him if MacLeod finds out are much worse. But it won't come to that. We're going to show him there's another way to live that he never knew existed before."

"You're very sure of yourself." Kaelyn pulled on her own borrowed clothes. "It's difficult to unlearn cultural norms. This world is the only one he knows, and he's willing to kill without thought of consequence. What makes you think he'll change?"

"Everyone deserves the opportunity to change. It's just that people aren't often given that opportunity. They're bogged down with what people expect from them, what the world expects from them. I'm giving him the opportunity to be something else because I'm allowing for the space that's necessary for growth."

"And what if he is exactly who he says he is?" Understanding Arrow's thought process on the matter felt incredibly important.

She pulled on her vest and checked her weapons. "Then I'll let him go, but he won't be able to do any damage to us at that point. If he wants to die, he'll need to find another way of doing it."

Kaelyn smiled. "So you're capable of lying?"

Arrow smiled, and then her expression became serious. "Not to you."

Kaelyn put her hand on Arrow's cheek, and a feeling of warmth swept through her body. "I don't know why, but I believe you."

Kaelyn watched Arrow walk away and wondered how that kind of idealism bloomed in an environment of darkness. There was no reason to believe that this soldier would change his fundamental thinking after a brief stint with the four of them. Deprogramming could take months if not years, and it was even harder to do when your whole family was inculcated as well. But there was Arrow with her untarnished belief that good would always overcome evil. Admittedly, her optimism was contagious, if not intoxicating.

One thing was glaringly clear. She wanted more of Arrow.

CHAPTER NINETEEN

A rrow entered the coordinates into the transport vehicle. They were at a disadvantage, unable to travel the most direct route since that's exactly where they'd be looking. Taking the wrong route would be problematic, to say the least. She'd run through a thousand different scenarios for possible routes and was grateful she had, even if people had teased her at the time. They would need to head north and then east.

She adjusted the reanimation unit on her shoulder. It would only take a few hours and her shoulder would be good as new. The device fastened small pins into her shoulder and began to vibrate, reconstructing the afflicted areas. If she'd been back at base, she would be lying in a capsule while the technology worked its magic, and it would've taken half the time. But this was the best she could do at the moment.

She glanced in the rearview mirror to see a very uncomfortable looking mother, prisoner, and Phoenix all glaring in her direction. It wasn't because of lack of space as much as it was about their forced proximity to each other. If looks could kill, she would be in the process of perishing in this moment.

They had released Corporal Clayton thirty minutes before, and Arrow wanted to wait longer to ensure he wouldn't return to do harm to Lily or anyone else in the village. Valor had driven him out and left him about an hour from the village, but she wasn't taking any chances. Keeping everyone in the transport in the meantime was her way of safeguarding against the myriad of circumstances that could possibly unfold without any warning.

"Do you have music in these things?" Kaelyn's voice broke the silence.

Arrow glanced at Valor, who looked as confused as she felt. "What do you mean?"

Kaelyn seemed surprised by the answer. She leaned forward in her seat. "You know, like a radio that doesn't just transmit signals to and from bases. A little box, that when turned to a specific station, spews out beats to dance along with."

Of course, Arrow knew what she was referring to; she'd studied Kaelyn's time ferociously. It just wasn't an amenity her world had embraced. Or at least not her life back at Resistance headquarters. "No, we don't have anything like that in our transports."

Kaelyn's eyes grew incredibly large and her mouth gaped open. "You have music, right?"

"Yes." Arrow was feeling slightly defensive. "You heard them playing it last night. It might not be as sophisticated as what you're used to, but we enjoy it. Most of our time resources are spent on survival. People aren't looking to sign recording contracts out here, so the music they make is for themselves with whatever instruments they make or what they've inherited."

"But that's it?" Kaelyn asked.

Johnson spoke next. "We have Gospel music in Eden."

Kaelyn turned slowly to look at him. "You guys can blow up an entire building with some sort of laser, but all you have is Gospel music?"

Johnson shrugged. "What your kind listened to was the devil's work."

Kaelyn pulled out her computer from her bag and pushed the screen open. "It's rude to say 'your kind.' We're the same species, whether you like it or not." She pushed a couple of buttons, and sounds Arrow had never heard started to fill the car.

Arrow marveled at the flow of sounds. They seemed to encapsulate emotions, both good and bad. She could feel the thumping rhythm in her body, and it was almost magical. She knew the music of Kaelyn's time. She'd even listened to it as a point of reference. But it wasn't until right now that she ever really heard it. She was lost in thought when the transport began to roll forward. She hadn't taken it off auto when she programmed in their destination and was about to switch to manual when she changed her mind. She wanted to enjoy this feeling and these sounds for a bit longer.

Maybe it was only a few minutes, or maybe several dozen. Arrow was caught in the beauty of the range of sounds and didn't pay attention to the time passing. She didn't understand why this practice had ever been abandoned. Music should have been kept like the treasure it was, built upon, spread around. She'd always been impressed with the guitars the villagers used, and at times they would pound on items they found to follow the different beats, but it was nothing like this. For a moment, she was mad at her mother for never exposing her to this simple pleasure. She was going to say something and looked in the rearview to catch her eyes. But her mother looked as transfixed on the moment as she was, lost in the words and the sounds.

The moment of magic was short-lived. Valor pulled the beeping transmitter from his side pocket. Apparently, it hadn't taken Clayton twelve hours to be picked up. It only took two. There were alerts flashing on the screen, offering a bounty for their capture.

"That didn't take long," Valor said.

Arrow sat up straighter in the seat and switched to manual drive. "There must've been more drones out then we had anticipated. He said they'd been told to double patrols, so one must have been closer than we thought. Things are going to go south very quickly if they figure out our location."

"We can take the tunnels," Valor said.

The tunnels had been built long before the Resistance had formed, but they utilized them as a lifeline. It was a way out for people, a network of hope and possibility. But certain areas were anything but structurally sound. It would be a risk as well. But what was the other choice? Allow the drones to find them by remaining out in the open? Arrow didn't like either of these options. But a choice was going to have to be made.

She looked at her mom. "What do you think, stay on the roads or head to the tunnels?"

Her mom stared out the window, undoubtedly turning over the different possibilities in her head. "We don't want to take the tunnels from here. We need to switch direction and head toward Denver. The tunnel structure from there is sound. If we enter it from here, it might not hold up, and we'll wind up dead."

Arrow bristled at the suggestion. "If we head toward Denver we'll wind up dead. We won't make it through that area without being recognized."

Valor rubbed his hand over his face, then rested it on his chin. "The president is right. The tunnels won't do us any good if they don't hold up. At least we have some friendlies through the Denver path."

"There has to be another way," Arrow said.

Kaelyn leaned forward in her seat. She put her hand on Arrow's arm. It didn't seem intentional. It seemed an unconscious action that added to the haze in Arrow's head. "I don't understand what you're trying to figure out. I'd like to help."

Arrow thought about it for a minute. Kaelyn had just as much right to weigh in on the subject as the rest of them. If anyone would see reason, it would be Kaelyn. "There are ten entry points to the old military underground base system. The one we'd like to take is at what used to be the Denver International Airport."

Kaelyn looked surprised by the information. "Bullshit. That's just an old conspiracy theory."

Valor shook his head. "No, it's very real. When the older MacLeod started his takeover, the Resistance started to use those tunnels to funnel people out, before his army could round them up completely. The Resistance made several others, but the one we're speaking of is the most structurally sound."

Kaelyn leaned back in her seat looking as if she was trying to put pieces of a puzzle together that didn't quite fit. "I still can't believe that our military couldn't isolate him to keep him from taking over that way."

Her mom shook her head. "It wasn't like that. It started slowly. First, he paid off a major media organization. Its sole purpose was to discredit the others until people who were loyal to him only tuned in to that outlet. Next, he used them to discredit all our intelligence branches. I know it seems ridiculous, but when people want to believe something, they'll hang on to any little bit of information they receive that justifies what they already think. Next, he started to discredit our FBI. Once they fell, the other agencies went down like dominoes. About a quarter came over to the Resistance, the rest...well, you can see what happened."

Kaelyn turned to Johnson, who looked as confused as Kaelyn had moments before. "Does the Hand of God patrol the tunnels?"

He just kept staring in front of him, looking like he was trying to understand things beyond him. Kaelyn waited another moment and smacked his arm.

He looked at her and shook his head. "Not that I know of, but I don't know a whole lot."

Arrow saw by the way Kaelyn's face changed she was going to take Valor and her mother's side on the issue. "If we get trapped down there, if they do patrol it because they're looking for us, there'll be nowhere to hide."

"There's nowhere to hide out here either, and we already have plenty working against us, and you don't want the integrity of our passage to be one of the issues. We need to control what we can, and this seems like the best option," Kaelyn said. Her voice was softer than Arrow had expected.

Arrow sighed, knowing the final decision was hers, but that she'd also been outvoted. "Denver it is." She punched in the coordinates and prayed they'd make it to friendly territory before getting picked up.

Once Arrow turned the transport toward Denver, everyone was eerily quiet. Not the comfortable kind of silence Kaelyn enjoyed. No, this was like a heavy, wet blanket smothering the people it had been placed upon. Kaelyn knew she'd made the right decision, but she'd also disappointed Arrow. That thought alone made her even more uncomfortable.

She took time to stare out the window. Barren landscape as far as the eye could see showed the ravages of climate change. The soil was so arid nothing could survive there. No people, no plants, not even a cactus. They passed areas that had once been bustling with people, offices, parks, day-to-day life. Now, everything was abandoned. The sides of buildings and houses were crumbling, parts scorched from what she could only assume was the sun. Playground equipment was half bent over, twisted, looking as if it was weeping from the loneliness of being long forgotten. The sky was a shade of red that Kaelyn had no word to describe. It looked like an open gash, festering with infection. There were no clouds, just decomposing sky, as far as she could see.

Arrow spoke to her from the front seat. "This is what it looks like when we leave a weather bubble."

"So, this is their doing?" Kaelyn thought back to what she'd seen within the protection of the bubbles. The sky looked the same as it had during her time. Blue skies, billowing clouds, and even a tinge of humidity at certain times of the day. If it hadn't been a ruse, it would've been lovely.

"No. This is what climate change did. They just picked which areas to rehabilitate."

Kaelyn was beginning to understand better now. Controlling people's access to water and healthy soil was the most powerful weapon anyone could ever employ. A person could wield it like a sword that had the power to devastate thousands of people at a time. The Hand of God had allowed people to live outside Eden, but they still controlled them through the bubbles, so it wasn't a huge risk.

"How hot is it out there right now?" She couldn't imagine the temperature number this atmosphere would create.

Valor pushed a button on the middle console of the transport. "One hundred and forty-seven degrees."

Kaelyn turned her music back on, hoping the familiar words and instruments would ward off the blatant malice of the world she no longer recognized. She tried closing her eyes, but the need to witness the horror firsthand forced her gaze back to the landscape. The long-forgotten bones of a suburban area whizzed past her line of sight. Dried up riverbeds, cracked and broken trees, old cars abandoned on the side of the road, served as nothing more than empty shells of a civilization that once thrived.

A loud beeping sound filled the car, startling her from her blistering anger at what the world had become. Valor touched a few buttons on the screen, and a video image of what Kaelyn assumed was the sky above them came into view.

"Incoming drone," Valor said as he started pressing a different series of buttons.

Kaelyn wasn't sure what that meant, but she knew instinctually that it couldn't be good. She sucked in a breath and turned off her music, not knowing what to do to help and not wanting to do anything that would add to the tension.

"Deploy the reflection barrier," Arrow ordered Valor in a calm and focused voice.

"Reflection barrier is up." He pulled at a different screen on the console. "EMP is charging."

Arrow flipped a switch on her steering wheel. "Everyone hold on."

Kaelyn wanted to ask what the plan was, but before she had the chance the vehicle swung around in a tight circle. She felt the tires skid from underneath them and her body pushed up against the door. The car skidded to a stop, and Valor flung open the door. The wave of heat that flooded the car was like nothing Kaelyn had ever felt. The air was scorching; she could feel it in her lungs, pinpricks punishing her species for having wreaked havoc on the only planet they'd been awarded.

Valor shut the door and ran a few feet from the vehicle. He pushed a button, and a few moments later started running in a different direction. Kaelyn squirmed to see what was happening. Arrow hopped out next and met Valor at the back of the vehicle. She wasn't expecting the urge to tell her to get her ass back in the car. She hated Arrow being outside and vulnerable, even if it was only for a few moments, and even if it wasn't her decision to make.

Before she could force her mouth to form words, the back gate to the transport opened and a weird looking machine was tossed inside. A moment later, they were back in the transport. Sweat was rolling down their necks, and she could see it shimmering off their arms. Valor downed a bottle of water, and Arrow hit the gas so hard the tires squealed.

"Do you think we got it before it sent the transmission back?" Valor asked Arrow.

Arrow shook her head. "I don't know, but we need to get out of here."

"Is that the drone?" Kaelyn tried to get a better look, but there was a metal screen blocking her view.

"Yes," Valor and Arrow answered in unison.

She couldn't see it, but she could hear the hissing and popping the electrical components were making from the machine behind her. It sounded like it was dying, a perfect representation of the world around them.

CHAPTER TWENTY

MacLeod paced the large conference room. He felt the familiar sensation of rage start to pump through his body. It was invigorating, and he wanted to punch the glass window in front of him, or better yet, the commander who had just given him the news.

People were talking to him, throwing out information, ideas, and worse, excuses. Finally, a voice broke through that soothed his inner devil. Nora inspired many emotions in him, but right now, her presence was like a piece of ice to his scorching temper.

"If you *had* to guess, which direction would they have headed?" she said, hands flat on the table, her body angled toward the commander.

The commander squirmed under her scrutiny. No one was used to having to discuss anything with a woman. It forced them out of their comfort zone, and MacLeod loved watching them try to navigate the correct amount of respect balanced with their knowledge that men were the superior gender.

The commander turned his hat over in his hands. "North would be their best option. There's another Resistance base in that area, and they'll want to stay in friendly territory. But there's more. The corporal that escaped has some information for you."

He hated that name, *Resistance*. He tried not to fly over the table at him. "Don't call them that." He gripped to top of his chair. "They're traitors, pure and simple."

The commander, to his credit, knew better than to argue. "Yes, sir."

"Where's that corporal? I want to get this over with."

The commander went to the door and motioned at someone to enter. A moment later, a kid who couldn't have been a day over seventeen walked through the door. His hands were shaking, and he stared at the ground. He loved to inspire this kind of respect from his people. It helped to dull the anger he was feeling.

The commander pushed him forward. "Tell him about the Phoenix."

He looked like he was about to vomit all over the table. "Phoenix isn't just a project, it's a person. Her name is Kaelyn Trapp."

MacLeod felt the blood in his body pool in his head. He must have heard wrong. Not only was it impossible, it didn't make any sense. "What did you say?"

The corporal looked up at him now, fear etched around his eyes. "Kaelyn Trapp, sir. She was with them, and she isn't old the way she should be."

He rubbed his hands together, a motion to help control the rage that was making them shake. "Commander, triple the drones. I want all of them dead, except this person who claims to be Kaelyn Trapp. I want her brought to me, alive."

The commander stood a little straighter. "Sir, if this is really Kaelyn Trapp, keeping her alive is not a good idea."

MacLeod slid his hand over the top of his gun. He didn't have the patience or the inclination to deal with insubordination. He said what he wanted, and there was no room for argument. This commander would be easily replaced, and it would be a warning shot to the rest of the morons in his army.

Nora's hand came to rest on his shoulder, and he relaxed slightly. She squeezed him a bit as she spoke. "Commander, surely you understand the importance of needing to talk to someone who claims to be Kaelyn Trapp. If this were true, she would be in her mid nineties, and it sounds like that isn't the case. We need to know what's happening to protect our people."

"It just doesn't seem possible," the commander muttered under his breath.

MacLeod was impressed with Nora's deductive reasoning. He hadn't thought of questioning the imposter, he simply wanted to see her tortured, but he liked where her line of thinking was heading.

"Go on, Nora." He relaxed and took a seat.

Nora looked over to the corporal who looked as if he might pass out. She crossed her arms and looked out the window. "How old was this person who claimed to be Kaelyn Trapp?"

"Probably around thirty, ma'am." He sounded convinced, a direct contrast to his expression.

Nora pulled up an image on the projection screen. "Is that her?"

The corporal nodded vigorously. "Yes, that's her."

"Fascinating," she said thoughtfully. "There might be others."

MacLeod stood, his emotions pounding in his head. "Others? Like who?"

Nora shook her head. "I'm not sure, but if they somehow developed the technology to keep her in some kind of preserved state, wouldn't they do it with others?"

The thought was preposterous. The very idea that something like this could be happening without his knowledge was a betrayal. He wanted every single person responsible. He wanted to hang them from columns in the center of Eden. He wanted everyone to witness his crowning achievement, the final annihilation of the Resistance.

He grabbed the commander by the collar and pushed him against the wall. "Find them all and bring them to me. Go to all the bases, all the Resistance villages, and find out where they are. If they won't talk, start killing at random. I don't care what it takes, I want them all."

The commander straightened his shirt when he finally let him out of his grasp. He nodded to the corporal, and they speedily exited the room. Nora was beside him instantly. She rubbed his back and led him to his chair.

She pushed the call button on his desk. "Please bring in some tea with extra sugar."

The fondness he felt for Nora wasn't shared with anyone else in the world. Not any of his wives or mistresses could hold a candle to his daughter. "You always know what I need."

CHAPTER TWENTY-ONE

Arrow opened the trunk of the transport. Valor had managed to take down the drone with the EMP, but they still didn't know if it had sent their location before it had fallen. She pulled it out and turned it over. She pulled the hatch and looked at the smoldering innards. She took the detection device from her pocket and scanned the drone. After a few moments, the message scrolled across the screen, *NOT REPAIRABLE.*

"Shit." She dropped the detection device back into her pocket.

Valor was leaning against the transport. "What did you think would happen? The EMP is supposed to wipe it out."

"I know. I was just hoping we would be able to download some of the information." She dropped the drone on the ground.

She looked around the area and used her shirt to wipe the sweat from her forehead. "Any word from the other Phoenixes?"

Valor leaned closer, keeping his voice down. "No, but we aren't supposed to, unless it's an emergency."

"I know. That's why I asked." She shut the back of the transport. "Let's see if we can get in there without drawing too much attention to ourselves."

Kaelyn jogged up from the tree where she'd just relieved herself. "Thanks for stopping."

Arrow gestured to get back in the car. "We just needed to get inside a weather bubble."

Once inside the transport, Arrow pulled the device off her shoulder and rotated her arm. The pain was gone and she felt good as new. She turned and looked at Johnson. "What's the protocol for a full search?"

Johnson shrugged. "Send out all available drones."

"How many is that?" Arrow asked, happy she didn't have to badger him for an answer.

"I don't know for sure, but thousands."

Arrow had assumed as much, but she didn't like the answer all the same. "They're going to flood all the emergency broadcast frequencies."

Her mom leaned forward. "That's what we wanted. Our people don't usually fight back. If they know MacLeod is looking for the Phoenix, they will. He'll have to start fighting battles all over the colonies. It will weaken them in Eden."

She was right, but it did nothing to squelch the fear Arrow had pumping through her. They were making the best decisions possible for the circumstances they were in, but that meant nothing if things went south.

She put the coordinates into the transport. "We'll stop in the village right outside Denver for a few hours. Then we'll trade out the transport and get into the tunnels before sunrise."

"Will we be safe there?" Kaelyn asked.

Arrow shrugged. "I don't think we're safe anywhere. We just need to get as close to the tunnels as possible."

❖

This village wasn't like the last one they had visited. Kaelyn strained to see out the window as they pulled the transport into a series of makeshift carports that sat alongside a large warehouse. There was nothing else of distinction, and Kaelyn struggled to understand how this was a village at all. There was nowhere to sleep, no center to the community. It seemed like they just stumbled on a warehouse that a passerby might use as shelter. There was an old light rail car in the distance. It had fallen over on its side; the windows were shattered and there were branches winding through whatever openings they could find. She could barely make out the *RTD* on the side.

Arrow and Valor pulled a large tarp over the transport. It wouldn't prevent people from peaking under it, but it was inconspicuous enough to not draw attention. Although, Kaelyn wasn't sure there was anyone around to see it. Johnson's pleas for a bathroom were answered by Valor, who pulled him back into a wooded area.

Macy kept herself busy by arranging her pack for what must have been the third time that day. Kaelyn assumed this was probably a nervous habit of sorts, needing to organize in a sea of chaos.

The lonely sounds of a zipper opening and a piece of paper moving was all she could hear. There was no hum of people near them or machines working. She watched Arrow scour the paper maps, seemingly trying to etch them into her mind on the chance they weren't available to her at a later time. At first glance, she seemed relaxed, body leaning against the transport with one foot propping her up her weight. But her eyes were laser focused on the information she held. The tips of her hair that fell against the edge of her ears and face were damp with perspiration, and Kaelyn thought of how they would feel, slick and smooth under her fingertips. She imagined touching the side of her face and how it would feel to have Arrow lean into her palm.

Valor interrupted her internal lusting. "We should get inside."

Kaelyn could only assume that inside meant the warehouse, but she couldn't imagine an entire village of people calling this their residence. Then again, she couldn't have imagined most of this when she'd been put into her suspended state. She was going to ask him to explain but changed her mind. She'd learned over the last several days that there was no explanation that could properly prepare her for what she was about to see.

The inside of the warehouse was well lit with high ceilings. It would have looked just like any other warehouse she remembered from her time before if it weren't for the hundreds of people moving about inside. They had divided their personal spaces with makeshift walls, mostly constructed out of old pallets and cinder blocks. She was doing her best to take in the ways people had arranged their designated areas as they moved through the expanse, but it was becoming more difficult the farther they made their way to the center of the building.

The loud sounds of chatter and noises quickly faded as people turned to gawk at their arrival. She watched as older people grabbed hold of children, pulling them closer. She wanted to stop and tell them she meant them no harm, they were here to help, but she didn't. She realized that this might be their intention, but it wasn't something she could guarantee. Their very presence was putting all these people at risk, and the weight of that truth started to squeeze at her throat making it more difficult to breathe.

Arrow was a few feet in front of her, and she wanted to grab her hand. She needed assurance that this was the best option, she needed grounding, but she also needed the closeness of Arrow. Instead, she resolved to try to make eye contact with as many people as possible. To smile at them, trying to offer assurances she had no business making.

A very tall, very muscular woman stepped out in front of them. Her arms were crossed and she looked angry. But her stern expression was replaced with a welcoming smile and outreached arms when she saw who was in front of her.

Arrow walked directly into the woman's embrace. "Angela, it's so good to see you."

Angela stepped back, her hands still on Arrow's arms. "Arrow, it's been too long, my friend." She shook Valor's hand and then saluted Macy. "Madam President, it's an honor to have you here." When her eyes fell on Kaelyn, they brightened. She walked directly to her and put out her hand. "Phoenix One, we've been waiting for you."

Kaelyn didn't understand how they could have known they were coming, but she took her hand anyway. "I'm sorry. Plans have been changing regularly."

Angela put her hands on her hips and smiled. "No, Ms. Trapp. We've been waiting on you for nearly seventy years, not just today."

Arrow pointed to Johnson. "He's our insurance policy."

Angela looked at him intensely, and hatred flared in her eyes. "I see."

"What have you heard?" Arrow asked.

Angela pulled her stare away from Johnson and focused again on Arrow. "They sent out an emergency broadcast. They know about the Phoenix and they want her, bad. There's a fifty-million-dollar reward, along with immunity to whoever delivers her alive."

Arrow ran her hand through her hair. "They'll be checking all the villages. We won't stay long. Can we get a secure connection with the other Resistance divisions from here?"

Angela looked to the tallest of the three men behind her. "Take the soldier to get something to eat, then stay with him until we're done."

The tall man nodded and took Johnson by the arm, leading him in a different direction.

Angela showed them into an ancient, large RV. There were more monitors on the walls and radio equipment than what Kaelyn remembered RVs having, but it was a brief trip down memory lane. They took their seats on the couch and waited as Angela went to work typing into a keyboard that was also from Kaelyn's own time, not like the floating consoles and translucent screens that she'd seen back at the Guardian base.

Kaelyn bumped Arrow, who was sitting next to her. "You guys should do her a solid and upgrade her machinery."

Angela answered instead of Arrow. "We communicate on a different frequency with these machines than what's monitored by the Hand of God. We're not considered a lost city, and they've pretty much forgotten we're here. We try not to go outside very often, and we keep our tech to a minimum."

Kaelyn realized her joke had fallen flat on her audience and decided not to interject any other little tidbits. "All the Resistance bases have these?"

Angela turned around in her seat after pressing a final button. "In some form or another." She angled the webcam so the screen included Kaelyn and Macy.

After a few moments, twelve different pictures popped up on the screen. It took Kaelyn a moment to realize that every one of them was a picture of a woman. It was a moment of pride in a whirlwind of danger and unease.

All of them greeted President Steele and were then silent for a long moment. Finally, the woman with the letters MTA 3 listed under her frame spoke again. "Phoenix One, it's our honor."

Kaelyn nodded while the rest echoed the first woman's sentiments. "The honor is mine."

Arrow leaned forward to speak to the camera. "I know this is all happening slightly differently than we'd previously discussed. We need to know that your forces are ready to move forward. I'm afraid we're running out of time."

Each of the women began to report with what sounded like rather impressive numbers. Arrow wrote down the details. Kaelyn watched intently as the totals were being figured. In all, the Resistance had a complete fighting force of just over eleven thousand able bodies.

Arrow glanced over at Macy who nodded to her; they obviously had shorthand between them that no one else was privy to. "Have Phoenixes Two, Three, and Four started making their way to Eden?"

"Yes, everything is in motion. We have no contact with them unless they arrive at a secured location, as you have. So we can't confirm their status at this point. But has the final destination changed? You're off track for Eden."

"Our route had to change. We're using the underground tunnels. The Hand of God is looking for us, but as far as we know, they aren't looking for any other Phoenix, nor do we think they're even aware of their existence. If they stick to the plan, they should be fine. Our final landing spot is still Mt. Weather, just inside Eden, in approximately one week."

"How should the fighting forces proceed?" one of the women asked.

Macy put her hand on Arrow's shoulder. "Start loading equipment into transports. You'll need to be ready to move. When the Hand of God shows up, fight back. Once you've overthrown their soldiers, start moving forward. We'll have four key fronts, just as we had discussed. You should have the coordinates, but they'll line the outer limits of Eden. The coordinates reflect what were once known as Erie, Pennsylvania; Buffalo, New York; Morgantown, West Virginia; and Fredericksburg, Virginia. If we can enter at these points, we'll be able to surround them. It's also where they make all their water and food transfers. If we can isolate these areas, the fact that we're outnumbered won't matter. We can starve them out."

"We'll post at all their main exit routes. President Steele and Captain Valor Markinson will be at Fredericksburg once they've replaced the general that needed to remain at his headquarters to deal with the government showing up. Phoenix Two will be at the Buffalo location, Phoenix Three at Morgantown, and Phoenix Four at Erie. Phoenix One will go directly to MacLeod." Arrow counted them off on her fingers as she spoke.

"And if you don't make it to Mt. Weather by the time all the forces are in place?" another of the women asked.

Arrow shot Kaelyn a half-smile. "Then all command will revert to President Steele."

Angela turned back around in the chair. "We'll have the Phoenix record a message to show to your people. I'll send it over as soon as it's ready." She ended the communication.

Kaelyn was still trying to let her mind catch up to what was clear—they were on the brink of war, and it was up to her to get people ready for it. She needed to get out of this enclosed space. She needed to walk around; she needed to process.

She stood and pushed open the door. She was sure she mumbled some excuse, but she wasn't sure what she said. She wandered out into the warehouse, taking several deep breaths and trying not to bend over with her hands on her knees. People needed her to be strong, unflappable, and right now, she felt anything but.

She remembered the general direction she'd come from and tried to retrace her steps. People were still staring at her, whispering to each other. She found what looked to be the main section of the building and started down that direction. Three small children ran past her, kicking a soccer ball. They didn't seem to notice who or what she was, and that made her want to follow them, to hide with them for just a little bit.

She was going to follow them when she felt a hand on her arm. She looked down and noticed the familiar fingers. Only a brief moment of wonder passed as she realized how intimate it was to recognize a person's fingers. Arrow pulled her close and then tugged her around a corner.

"Are you okay?" Arrow's eyes were inspecting every part of her face, like she was looking for a secret tucked away in plain sight on her facial features.

Kaelyn put her hands against Arrow's chest, allowing her presence to settle her. "Yes. I just needed to take everything in. You've been planning this since you were old enough to understand war strategy, but I haven't had the opportunity. It was overwhelming."

Arrow looked concerned. "I know it's a lot. But we can't put this off."

"I know," Kaelyn said. She moved closer to Arrow, trying to steal her strength. "It's just hard to make peace with the thought of putting so many people in harm's way."

"People are in harm's way now, whether you do anything or not. The moment the Phoenix Project went live, everyone's life changed." Arrow leaned into Kaelyn more.

She put her arms around Arrow's waist, needing to be held. "I know. I just don't want to mess any of this up. I want to do right by all of this, by all of you."

Arrow hugged her back. "You won't mess anything up."

"How do you know that?"

Arrow leaned her head down so it hovered right next to Kaelyn's ear. "You were chosen because you have a deep understanding for this country and its history. You wrote dozens of papers on how the Founding Fathers came to the decisions they did, their reasons for fighting off tyranny, and their devotion to a free people. You articulated how those initial thoughts and actions morphed into a growing and developing country. You described the lessons that could be taken from their mistakes and the mistakes that were made along the way. Once all of this is over and we have placed you in power, these people will need someone to lead them. Someone who not only has a vast understanding of where we came from but where we need to go after. You studied history and strategy your entire adult life, you researched military operations, their effect on the world, and what could've and should've been done differently. You're an expert in leadership in a globalized world. You understand and helped to develop the benchmarks for peaceful leadership around the globe. You quite literally wrote the book on why governments place profit over people and how to rectify that. During your time, you were chosen for this for all of those reasons. That hasn't changed. These people already believe in you, in what you stand for, and the world you once represented. Now, they just need to hear that you believe in them too."

"You'll be with me until the end?" This seemed just as important to her success as anything else.

"Yes, of course. I'm not going anywhere." Arrow squeezed her tighter.

Kaelyn wondered if Arrow was comfortable making promises she had no way of knowing she could keep.

CHAPTER TWENTY-TWO

Valor brought Kaelyn her computer. She sat down on an old ammunition box and started scrolling through documents. Arrow was amazed at the speed she flipped through documents without the assistance of CAM. She'd taken several notes and then stared up at the ceiling several times as though thinking things through.

Arrow noticed Angela pacing from about twenty feet away and put her hands up, motioning her to relax. Kaelyn was putting enough pressure on herself and didn't need anyone adding to it.

"How's it going?" her mother asked, appearing by her side.

"Okay, I think. She's been writing for over an hour." Arrow chewed on her thumb.

Her mother pushed her hand away from her mouth, momentarily breaking the bad habit she had since childhood "You should eat something. Hovering isn't going to make it go any faster."

"I'll eat when she's done." Kaelyn hadn't asked her to stay, but she wanted to be close by if she needed her.

Kaelyn closed her computer and smiled. Arrow felt her heart rate pick up as Kaelyn approached her.

"I'm ready," Kaelyn said.

"I'll take you over." Arrow motioned in the direction of the RV.

Once inside, Angela arranged the equipment to record Kaelyn. After a few moments, she sat down. "Let me know when you're ready to begin."

Arrow didn't understand why she was so nervous. She was trying to keep herself from fidgeting as Kaelyn arranged her computer off to the left so she could scan the words she'd just written. She wanted this to go well for the Resistance, for the thousands of people who were counting on their success, but more than that, for Kaelyn. She wanted her to feel good about the outcome, about her decision to do this, about her destiny.

Kaelyn nodded, and Angela pushed a button and then pointed at her. Kaelyn looked calm, resigned to the magnitude of the endeavor she was taking ownership for in this moment. "Hello, everyone. My name is Kaelyn Trapp, but some of you might know me as Phoenix One. You might have thought the story of the Phoenix was a fairytale, a legend of sorts. I can tell you it's absolutely true. I was cryogenically frozen because we thought, even back then, that we might need someone in the future who knew how beautiful and how inclusive the country could be.

"I come from a time that was tremendously different from the one we find ourselves in now. My time was riddled with injustices for many people, our planet was in a terrible state, and our country was in crisis. I was sad when I woke up to find those aspects hadn't changed. But that's not all I saw when I started to learn more about what our people had become. I discovered all of you. I found that the Resistance is stronger than ever. I found that you have persevered through conditions and tribulations that you should've never had to endure. I found kindness, compassion, and a desire to help your neighbors, even in the face of poverty, forced labor, and cruelty. I found you all to be a better version of us than during my time. The desire you feel to fight comes from the long-enduring spirit that once created America. It comes from your ancestors, who were willing to risk everything for the simple promise that life would be better for their children and grandchildren. It comes from your faith in not only your own spirit, but in that of your fellow compatriots."

Arrow saw Kaelyn's hand tremble as she smoothly pressed a button on her computer to scroll down. She looked totally calm, but she clearly didn't feel that way. Arrow wished she could go to her, give her support. But this was something she had to do on her own.

"The people living in Eden have been lied to about who we are and our intentions. We don't want to destroy them; we want to be together again. We want to begin the process of putting our country back together the way it was always meant to be, with the will of the people at the helm. MacLeod keeps them sedated, uninformed, and angry. He whispers deceit into their ears to keep them bitter; he uses us as the enemy. He wants them to hate us, so they don't see the magnitude of what is happening. He tells them we're to blame so they don't turn their attention toward him. My father used to say that it's easy to be against something, but what are you *for*? Well, the Resistance stands for equality, unity, and freedom."

Arrow was aware of the gathering crowd behind her, and the feeling of expectation and energy filled the air. She could feel people responding to Kaelyn's words.

"We will fight for what is ours, and we will fight to free the people of Eden of the mind control they have been enduring for decades. We will fight because it's right, it's just, and because it's our duty. Many of you have been waiting for this day all your life. Others are unsure of the change that is coming. But change is necessary. Taking back our country and restoring freedom is the only solution to this authoritarian government. People will try to stop us, but they won't succeed. It is impossible to kill an idea that lives in the hearts of each and every one of us. It is impossible to extinguish a fire that burns so deep within you that it makes up part of your DNA. It is impossible to turn back. I'll be there with you, to fight, to create, and to once again bring us all together."

Arrow shivered as the goose bumps that had begun at her legs raced up her body, up to her neck. Reading about Kaelyn, watching her lectures, was nothing like witnessing her in action, in real life. Kaelyn was everything Arrow hoped she would be and more. Arrow glanced over and saw Angela wiping a tear out of her eye, and the looks on everyone's faces said what Arrow felt in her heart as well; they would follow Kaelyn anywhere.

"Was that okay?" Kaelyn asked a moment later, holding her computer against her chest.

Arrow couldn't believe she was asking the question. Could she not see the effect she had on everyone in this room? Could she not see their eyes on her, waiting for their next direction? How could she not feel it?

"You were perfect," Arrow said. She wanted to say more to give credence to her words, but that was all she could manage.

"It will broadcast everywhere when you give the word," Angela said.

"Send it to the Resistance first, and then air it everywhere in three days. Most of the troops should be in position by then," Arrow answered, but she couldn't pull her eyes away from Kaelyn.

Kaelyn's cheeks flushed red under Arrow's intense scrutiny. "Everywhere?"

"Yes, even Eden will see it once we're in place." Arrow took her hand.

"We won't be to Mt. Weather in three days." Kaelyn squeezed her hand.

"No, but we'll be close, and we need them to know we're coming. If we have any chance of uniting the skeptics inside Eden and ourselves, we can't ambush them." Arrow practically choked on her words, wanting so badly to kiss her.

A moment later, she heard the speech Kaelyn had just given pouring out of the speaker system inside the warehouse. Luckily, it was enough to get her to focus on why they were there in the first place.

"Let's go get some food and then a few hours of sleep before we head out."

"Okay," Kaelyn said.

❖

Kaelyn watched from the back seat of their new transport vehicle as Arrow and Valor loaded the last few bags. Arrow told her they'd switched in case the soldiers managed to hack the system back at the Guardian base and were able to track their location. They wouldn't be able to trace them completely with the encryption software they'd administered, but switching was the safest bet going forward.

Kaelyn hadn't been able to sleep after they'd eaten. So many people wanted to talk to her, touch her, and be near her. She'd forgotten how exhausting it was being a talisman for people in need. But it was also invigorating to see their excitement, to feel their loyalty, and to sense the change they all knew was coming.

When she had finally lain down, she stayed awake, hoping Arrow would come to her, but she never did. The longing she'd felt to have Arrow near her almost eclipsed all the other emotions she'd experienced right before. But she also knew that it was for the best. Arrow had to focus and so did she. Any mistake or minor slipup could cost thousands of people their lives.

"Did you mean everything you said?" Johnson asked from his small seat in the middle. She hadn't been expecting to hear his voice, and since the only thing he had projected until now was contempt, she was surprised by his earnest tone.

"Yes, every word," she answered.

"What did you mean by," he leaned in closer to whisper, as if he'd be in trouble for his thoughts, "he keeps us sedated?"

She answered him without hesitation, not to make him feel guilty or to rub it in his face, but because his question was a big step and probably difficult and scary to ask. "MacLeod adds sedatives to the water supply in Eden. He keeps your minds dull to help keep you in line."

His face turned a ghostly white and then transformed into a red of fury. "That can't be true."

"Tell me something then. Do you feel different after being outside the wall for so long?" She made sure her tone was careful and comforting. She had no desire to be combative.

"Yes, but I thought it was because I've been here with all of you, eating different types of foods and being in and out of the weather bubbles." He was pressing his thumb into his palm hard, almost as if he were trying to inflict pain. Or maybe he just wanted to be sure he wasn't dreaming.

"All of the food you eat in Eden is provided by the farmers in the Resistance," Macy added. "It's the drug from the water wearing off that allows you some clarity." Her voice was calm and sure.

"But why?" His voice cracked.

"To control you," Macy said. "People under control are easier to spoon-feed propaganda to, and it's easier to get them to fight for that propaganda."

Arrow and Valor got back into the car. Kaelyn got a whiff of the soap on her skin as she sat down. She wondered if she'd ever been so attuned to the way a person smelled before. She'd put on a black hat for this part of the journey; it made her look even fiercer, stronger somehow. Kaelyn knew Arrow had probably done it for a pragmatic reason, but she didn't care. She was going to enjoy it all the same.

Arrow adjusted her mirror. "You okay, Johnson?"

Johnson shifted in his seat, probably an unconscious action to help settle the information into his mind. "Yeah, I'm fine."

Arrow caught Kaelyn's eyes in the mirror while checking to see if Johnson was telling the truth. Kaelyn winked at her, and although she couldn't see her mouth fully, she knew by her eyes that Arrow was smiling.

"We'll be at the tunnels in about twenty minutes." She finished pushing the buttons and the transport started moving.

Kaelyn turned and looked at the warehouse they had called home for a few short hours. Inside, people were busying themselves, preparing for battle. The fighting units were polishing their weapons and writing letters to anyone they were leaving behind. Kaelyn ruminated on the fact that no matter how many things changed, some things would always remain the same.

Twenty minutes later, Arrow slowed the transport until it came to a stop. There was another vehicle parked nearby. Arrow pulled out a set of binoculars from the console.

"Shit." She handed the binoculars to Valor.

"They can't be here waiting for us, can they?" he asked.

She shook her head. "They would've sent more than one transport if they knew we were heading here. But it's probably a general search unit since they're watching for us."

Arrow turned in her seat and faced Macy. "Take the two of them and hide behind that wall over there. We'll go take care of this. If they see the transport, it's the first place they'll head, and I don't want you to be sitting ducks."

Macy nodded and pulled a large gun from under the seat. "Let us know when it's clear."

Johnson looked panicked. "Can you undo these?" He put his bound wrists forward. "I can't run very well like this."

Valor and Arrow looked at each other and then Valor reached forward to undo the bindings. "One funny move and she'll kill you." He nodded at Macy.

Johnson nodded his understanding and rubbed his wrists as the mechanisms slid back off him. Macy opened her door and Kaelyn did the same.

She was about to follow Macy out of the transport when Kaelyn leaned forward and put her hand on Arrow's shoulder. "Please be careful."

Arrow smiled at her. "I'm always careful."

Kaelyn wasn't sure if that was true or not, but she had no choice but to believe her right now. She slipped out of the back seat and followed Macy to the wall alongside a building, long forgotten like most things in this world.

She thought it had taken them an eternity to get there, and the relief she felt when they rounded the corner was squelched when she peeked around and saw Arrow and Valor moving in tandem between abandoned vehicles. She heard movement from behind her and the sound of rocks rolling down a hill. Then, the definite sound of footsteps.

Macy turned with her gun trained on the direction the steps were coming from. She tapped Kaelyn on the shoulder, pointed to her eyes, and then to another wall. Kaelyn thought back to all the war movies she'd seen as a child, a favorite genre of her father's and thanked him silently for that now. She held Johnson's arm as they moved over to the adjacent wall together, Macy walking backward to protect them from whoever the footsteps belonged to.

Once at the wall, Macy pulled a thin pipe from her pocket, extended it, and turned the head of it around the corner. She attached it to a small device, and a moment later, a picture came into focus in a hologram in front of them. They could see the man inspecting their transport. He pulled open the doors and started tossing their bags onto the ground. He must have radioed for someone because a few moments later, another man came down over the hill.

Kaelyn felt her palms sweating and her neck flush. She wasn't sure where Arrow and Valor were, but she hoped it was nearby and that they were witnessing this. Johnson shifted next to her.

She looked at him and shook her head. "Don't even think about it."

She realized that he wasn't shifting to run away; he was shielding her from the opposite side. She wanted to show her appreciation, but their time was up. Another man had appeared from a different direction and had his gun trained on the three of them.

"Stand up and put your hands against the wall." The Eden soldier took another step forward.

Kaelyn glanced over at Macy, wanting to take her lead, and saw her push a button on the bracelet she was wearing before Macy turned and did as she was told. The small amount of relief that flushed through her system was short-lived as the soldier pressed the gun against her chest.

He called out to whoever was there with him. "I have prisoners!"

The word bristled against her senses. *Prisoners.* Is that what they would become if they couldn't find a way out of these circumstances?

Johnson and Macy had put their hands against the wall while she stood eye-to-eye with a man who couldn't have been more than nineteen years old. She'd always assumed in a situation like this her emotions would get the best of her and it would lead to tears. But that's not what she felt now; she felt anger, the need to survive, and conviction pumped through her body.

"You're making a huge mistake." She searched for the right words to say, the ones that would create the gap they needed.

He pushed the gun into her chest harder. "Don't make eye contact with me, female."

Johnson spoke from beside her. "My name is Corporal Lawrence Johnson, I'm with the One Hundred and Third Division. I was transporting these two to Eden."

"Bullshit!" the soldier practically yelled. "One female is armed. Who are you?"

He reached to turn Johnson around, and in doing so, broke contact with her chest for a second. But that was long enough. Kaelyn pushed the gun straight up and away from her. A single shot was fired, and as the soldier tried to reclaim his control of the weapon, Macy managed to hit him in the side of the head. He fell over backward, unconscious.

There was no time to celebrate the small victory. The other two soldiers had closed the distance and had their guns aimed directly at them. The soldiers looked at their colleague on the ground and gripped the guns harder, seeming to aim at them with more focus.

Johnson put his hands forward, a sign of surrender. "Just put the guns down. We'll go with you."

The older looking of the two soldiers looked past Johnson.

"No one is going anywhere."

Kaelyn saw Arrow before she heard her, but only by a second. She ran up behind the two soldiers, almost in a crouched position, and Kaelyn felt herself, once again, in awe of Arrow's capabilities. As Arrow moved, she retrieved a knife from somewhere behind her back. Once she was within striking distance, she made her move, sliding the knife into the side of the soldier closest to the wall.

The other soldier, seeing the man next to him fall to the ground, turned his gun on Arrow. Arrow had already pulled her sidearm and they now stood face-to-face, weapons on each other.

Valor's voice echoed from on top of the wall. "Drop your weapon. You're surrounded."

The soldier glanced up at the top of the wall and smiled. "That's what you think."

A gunshot from a building off in the distance rang out, and the dirt around Arrow's feet fumed up in a cloud of dust. Another gunshot reverberated in her ears, and Valor pushed himself over the top of the wall and landed on the ground. Macy reached for her weapon on the ground, only a few feet away.

"Touch it and she dies," the soldier said, moving closer to Arrow.

The chaos was closing in on the soldier. Sweat dripped down the side of his face in a long bead, and his hand was shaking. Valor was now behind Arrow with his back against the wall, gun drawn.

"You're running out of options. Your sniper friend can't get us all before we get you," Arrow said.

Kaelyn did the mental math, and there was no way they got out of this alive with a sniper in an undisclosed location. She also knew that Arrow and Valor weren't going to budge, which would lead to someone dying. The only way out was to do the unexpected, cause a distraction that would leave this soldier vulnerable.

Kaelyn pushed herself off the wall. "Take me. Trust me when I say I'm the one you want."

The soldier didn't take his eyes off Arrow. "What are you talking about?"

"I'm Phoenix One." She took a step closer, her hands out in front of her. "Check your transmitter. Your government is looking for me."

"Be quiet, Kaelyn." Arrow's voice calm, but her eyes were frantic.

The soldier must have noticed her reaction because he reached into his pocket and pulled out his transmitter. He pushed a few buttons and then dropped the piece of communication equipment on the ground.

He turned, gun aimed on Kaelyn. "By order of President MacLeod, you're under arrest."

Kaelyn put her wrists out in front of her. "I'll go with you quietly, but I need to know that my friends will be safe. Call down the sniper."

He took a step toward Kaelyn and then hesitated. His hand shook with more ferocity, and he blinked the sweat out of his eyes. "No."

Arrow reached for her gun, and he moved closer to Kaelyn. "Make one more move and I'll shoot her. I swear I will."

Kaelyn got on her knees and put her hands behind her head. "You'll be a hero. You have no idea what I mean to your president. Just call down your sniper and we can end all of this."

The soldier only took another second to make up his mind. He pushed a button in his ear that Kaelyn couldn't see. "Come down from your post."

He tossed the restraints to Kaelyn and then turned his gun back on Arrow. "Put your weapons on the ground."

Johnson moved so quickly, Kaelyn didn't have time to string the movements together. Johnson tackled the soldier from the side. There were punches and billows of dirt. Out of the corner of her eye, she saw Valor go back up and over the wall. Then three gunshots were fired. Two were very close and another was far away. Macy was on top of her a moment later, shielding Kaelyn with her body. She could taste dirt and sweat mixed together as she tried to breathe. Kaelyn wasn't sure if it was fear or the granulated mixture in her mouth that was impeding her efforts. She wasn't sure who was alive and who was dead. She closed her eyes and prayed to whatever God existed that it wasn't Arrow, while asking for forgiveness that by doing so, she hoped it was someone else.

CHAPTER TWENTY-THREE

Arrow turned Johnson over. There were tears streaking his cheeks, leaving a clean wake through the dirt that covered his face. He wasn't going to make it; the soldier had shot him in the gut after he was tackled. The blood loss was already too severe. So she did the only thing she could, she held his hand.

"I'm here with you, Johnson."

"Is Kaelyn okay?" He choked, blood bubbling at his lips.

"Yes, thanks to you," she said.

His body was shivering from the blood loss and his voice was cracked from the pain. "I'm sorry."

She gripped his hand tighter. "You have nothing to be sorry for. We're still here because of you."

"You have my information. Please, find my parents and tell them I did the right thing."

"I promise." She put her other hand on his shoulder. "I'll make sure they're okay, and I'll take care of them."

His eyes closed and his chest stopped moving. She sat there for a second longer, making sure to tuck away in her heart the promise she made. She pulled one of the Guardian patches off her shoulder and put it in Johnson's hand, closing his lifeless fingers around it.

Valor appeared a moment later, a body draped over his shoulders. "We're all clear."

"I'll go grab some shovels. We need to bury Johnson." She didn't know if Valor agreed and she didn't care. Johnson had given his life to protect them, and as far as she was concerned he was as good of a Guardian as any of the people she'd trained with.

It wasn't until the last bit of dirt covered Johnson that she allowed herself to make eye contact with Kaelyn. Kaelyn looked on, her arms crossed and tears on her cheeks.

Arrow hadn't known until Kaelyn had stepped forward and volunteered herself that she'd never experienced true fear before. The sensation was crippling, and even now, the last remnants were working their way out of her system.

"Don't ever do that again," she said to Kaelyn.

Kaelyn took a step forward and buried her head into Arrow's chest. "I had to do something. I did the mental math, and the only plausible solution was to do something that no one expected. When the unexpected arises, people don't know how to react, so they improvise. It leaves them vulnerable."

Arrow instinctively put her arms around her. "You could've gotten yourself killed."

Kaelyn sniffed. "Better than getting us all killed."

Arrow wondered if Kaelyn could hear her heart slamming against her chest with those words. "Promise me you won't ever do something like that again."

Kaelyn looked up at her now. Her bright green eyes reminded her of fresh grass. The way it felt to be a child, rolling down hills without a care in the world. But the innocence of childhood wasn't what stared back. Her eyes were tinted with desire and need.

"I promise," Kaelyn said in a breath.

But even as she said it, Arrow knew Kaelyn would do whatever necessary if the situation presented itself. Arrow marveled at the lies she and Kaelyn continued to exchange. Promises to always be there and to stay out of harm's way, lies they told to extinguish the pain in the moment.

Her mother's voice pulled at her, bringing her back to reality. "We need to get going. It won't be long before they realize there are soldiers missing."

All Arrow wanted to do was stay beside Kaelyn, but her mother was right. Time wasn't on their side, and giving in to her desire for Kaelyn wasn't her choice to make. It wasn't fair to the Resistance to risk it all on feelings. Who would she be if she gave in to such selfish desires?

She stepped back from Kaelyn. "Let's get going."

Kaelyn nodded her agreement. "Okay, let's go."

They found the entrance for emergency vehicles within a few minutes. It wasn't very well hidden, but that was part of the idea of placing one of the entrances within the confines of an airport. Arrow pulled the car up and hopped out. She found the small screen on the outside of the heavy door and hooked her transmitter into it. Within a few seconds, it isolated the code and the door slid open.

Once the transport was inside the lift, the door slid shut behind them, and the lift automatically started moving down. When it reached the bottom level, the overhead fluorescent lights started turning on in sequence, lighting the way into the darkness ahead. Arrow hesitated; the tunnel was only big enough for the transport plus a person on each side. There would be nowhere to go if they were to encounter soldiers from Eden anywhere along the way.

"What's wrong?" Valor asked from the seat next to her.

"There's no turning back once we get in here. I'm just running through it one more time in my head."

Valor opened the paper map and measured their distance for the fourth time since they devised their plan. "It's four hundred and fifty-five miles to Hutchinson, Kansas. That's the closest entry or exit point. Chances are, if anyone is coming, they're going to start here. The sooner we get moving, the sooner we can reevaluate at the next point."

Arrow knew the numbers, and she had all the routes memorized. "I'm programming the cruising speed for ninety-two miles per hour. That's the fastest speed we can safely travel through the tunnel. It should take us four hours and fifty-six minutes."

Valor folded the map. "Then we better get going."

Arrow double-checked the sensors and turned their sensitivity levels up. If anything got in their path, the autopilot features would notify her. The transport started moving, and Arrow pushed down the large lump that had grown in her throat. She couldn't believe how relaxed Valor and her mother were in this moment. They both had their heads against the windows of the transport, taking this opportunity to get some rest.

Kaelyn handed her a book from the back seat. "I think you'll enjoy looking through this. Plus, it will help pass the time."

Arrow took the book, amazed by the worn binding and the glossy cover. She wasn't sure if she'd ever held an actual book other than the one of the Louvre she'd found in Kaelyn's things. The heft of it weighed her hand down, and the smell wasn't like anything she'd ever experienced. It smelled musty, like some of the old buildings she'd entered from the time before. But it wasn't musty in an offensive way. It was pleasant, like people had poured their best emotions onto the pages like a perfume.

She read the cover. *A People's Art History of the United States* by Nicolas Lampert. She flipped through the pages, amazed with each turn of the page. It was the same history she'd learned, but it was told from a different viewpoint. The political and social struggles, and the fight for injustice, were told by artists and activists. The pictures, paintings, and photographs clung to her. They seemed to sit down on her skin and seep into her soul. The consistent theme throughout the book was that the Resistance wasn't new. It had just taken on several names and meanings throughout the tumultuous life-span of the country's history. With each new enemy or opposition, rose the people who were determined to change what was happening, to make their voices heard. They were the last barriers that stood between good and evil. These people on the pages, they were her kindred spirits. They were all linked, for different reasons, for different promises, but they were the same.

"See something you recognize?" Kaelyn asked from the back seat. In the quiet of the car, her voice was like velvet wrapping itself around Arrow.

"Thank you for this. I had no idea. We've always been here, emerging when needed. Speaking out for the people who had no voice and protecting those that were the most vulnerable." Arrow knew she sounded idealistic, if not poetic, but she didn't care. It was how she felt.

"Keep it," Kaelyn said.

"But it's yours." Even as she said the words, Arrow knew this book would be her most cherished possession.

"I've gotten everything I need from it. It's yours now."

"Thank you, Kaelyn." She hoped Kaelyn could hear the sincerity in her voice.

Kaelyn leaned back against the seat and drifted off into sleep again. Arrow was left to her own devices for the next several hours. She stared out her window as the steel bulkheads whizzed by, creating the illusion the tunnel was moving instead of the transport. She thought about the upcoming days, the problems they might face, and what was at stake. She'd trained for this mission her entire life, and now that it was happening, she was overwhelmed by the need to get it right. Everything hinged on her ability to do her job.

She glanced in the rearview at Kaelyn sleeping. Her feelings for her were growing by the day. It wasn't what she'd expected or even what she wanted, but that didn't matter. She also understood that those feelings were going to be sacrificed for the well-being of her people, and it didn't matter what she wanted or how she felt. She drifted to sleep like the others had, and her dreams were sliced through with chaos and smoke.

The transport slowed, and the screen indicated that they were arriving at their destination. The rusted doors to the lift had been left unattended for a lifetime, and the transport idled in front of it as everyone woke.

"So, what's the plan? We can't see this village like we could the other from down here," Valor said as he motioned to the lift.

"We're going up, but we're leaving the transport down here. We don't know what's up there waiting for us, and I don't want to draw attention to ourselves. For all we know, the government has the village surrounded and we'll need the element of surprise on our side."

"Let's grab the bags." Valor opened the door and got out of the transport and Arrow followed.

She hoped that whatever was waiting for them topside had nothing to do with the Hand of God.

CHAPTER TWENTY-FOUR

We should go up the ladder. That way we can see what's out there instead of just being vulnerable once the door to the lift opens. Plus, it won't make nearly as much noise as that old lift." Kaelyn pointed to the rusted old ladder that led up to a metal disc that looked like an old manhole cover.

Arrow nodded, holstered her sidearm, and started up. Macy and Kaelyn were in the middle, with Valor behind. At the top, Arrow forced the metal disc away from the opening and slowly looked above it before she climbed out. Once Arrow was out, she turned and helped the others out. The sudden onset of sunlight was a surprising contrast to the tunnel they'd just left. They seemed to have surfaced next to an old parking structure. She looked at what used to be streetlights, now hunched over like old men who had far exceeded their prime. There was a replica of an early space shuttle a few yards away, the top broken off and swinging next to the structure. The sides had started to rust, leaving holes you could fit an adult through. The sidewalks had buckled ages ago, their ragged edges now being cradled by determined weeds, desperate to retake the area. Kaelyn looked at the large building to their left. *Cosmosphere*, the large sign on the front read. Kaelyn shook her head. The people of her time hadn't been very creative. Building a secret underground tunnel system that led to a space museum was pretty cliché.

Arrow looked worried as she checked her watch. She squinted. Kaelyn couldn't tell if it was from the sunlight or anxiety.

"What's wrong?" Kaelyn asked.

Arrow jogged over to the side of the building and pulled out the same long tube Macy had used in Colorado. "It shouldn't be this quiet. It's not curfew time yet. There should be people in the streets."

Kaelyn looked over Arrow's shoulder as the picture came into focus. There were dozens of bodies scattered in the streets, and no one was moving. Blood pooled around them, becoming part of the black asphalt, making it difficult to distinguish where the liquid stopped and the ground began. Arrow pulled a small orb from her pocket and typed in a code on the video device. Then she tossed it up in the air and it disappeared around the corner.

The picture came through on the transmitter. Bodies, bloody and mangled, littered the streets. The orb took a right turn, and more bodies came into sight. But these were different; they were wearing Army of Eden uniforms. Arrow pushed another button, and the orb landed back in her palm a minute later.

"What do we think?" Valor asked.

"I think the first wave of the Resistance is in full effect." She grabbed both her side arms and leaned up against the wall. "Stay close."

Macy and Valor drew their weapons and got behind Kaelyn as she followed Arrow through the streets. Kaelyn tried not to stare at the carnage, but it was hard as they passed by not to wonder about the people they had left behind. They were casualties, not just in this war but of their circumstances as well. They lived inside a civilization that had been poisoned with lies, half-truths, and ignorance. The smell almost made her knees buckle, and it was so strong she thought it might singe the hairs inside her nose. She fought the urge to run her hands over her arms, not wanting the smell to cling to her, a reminder for later of what she'd seen.

There were three people kneeling over a pair of bodies at the end of street, and when they saw them approach, they jumped up, guns aimed at the four of them.

"Stand down. We're Guardians," Arrow yelled at them.

The three people didn't put their guns down. "Identify yourselves."

Arrow pulled her bracelet off her wrist and tossed it the group as they continued moving toward them. "I'm Major Steele. This is Captain Markinson, President Steele, and Phoenix One."

The woman in the front of the group plugged the bracelet into a transmitter, and after a moment unplugged it. She nodded to the other two who were with her and tossed the bracelet back to Arrow.

"Sorry, Major, we can't be too careful right now." She motioned for everyone to enter the building to their right.

"I understand," Arrow said. She holstered her weapon and moved toward the doorway.

Inside, there were at least twelve people sitting around a table. They were all talking over each other. Some were standing, others were shouting, but all of that came to an abrupt halt once they entered the room. Several of them must have recognized Macy because they stood and looked in her direction.

Kaelyn didn't realize it was her they were standing for until the first woman approached her.

"Phoenix One, it's an honor to meet you. I'm Olivia, and we're here to assist you on your way." She nodded to Macy. "President Steele, it's an honor to have you here as well."

Kaelyn shook Olivia's hand. "Thank you for helping us. What happened?"

Olivia's face flushed red. "The soldiers from Eden arrived, demanding we help them trap all of you. As directed, our Resistance forces fought back. Unfortunately, there were casualties, but we managed to overtake them. Our troops left about an hour ago, after we checked in with Guardian headquarters. As ordered, they're on their way to Morgantown. The Guardians sent out drones to help with air coverage and protection. They're also dispatching several platoons of Guardians to the front lines."

"You have a secure line to Guardian headquarters?" Macy asked.

"Yes, Madam President. Would you like us to set up a line for you?"

"Yes, immediately," Macy said.

Olivia motioned to one of the people sitting at the table who pulled up a screen. A few keystrokes later, and they were connected to Guardian headquarters.

CAM acted as the automatic answering system. "Good evening, H-one. How may I be of assistance?"

Macy didn't give anyone else the opportunity to answer. "CAM, this is President Steele. I need to speak with General Steele."

"Right away, ma'am."

The screen was black for almost three minutes, and Kaelyn could feel Arrow growing more agitated next to her. Her body was stiff, and she shoved her hands into her pockets. Kaelyn knew it was out of worry and not impatience that was causing her shift. She wanted to touch her, to let her know that she was here, but she wasn't sure it would be welcomed among all these people.

Finally, the general appeared on the screen. He looked exhausted and concerned. There were black smudges on his cheeks, and it looked like he had a large cut on his chin. The look on Macy's face said she wanted to crawl through the screen and look him over herself.

Despite her body language and facial expression, Macy's tone remained professional. "What is the current situation back at headquarters?"

The general gave a half-smile, looking as if he appreciated his wife's adherence to protocol while still being able to see the worry etched on her face. "All Guardian forces are heading to the front lines as we speak. We have received several calls for backup. The villages are being attacked everywhere. We're doing what we can. We have sustained minimal casualties here at headquarters, but there have been a few. We believe there are more coming as MacLeod attempts to isolate our forces."

Macy looked at Arrow, almost as if she needed an anchor. "How many casualties?"

The general looked off to the side, searching for information. "According to CAM's calculations per the life force bracelets, two hundred people in all have been killed."

Arrow leaned toward the display, her knuckles white on the edge of the table. "In all of the Resistance or just at headquarters?"

"In all, Major." The general took a deep breath. "But our numbers are holding strong, and we aren't worried about our forces' capability once at the front line. Most of those casualties can be chalked up to ambushes from soldiers."

The general made a valid point, but it didn't seem to sit well with Arrow. She focused on a spot on the floor instead of her father.

"We have several civilian casualties here. Are there any there?" Valor asked.

"Yes, but we don't have the final numbers, as reports are still coming in." He looked down for a moment. "But I can tell you this, Captain. Your wife is alive and well." He looked to a part of the room that none of them could see. "I have to go, but I'll make an emergency transmission if anything vital changes. Be careful out there." The screen went black.

Kaelyn had a brief glimpse of what her life could potentially be like if she were to ever be with Arrow. Cordial calls in front of dozens of people didn't allow for any form of caring or intimacy. There would be months apart while they both did their best to play the protectors of the world. Moments where all they were allowed to see was that the other was still alive and well without being given the opportunity to show their vulnerable state. The thought terrified her. She'd watched her parents live like that for years. She knew they loved each other and that their work was important, but they always belonged more to the world than each other. It wasn't the kind of life she wanted for herself or for Arrow.

Arrow grabbed her hand and squeezed it gently. Her heart pounded at the touch, sending a jolt through her from where their fingers intertwined all through her body. She didn't know what these conflicting messages meant, and now wasn't the time to wade through them. There was still so much at stake, so many people depending on them.

Arrow turned toward Olivia. "I know you have your hands full right now, but we need to eat, sleep for a few hours, and then be on our way."

"I understand. Please, follow me to the dining hall. We don't have much, but you're welcome to whatever we have." She started toward the front entrance. "After you leave, those of us that remain will take refuge in our underground bunkers. It won't be long now until MacLeod turns off the weather bubbles."

"Do you have enough to survive?" Macy asked as she matched Olivia's steps.

"We'll be okay for about a month, maybe a month and a half."

No one said what they were thinking, that there were no guarantees this would be over by then. Kaelyn didn't want to think about what would happen to all these people if they couldn't get them help in time. She'd never be able to clean their blood from her hands.

CHAPTER TWENTY-FIVE

A don stared out his window. He had the weather adjusted to a perfect seventy-eight degrees. Typically, they followed the seasons, and today would've been unseasonably warm for the month of November, but he didn't care. He wanted to keep his people happy and quiet. He needed to remind them why they needed someone to oversee these situations and why he was the perfect person for the job. The happier people were, the more loyal they were. Fear worked well too, though.

He'd also promised that he'd deliver a lower class, giving his people more free time, and more opportunity for bliss and leisure. The Resistance wasn't being cooperative. They thought they were entitled to his country. Those treasonous bastards thought they could undo everything his family had worked so hard to construct, the life they had made. Well, it wasn't going to happen. He'd see every single one of their leaders hanged in the square, and the remaining scum would work in servitude.

These grand ideas of freedom were ridiculous. People needed to be told what to like, who to worship, and who was in charge. They'd tried it the other way for several hundred years and where did that get them? The white race was almost obsolete, people were worshiping false idols, and women thought they were the superior sex. It was no wonder so many clamored to his father. He represented the values the country was based on and that others were trying to steal. He wasn't afraid to tell people the enemy was right there in front of them. He didn't care what the critics said about the need for protection for the racial classes. He understood that great men were going to be hated at times for the good of the people. He gave this country back to the true believers, the real countrymen.

"We've lost communication with all the soldiers we deployed to Kansas," a hesitant voice from behind him stammered.

Adon turned and gripped the top of his chair instead of grabbing the general by the neck. "What does 'lost communication' mean? Are they dead or alive?"

The general turned his hat over several time in his hands. "They're dead, sir."

Adon clenched his teeth, trying to remember what Nora had told him about his blood pressure. "How is that possible?"

"We reviewed the feeds, and it seems that the villagers fought back. We're deploying more troops now."

"No, you're not." Nora shut the door behind her. "We're going to consolidate our forces. They're clearly coming here."

The general rolled his eyes. "I don't think you can make that assumption. And with all due respect, this isn't your call to make."

Adon ignored the man and focused on Nora. "Why do you say that?"

Nora pulled a cigarette from the tray he kept on his desk and lit it, inhaling deeply. "They aren't going to make a show of force unless they already have a plan. Factor in this, along with the Phoenix, and I think it's pretty clear what they're doing."

"Women aren't supposed to smoke," the general said, straightening his back.

She tapped the side of the cigarette on the ashtray. "And we aren't supposed to lose soldiers to disloyal hacks who have no military training, but here we are."

The general took a step forward. "It's unwise of you to question our capabilities. It's only us that stands in the way of them overthrowing your regime."

Adon felt contempt roll through his belly. "You speak of protection as if you're doing something to stop this, yet I've seen no results from you or anyone in your position. Perhaps, it would be better for Eden if Nora took control of the military forces."

The general squeezed his hat together. "Sir, no one will take orders from a female."

Adon slammed his hands on the desk. "You'll take orders from whomever I tell you to take fucking orders from! Is that clear?"

"Sir, if I can just—"

"Is that clear?"

"Yes, sir." The general bowed his head, his jaw clenching.

Nora put out her cigarette and placed a hand on his back. "Turn on the emergency notification system inside all the villages. Tell them their weather bubbles are being turned off in twenty-four hours. For those that want to come to Eden, we will welcome them with open arms. Everyone else will be considered an imminent threat against President MacLeod."

The general still had his head down, but his tone was acerbic. "Wouldn't it be more efficient to just turn them off without warning?"

Nora shook her head and smiled. "We're playing the long game here, General. We still need these people to *want* to come here. They need to feel as if we're being lenient and accepting. If we just kill them all, where would that leave us? That's the problem with men; you think everything is obtained with brute force. But you catch more flies with honey. Plus, if there are people that start to turn within the ranks of these traitors, it will send a shockwave through their little organization. And it will put them on our timeline. Do you really think they can survive without the weather bubbles? No, they'll have to make their move, and we have them beat based on sheer numbers. They'll come to us or they'll starve or die from dehydration. Simple."

The general straightened and saluted the president, never making eye contact with Nora. "I'll take care of it, sir."

Adon wrapped his arm around Nora's waist, just to get under the general's skin. "And for the last time, bring me Kaelyn Trapp."

He dropped his salute and went out the door.

THE RISE OF THE RESISTANCE: PHOENIX ONE

CHAPTER TWENTY-SIX

Arrow's internal clock started to sound in her head. She checked her watch to confirm that she was correct. Three hours of sleep was all she was allowing herself, and that time had come to an end. She tried to slide her arm out from underneath Kaelyn. At some point in the middle of the night, she'd managed to pull her close.

Kaelyn noticed her movements and pulled her arm back down on top of her. "Ten more minutes."

Arrow was going to protest, but really, what would ten more minutes hurt? Plus, she didn't want to leave this place. The way Kaelyn's hair fell over her face, the way she smelled of springtime and happiness, was enough to make her stay here like this for as long as Kaelyn would allow.

Kaelyn rolled over, tucking her head in Arrow's neck. She wrapped her arms around her and started to rub her back. Kaelyn shifted her leg so that it rested between Arrow's. "Where is everyone?"

"They're in the next room over. Someone has to stay with you at all times." Arrow tried to keep her voice as quiet as possible. She was worried that any disturbance to this moment would make it go away.

Kaelyn's hand moved up Arrow's back and into her hair. "Can this ten minutes just be us? I don't want to think about anything else right now."

The breath against her neck sent shivers throughout Arrow's body. She wanted to be closer to Kaelyn, but she didn't think that was physically possible. "Yes, whatever you want."

"And if I want you?" Kaelyn's lips traced the words along Arrow's ear.

Arrow spoke before she allowed herself the opportunity to think about it. "Would you still want me if it could only ever be these ten minutes?"

Kaelyn ran her fingers along Arrow's stomach and to her belt buckle, pulling it open. Arrow looked down to see if what she thought was happening was actually happening. Her movement was met with Kaelyn's lips against hers. The softness and urgency in Kaelyn's lips was enough to make Arrow forget any apprehension she had a second before.

Arrow lifted her hands into Kaelyn's hair, her palms resting against the sides of her face. Kaelyn bit down on Arrow's lip and tugged her closer. Arrow felt as if her body were plugged into an energy source, awakened from a sleep she never realized she was in. She slid under Kaelyn's shirt, desperate to take it off but wanting to make this moment last as long as possible.

Kaelyn moved into her with every stroke of Arrow's fingertips against her ribs. Kaelyn's mouth moved rapidly down to Arrow's collarbone. Kaelyn didn't appear to have the same need to savor the excruciatingly blissful moment as she pulled Arrow's shirt over her head and then took off her own. When their bodies came back together, the sensation of Kaelyn's bare skin against hers broke the last thread of Arrow's conscious ability to carefully navigate their relationship.

Arrow closed her eyes and breathed Kaelyn in, felt her hands slide down her pants, forcing them lower until Arrow was completely free from them. Kaelyn didn't make quick work of her boxer briefs as she'd expected, though. Instead, she ran her fingers slowly down Arrow's center, using the material that remained as a veiled promise of what was to come. The friction of the soft fabric against Arrow's sensitive skin changed the pace of her breathing. She was desperately trying to hang on to the present as the sensation of desire, longing, and urgency took form in her hands raking down Kaelyn's bare back.

Kaelyn let out a soft groan and bucked against her, pushing her hand harder against Arrow's slick center. Arrow removed one of her hands from Kaelyn's back, letting her fingertips slide along Kaelyn's sweating stomach and down below the waistband of her underwear. Kaelyn forced her hips harder into Arrow, urging her hand lower.

When Arrow's fingertips met the warm wetness between Kaelyn's legs, Kaelyn tightened her grip around Arrow's neck, pulling her closer until there was no space left between them. Arrow was mesmerized by the way Kaelyn's body moved against her hand in perfect rhythm. Her breath and the soft noises that were coming from the back of Kaelyn's throat urged her along, stroke by stroke.

Kaelyn abandoned the fabric and moved her hand underneath, causing Arrow's vision to blur and a warm, tingling wave radiated out from between her legs. Arrow knew she was close but wanted to make this last for as long as possible.

She pushed her fingers harder against Kaelyn's center and felt her begin to twitch against her, rocking her hips harder and faster. She felt Kaelyn's fingers dig into her back, and her breathing became more ragged and desperate. Arrow felt the first wave of her orgasm beginning and wanted Kaelyn to experience it at the same time.

Kaelyn pushed her fingertips against Arrow's clit and lightly squeezed, pushing up and down. Arrow slid her fingers inside and felt Kaelyn come around her. Arrow tipped over the edge, the tsunami of pleasure crashing against all her senses.

The waves of pleasure were overwhelming her senses, and she started to shake, an unintentional outcome of the cascade of emotions and pleasure she was feeling. Against her neck, she could feel Kaelyn smiling, lightly kissing the dampness she'd caused.

"You're amazing," Kaelyn said between breaths.

Arrow wasn't sure how much she had to do with it. She'd never had a sexual encounter with this much intensity, this much emotion, or that ended with this level of satisfaction.

"That was amazing." She put her forehead against Kaelyn's.

"Ten minutes isn't long enough." Kaelyn pushed the hair out of Arrow's eyes.

Arrow didn't need to look at her watch to know that it had been longer than ten minutes. But it didn't matter. For this brief period, all that mattered was Kaelyn. She knew it couldn't last, that fate wasn't built that way. But she was going to hang on to it for as long as she could.

❖

Kaelyn had been protected by some of the most qualified and capable people in the world. But she'd never felt safer and more herself than she did right now, lying in Arrow's arms. Sure, the sex had been incredible, but that wasn't all that had transpired between them. If they were in a different place, if they were different people, this would've been the beginning of a promise, one she would have no problem keeping for the rest of her life.

She ran her hand over Arrow's face, wanting to memorize the way her stormy gray eyes looked at her as if she were the only person in the world. She needed to remember everything about this moment. It would be all she would have left after everything fell into place. Kaelyn already knew she would look back on these few stolen moments together as the best in her life. Arrow's skin was still flushed, and her lips were swollen from the fervor Kaelyn had needed and wanted from her. Now both were proof that they had happened, that what they felt was real. And Kaelyn would need that. She needed all of this, and it would be part of her forever.

She took Arrow's hand from where it rested on her waist and kissed her knuckles. Arrow's eyes grew dark, desire reigniting. Her heart beat faster and her head grew fuzzy. She felt intoxicated. But whatever her body was calling her to do was interrupted by a knock at the door.

"We need to get going." Valor's voice reverberated through the wood paneling.

"Time's up." Arrow tried to smile, but the sentiment didn't reach her eyes.

Kaelyn's heart wanted to protest. She wanted to say screw it all and stay right here with Arrow for as long as they could possibly manage. But there were too many people counting on them and the roles they were meant to play.

Kaelyn kissed her slowly. She needed one more memory to tuck away, something that only belonged to them, a part of themselves they didn't have to share with the rest of the world. Arrow put her hands on Kaelyn's face, seeming to understand the significance of that kiss. There were still so many things she wanted to experience with Arrow, things time didn't allow. So she did the only thing she could do; she kissed her harder, trying to articulate her thoughts and feelings into a single action. It wasn't enough. It would never be enough.

Arrow pulled away first, answering Valor. "We'll be down in a few."

Arrow moved away from her, sitting up in bed. The simple action hurt more than any physical injury Kaelyn had ever sustained. She fought the urge to pull her back down. Instead, Kaelyn watched as Arrow walked naked into the bathroom to take a shower. She thought back to her life before her cryo state. She would've moved mountains to find someone like Arrow. But this wasn't seventy years ago and this was her new life. It was a sick twist of fate to have found someone that made her feel like this, knowing she'd never really be hers. She pushed herself out of bed, needing to face a destiny that had been set in motion for her seventy years ago.

Chapter Twenty-seven

Olivia was saying her good-byes and giving her assurances to everyone when Kaelyn got to the transport. The tunnel here was well lit and there were lots of people milling around, most of whom stopped and watched as she made her way to her group.

"I hope to see you soon, Phoenix One." She shook Kaelyn's hand.

"Olivia, please, call me Kaelyn."

Olivia nodded. "Yes, of course, Kaelyn. Take care." She was being polite, but her face was etched with concern.

"We're going to do everything we can for your people." Kaelyn hoped it wasn't an empty promise.

"They're your people too, and they're counting on you." Olivia hugged her. "Stay safe."

Kaelyn got into the back seat of the transport, her normal seat. But there was nothing normal about today. Everything looked different, smelled different, even the instant coffee she'd choked down before coming outside tasted different. She'd read poetry about a single night changing your life. She'd heard songs about how colors seemed brighter, but she'd never experienced it. That is, until now.

Arrow programmed their next location into their navigation system, and Kaelyn couldn't take her eyes off her. The way her fingers moved, the way her forearm flexed in the sunlight. Everything about her seemed to deserve a moment of silence for appreciation. But no one else noticed, everyone was going about their day as if nothing had happened.

"We'll be in Kokomo, Indiana, in eight hours and four minutes if we maintain ninety-three miles per hour." Valor folded the map.

"A lot can happen in eight hours," Arrow said.

"We can't go any faster in the tunnel." Valor slid the map into the side compartment of the transport. "You should use that time to rest anyway."

"I'm fine." Arrow seemed annoyed with Valor's response.

Kaelyn didn't know what had been said while she wasn't with the others, but something had transpired. She'd been so caught up in her own thoughts she hadn't noticed the annoyance Arrow was emanating until now. She wanted to ask what the problem was, but she thought it better to simply remain quiet. She didn't know the inner workings of the Guardians, and she didn't want to make life any harder on Arrow.

The transport was painfully silent, and Kaelyn had a feeling that was the way Arrow and Valor wanted it. She pulled her headphones out of her bag and placed them over her head. She plugged her computer into the power supply that Arrow had given her and turned on her music. The familiar sounds pulsed through her ears, easing her into sleep that she hadn't been able to get the night before. The memory caused her to smile before she drifted off.

❖

Arrow and Valor had spent the last several hours in silence. Now, her annoyance had turned into agitation. She knew why Valor was mad at her, and she also knew it wasn't fair of him to feel that way.

She glanced back to see that her mother and Kaelyn were both still sleeping. "What is your problem?" she whispered.

He had been clearly waiting for this opportunity because he turned on her. "What are you thinking? She's the damn Phoenix! You need a clear head or you're putting us all at risk."

In all the years they had known each other, she couldn't remember a time when Valor had been angry with her. And now that the time had finally come it was because of something that had nothing to do with him. He was going to lash out at the most beautiful night of her life?

She leaned closer to him, forcing herself not to yell. "Nothing has changed. I can still do my job and she will do hers."

"That's not the point, Arrow. The Phoenix can't be in love with anyone. It will compromise her decision-making and yours too." He shook his head. "I shouldn't even have to tell you this."

The word love caught her off guard. She'd never been in love with anyone. "No one said anything about love. The plan stays the same. Nothing has changed."

"I'm not blind. I see the way you two look at each other. You have to break this off before you can't." His anger broke and his eyes softened. "Look, you of all people deserve to be happy. But it can't be with her. It just can't."

"It was one night." But she didn't believe her own words. It wasn't just a night. It had been everything.

He put his hand over hers. "I know it's not fair. But these are the sacrifices we make as Guardians. We put the well-being of the people above our own. I'm sorry, but you know I'm right. Your head won't be in the game, and neither will hers. It has to stop."

"I know." She ran her hand through her hair.

She'd known the gravity of the situation when she'd allowed herself to fall into Kaelyn. She'd never expected to walk away the next morning feeling the way she did. Even now, her stomach lurched as the memories of the night before flashed in her head. It was a type of cruel playback she would always live with. But she would accept a head full of memories, painful as they were, if it meant she could keep a piece of Kaelyn with her forever.

"We've been friends for our entire lives. If there was any other way, I'd be the first one to tell you."

To his credit, Valor looked like he really meant what he said, and despite the anger she felt at the unfairness of it all, she knew he was right.

The transport slowed, bringing this conversation to a close. Her mother stirred in the back. She glanced in the rearview to see her stretch and then tap Kaelyn to wake her as well. As Kaelyn came out of her slumber, she pulled off her headphones and made eye contact with Arrow. She smiled and Arrow forced herself to look away before her eyes betrayed her.

"We're under Kokomo Airport," Arrow said. She was surprised her voice sounded normal and wasn't cracking with the pain she felt in her stomach and chest.

"Well, let's get to it." Valor opened the transport door.

"I think we should keep pushing forward," Arrow said. "Stopping has too many risks."

Her mother grabbed her weapon. "It's important for the villagers to see Kaelyn. They need to know she's real. It gives them something to fight for. Plus, the transport needs to recharge itself, so that's three hours we have to wait around."

Kaelyn looked like she was going to say something too, but Arrow couldn't bear to hear it. She nodded at her mother's suggestion, walked over to the lift, and plugged in the transmitter.

The door slid open, and screams of pain flooded the small shaft. The wave of heat that crashed into them was enough to blur Arrow's vision. It was difficult to breathe, and sweat started to cover her body.

"Shit, they turned off the weather bubbles." She covered her face with her arm and looked at Valor. "We have to get as many people as we can into the tunnels."

Valor hopped out of the lift and pushed a few buttons on his bracelet. "It says the temperature out there is one hundred and sixty-eight degrees. We'd only be able to last eighteen minutes in that heat without the suits. If our internal body temperature passes one hundred and five degrees, our DNA will start to unravel and brain damage will occur."

Arrow shook her head. "The suits are too bulky. We can't carry anyone in those things."

"All this technology and you haven't created a suit more conducive to this kind of situation?" Kaelyn yelled.

Valor ran his hand over his face. "CAM has been working on it, and we should've taken the most recent prototypes before we left."

"There's nothing we can do to change that now," Arrow said as she programmed the timer on her wristband and switched it to show her body temperature.

Arrow stepped into the lift and Valor followed. "When we get up there, we'll grab who we can and send them down. When the first group arrives, send the lift back up."

Kaelyn looked like she was going to argue, but her mom pulled her away from the opening, allowing the doors to slide closed.

Arrow pointed to the right of Valor. "You take one thousand feet to the right. I'll take the left." She grabbed Valor's arm. "Eighteen minutes, that's it. And only the ones we can save."

Arrow jogged, counting her paces. The air was heavy with heat and thin with a dying landscape. She did a quick once-over of the people she passed, doing mental calculations of who could be saved, but there was no one alive.

She jogged several feet to her right, wanting to make a perimeter sweep. She finally came upon a man who was barely breathing. His breathing was shallow and his body was no longer producing any sweat. His skin was burning hot and dry as a bone.

She pulled a small pouch from her pocket and tipped it into his mouth, and though the water made it into his mouth, he made no effort to drink. "I'm Major Steele of the Guardian class, Level One. I'm here to help you, but you have to drink."

He opened bloodshot eyes and managed to get a bit of water down his throat and then fell unconscious. Arrow lifted his body and slung him over her shoulder. She moved as quickly as she could manage, but the extra weight and the thinned air caused her to need to stop and take a knee.

She looked out across the expanse. There were thick waves of heat dancing up from the scorched earth. Small white dots began to appear with moments of blackness. She looked down at her bracelet. Her internal body temperature was at one hundred and four degrees, and she'd been out here for sixteen minutes. She thought briefly of leaving him but changed her mind. Even if she survived, she would never be able to look at herself again.

She settled her breathing and hoisted him up, her legs shaking. She continued toward the lift. She couldn't see it yet, but she knew it was there. She had to make it back to Kaelyn. She had to protect Kaelyn. She couldn't leave that up to anyone else. It could only be her.

Her head was pounding, there was a loud screeching in her ears, she couldn't feel her feet, and her arms had gone numb. When she stumbled again, a set of hands removed the weight from her shoulders. She looked up to see Valor pulling the man toward the lift a few feet away.

She willed herself to follow him, to get to the lift, to get to Kaelyn. She tried to move her legs, but they had stopped working. She felt her face hit the hot ground. It burned and made her choke. Then everything was black.

CHAPTER TWENTY-EIGHT

I'm not leaving her." Kaelyn pushed Valor away from her for the third time.

"You need to eat. I'll sit with her. She's not going anywhere." Valor put his hand on her back.

"No. I need to be here when she wakes up." She continued to search Arrow's face for any sign of life.

Kaelyn could hear Macy and Valor whispering behind her. She couldn't hear what they were saying, but it was undoubtedly some plan to get her out of the room.

"I brought you some nutrients." Macy sat next to her. "I would say food, but that's not what this is, sorry."

"I'm not hungry," Kaelyn said. That wasn't true, but she couldn't bring herself to eat with Arrow lying there.

"She'd want you to eat. You've got to keep your strength up." Macy held the pouch out in front of her.

Kaelyn thought about it for only a moment longer, and then took the pouch and squeezed the ooze into her mouth. It had no taste, which was probably better than tasting whatever it was that ooze would taste like. From the corner of her eye, she could see Macy smiling at the small victory.

"She's going to be fine. Her vitals are steady." Macy leaned over and pushed Arrow's hair back. She adjusted the wet cloth that was around her neck.

"She could've died," Kaelyn whispered.

Macy turned Arrow's arm over and ran her fingers over a long scar that went across her forearm to her elbow. "She was only eight when she got this. A village child had climbed up a tree and couldn't get down. Arrow climbed up trying to help her and fell in the process." She pulled up the sheet that covered Arrow and pointed to another large scar. "She was sixteen when she hopped the fence of a restricted area because she could hear kittens crying and wanted to feed them." Next, she pointed to Arrow's chin, a small scar only an inch long peeked out from underneath. "She got into a fight with a soldier who pushed a young child down."

"She's a good person." Kaelyn didn't need the scars for proof, but she wanted Macy to know she thought it, all the same.

Macy moved another damp cloth on Arrow's wrist. "She's the best, but that's not the point. She'll always be on the verge of something bad happening because she's always trying to save someone or something. Today wasn't an isolated incident. This is who she is, fundamentally. She would've no sooner left that man behind than she would've died right there next to him. I'm not telling you that to scare you. I'm telling you this because it's a reality you have to live with."

Arrow groaned slightly and her eyes opened. The wave of relief that swept over Kaelyn sent tingles through her body. She wanted to tell her how foolish her actions were, how mad she was, but she said nothing. Macy's words bounced around in her head, rendering her voice silent.

"Is he okay?" Arrow croaked.

"He'll be okay. How are you feeling?" Macy asked.

"I'm fine." Arrow tried to sit up and fell back down. "A little dizzy, but fine. Where are we?"

Kaelyn tried to take Arrow's hand, but Arrow pulled it away as soon as their fingers touched. She tried not to wince. "We're in the village's underground bunker. Some of the villagers managed to get down here as soon as the bubble was turned off."

"We need to keep moving. They're waiting for us." Arrow tried to sit up again but couldn't get herself all the way up.

Kaelyn shook her head. "You need to rest."

Arrow looked at her but wouldn't make eye contact, which hurt more than she'd expected.

"I need to talk to Valor."

Macy stood, but Arrow stopped her. "Mom, you stay. Kaelyn, please go get him."

Kaelyn wasn't sure of what to make of Arrow's odd behavior toward her, but it stung and made her angry. "Okay."

"Just him. Thanks for sitting with me, but I don't want you in here."

Kaelyn was slightly dizzy as she walked out of the room. She put her hand against the cold, dirty wall to try to steady herself. There were people walking by, and each acknowledged her as she passed. Her mind was foggy, and the feeling of rejection slid through her like poison.

She made it to the main room and found Valor talking to the only village leadership that remained. He saw her coming and stood.

"Is everything okay?" Valor asked.

Kaelyn crossed her arms, trying to stop the pain in her stomach from showing on her face. "She wants you."

He hurried past her without another word. One of the women he had been speaking with called her over, and she gladly accepted the seat that was offered.

❖

Arrow allowed her mother to help her to her feet and move her into the chair to put on her shoes. Her mother tried to help her slide her boots on, but Arrow pushed her away. She'd seen the hurt in Kaelyn's eyes and the pain on her face, and it made her feel sick. But it was necessary. She didn't want anyone's help. She wanted to feel the physical pain, hoping it would mask the emotional pain, at least for the time being.

Valor pushed the door open. "You finally done with your nap?"

Her labored breathing continued as she laced up her left boot. "How much time did we lose?"

"About six hours, but we're okay. If you need more rest, you should take it." He sounded concerned, but he made no movement toward her.

"How many people are dead here?" She needed to know. The anger would be a good motivator to push her body into motion.

Her mother spoke before Valor could brush her off again. "The Resistance forces made it out, but the village has been almost completely decimated. A handful have left to join the Hand of God. They gave everyone the option to come with them or remain, and they said they'd give people twenty-four hours. But weather bubbles started being turned off well before that. Those who remained..." She shook her head, looking tired.

Arrow stood and almost fell over. Valor reached for her, but she pushed him away. "We go straight through now. We'll drop you two off so you can make it to Fredericksburg, but we can't lose any more time."

"You aren't in any condition—"

Arrow pulled her shirt over her head and fastened her utility belt. "We're leaving, Captain Markinson. I wasn't asking you. I was telling you."

Valor lifted his chin, and for a moment looked as if he was going to argue. "Fine. I'll go get the transport ready."

"Do you want me to go get Kaelyn?" her mom asked.

Arrow checked her weapons, pretending to be unfazed by the mention of Kaelyn. She was the reason she made it back. The thought of her had given her the last little push she needed. But when she'd woken up and seen her, the feelings of gratefulness had been replaced by Valor's words of warning. She needed to stay away. There were bigger issues at hand. Death could come at any moment, and there was no time for emotion. "No, I'll go with Valor to the transport. You can go get her and meet us there."

She made it to the transport and got into the passenger seat. She lay down on her side and closed her eyes. She didn't want to have to see Kaelyn when she got there, and she didn't want to talk to Valor. She wanted to be alone. She wanted to sit with her mistakes, her failures, and let them seep into her. She knew it would leave an emotional mark, a scar of sorts. But maybe that's what she needed. A painful reminder of what she should and shouldn't do in the future. If she had been focused on their mission instead of Kaelyn, they would've left the other village sooner. Even if they had made it here thirty minutes earlier, she could've gotten more people inside. Maybe not all, but some of those people would've survived. She'd known from the start that she could never be with Kaelyn, but she had tempted fate. Who would be at risk next for her own selfish reasons? Arrow couldn't live with the answer to that question. Valor was right. It had to stop.

CHAPTER TWENTY-NINE

Kaelyn knew what Raven Rock was and what it meant to the United States government, when an actual government had existed. Looking at it from the outside, no one would believe how big it was. The entrance looked like any tunnel someone would find going through a mountain. A large concrete entrance with a road big enough for a semitruck acted as the mouth for the base. There were four of these mouths to the complex in total; two were close to a helicopter landing pad and two close to the tunnel that led to Camp David. Inside, there were power plants, a dining hall, gym, barber shop, chapel, living quarters, and even a bowling alley. It had its own fire station, ventilation system, and even a Starbucks. If anyone managed to locate the complex, hidden in the forest, getting inside would be nearly impossible. It was the most secure facility she'd ever seen. It had been built during the Cold War as a bunker to protect top government officials in the event of a nuclear strike and was added on to with each presidential administration. It would've served as an underground Pentagon of sorts if the need were to ever arise. Things had changed since her time, but she found it hard to believe they would be able to just walk inside. This base had been so sophisticated, she doubted that MacLeod would willingly give it up or wasn't aware of its existence.

Arrow was still asleep in the front seat, and despite the anger Kaelyn felt toward her for having blown her off earlier, she knew she needed to rest.

She leaned forward to Valor who was flipping through several maps. "How do you expect to get into Raven Rock?"

He stopped what he was doing and turned to look at her. "You, of course. Your retina will gain us access."

"It can't be that simple. They would've updated the technology by now."

"The system is set up so that it saves every person who has ever been entered into the database. There is no deletion allowed because that would create an access point for people to hack into it. So, people can be entered but never removed. Every member of every First Family that has been around since 1978 is saved in the system. There's only one entrance you have access to enter, but it's better than nothing." He smiled at her, seemingly proud of himself.

"How do you know that? I didn't even know that."

"One of the founding members of the Resistance was responsible for IT work inside Raven Rock, and he put in a failsafe when the MacLeods were first taking over, hoping this day would eventually come."

Everything really did hang in the balance of her ability to be here in this moment. "Is it not guarded anymore?"

"Not the way it was during your father's time. MacLeod doesn't use it as a military installation anymore because there's a shield around the country, keeping people out whose homelands have otherwise been destroyed by climate change or civil war. We aren't accessible to the outside world, so he doesn't need it as a headquarters. It is, however, where they keep their biggest stockpile of food and a major gateway for their water supply." He pulled up the overhead image of it on the console. "See those two reservoirs there? We need to shut those down."

"Is there still a Starbucks inside?" She knew the answer but thought she'd throw it out there anyway.

He looked at her blankly, his eyebrows coming together. "I don't know what you mean."

"Never mind."

Arrow turned over in her seat and sat up, rubbing her face. She still looked worn out, and Kaelyn assumed she would be for a while. Arrow looked at her, and the gray eyes that stared back didn't hold the same anger they had several hours before. There was a softness in them that confused Kaelyn. She sat back in her seat, needing to break the connection.

Arrow turned away and started checking her weapons. "If there were more of us, I would say the Phoenix needed to stay in the transport. But I don't think that's an option."

Valor nodded. "It's not ideal, but we'll have to split up. It's really our only hope to take both reservoirs out. If we hit one and then go after the other, it gives them too much time to consolidate their forces and stop us. Kaelyn can come with me."

Kaelyn expected Arrow to protest. She tried not to take it personally when she agreed with him. She knew Arrow and Valor were the experts in this area, but that understanding did nothing to rid the feeling of rejection she was feeling again.

Arrow got out of the transport and Kaelyn followed her before she had the chance to change her mind.

Kaelyn grabbed Arrow by the shoulder and turned her around, forcing her to finally look at her. "What is your damn problem?"

Arrow put her hands on her hips and looked into the distance. "Now really isn't the time, Kaelyn."

Kaelyn grabbed Arrow's chin and turned it back toward her face. "Right now is all we might have. I need to know what I did to make you give me the cold shoulder."

Arrow's eyes didn't have their normal vibrant streaks of blue and gray. They seemed to have lost some of their shine. "I can't give you what you want. We can't be together."

Kaelyn's anger eclipsed all other conscious awareness of who was around or what they were doing. "Is that what your problem is? You thought I was getting attached? Jesus, Arrow, it was one night. I'm not some teenage girl who's going to follow you around. I knew what I was getting into. So, don't worry. You're off the hook." The sting of rejection had allowed her to say it, but none of it was true.

Arrow closed her eyes for a long moment and then she reached out to touch Kaelyn. "That's not what I meant."

Kaelyn pulled her hand away from the contact. "Oh, I know what you meant. You made it perfectly clear that we were temporary. Look, there are no hard feelings. We were exactly what the other needed in that moment. No more, no less."

Arrow's jaw tightened and she put her hands on her hips. "Fine, Kaelyn."

"Don't you *fine*, me. This was your decision. I'm just the only one with the balls to say it to the other's face." She walked backward a few steps, needing to get away but unable to divert her eyes. The pain on Arrow's face was so clear it seared a spot on Kaelyn's heart. She finally turned around, unable to handle the burning she felt in every part of her body.

She thought for a second that she might throw up, but she managed to push the feeling away. Valor and Macy were standing on the other side of the transport, pretending not to hear what was taking place only a few feet away.

"Let's do this." Kaelyn pointed to the large steel door.

Valor slung his gun over his shoulder and nodded. He was smart enough to not say anything and just led her toward the panel on the wall. He used his shirt to wipe off the dust that had accumulated over the last several decades. He pushed a button and the screen turned on, requesting authorization.

She put her face down in front and watched the beam scan her eye. The lights blinked for a few moments, and then the door started to open, screeching loudly as each foot of steel disappeared into the wall above them.

She turned and looked at Arrow who was standing next to Macy beside the transport. "Be careful." She turned away and headed into the complex before Arrow had a chance to say anything back. She didn't want to hear anything else from her right now, and she certainly didn't want to look at those damn eyes that seemed to see straight into her soul.

CHAPTER THIRTY

Arrow watched as Kaelyn and Valor disappeared into the complex. She pushed herself off the transport and started toward the open door. Her mother put her hand on her arm, wanting her to stop.

"I don't want to talk about this right now," Arrow said. "We have a limited amount of time. Let's just do what we came here for."

Arrow thought there would be a protest from her mother, but there wasn't. She pulled the gun from her back and fell in step behind her. The plan was a simple one; they'd come in from the residence side of the base, find the reservoirs on each side of the complex, and shut them down. The water supply would stop pumping into Eden. In just a few days, the sedatives would be completely worn off. There were only a handful of soldiers assigned to the complex, and they would be dealt with if needed. There was surveillance in the complex, but Valor and Kaelyn would see to that. Valor was going to clip a jamming wire into the mainframe, but it would take him about ten minutes to get there.

Arrow had memorized the maps of the interior of the base, just as Valor had. It wasn't a complex layout, and Arrow was thankful. It would be easy to get turned around in a maze of underground tunnels that all looked identical. They had to remain in the residence area to avoid surveillance until the ten minutes had passed.

She checked around the first corner. There was a solitary soldier about one hundred feet away, coming in their direction. She checked her watch. Six minutes. Sure, there was the possibility Valor had gotten there early, but she couldn't risk it based on a maybe. She signaled to her mom that someone was coming. Her mom ducked into a small alcove, just big enough for one person.

Arrow crouched down against the wall. It was possible that the soldier would walk past this tunnel and not notice them, but she pulled her knife from its sleeve, just to be sure. She closed her eyes, taking in the sounds around her. She could hear the hum of machinery echoing through the complex and the sound of the soldier's footsteps. Each thump drew him closer to her location…only a few feet away.

Now, he was so close she could hear his soft humming. She tightened her grip around the knife she held in her right hand. She didn't want to kill him, but she would if it came down to it. He walked in front of her, not looking down. He had almost made it past their tunnel opening when he stopped and turned.

There was only a split second to make these types of decisions, and Arrow was already prepared for hers. She got to her feet, moving toward him. There was a flash of panic on his face when he realized she wasn't supposed to be here. She took the butt of her knife and hit him in the side of the head. He collapsed into a pile on the ground. She put her hands under his arms and dragged him into the tunnel.

"I thought you were going to kill him," whispered her mother.

Arrow pushed the soldier's body into the alcove. "I would've if he hadn't gone down."

"What if he wakes up before we're done?"

Arrow pulled the transmitter from his belt and took his gun. She pulled a small vile from her pocket and pulled the top off with her teeth. She pushed his mouth open and dumped the contents into his mouth. "He'll be out for at least three hours, and we only need one."

She looked at her watch again. They needed to stay undetected for another two minutes. But in these circumstances, two minutes could be a lifetime. She decided it was best to use her time wisely. She opened the transmitter she'd taken from the soldier. Listed on the screen was the watch rotation and positions covered. There was a total of twenty-four people currently on duty, and of those people, there were four at each of the reservoir locations.

There was also an all-points bulletin for the capture of Kaelyn and the elimination of Valor, her mother, and herself. There was no mention of the other three Phoenixes, which was a good sign. At least a portion of their plan was still undiscovered. She checked her watch. Ten minutes.

Arrow peeked out around the corner again, and there was no one in sight. She motioned to her mother to follow close behind. The main tunnel was a half-dome shape, the insides of the mountain making up the walls and the ceiling. The industrial lighting did little to illuminate their path, but that was a good thing as well.

Arrow and her mother ducked behind one of the large transports when they heard two male soldiers talking and laughing a few yards away. Arrow moved behind one tire and her mother behind the other. Arrow flipped the switch on her gun from bullet to laser and waited.

The voices grew louder, the pair caught up in conversation about their latest sexual conquests. They were on the other side of the transport and Arrow pulled her gun close to her chest. They carried on, oblivious, and she watched as their banter continued well beyond their hiding spots.

Once they were gone, Arrow and her mom hurried along the back side of the long line of transports. When they finally reached the tunnel they'd been looking for, Arrow took the left turn and bent over, holding her knees. She only allowed herself a second to compose herself and take inventory of where they were. At the end of the tunnel was a large metal fence, and she could hear the water rushing just beyond it.

She checked her watch again. Assuming everything went according to plan, Kaelyn and Valor should be reaching the same spot on the other side of the complex about now as well. She only briefly thought of the consequences of their plan going sideways. If anything had happened to Kaelyn or Valor, the whole thing would be for nothing. She knew Kaelyn was safe with Valor, but she would've preferred to have been with her, to know she was okay. But being with Kaelyn now could've resulted in a mission failure. As mad as Kaelyn was at Arrow, she wasn't sure Kaelyn would've followed her directions or kept her composure. She had a brief flash of Kaelyn being in danger, and she felt it burn the back of her throat.

Beyond what it would mean for the Resistance, it would be personally catastrophic as well. Kaelyn's well-being, she realized, was more important than anything else in her life. Not just because of what she meant to their plan but what she meant to Arrow. She hated how things had transpired between them and how she'd left it. She'd wanted to take the time to explain everything to Kaelyn, but when given the opportunity, she'd stood there like a coward.

She stared down the expanse of the final tunnel and knew exactly where to find the machine room. She also knew where the soldiers would be…well, she knew where she would've placed them. She felt her mother behind her, tapping her shoulder to get her attention.

She pulled herself from her internal reflection. She had the rest of her life to hate herself for what she did. Right now, they needed to finish the mission and get back to the transport. She had to see for herself that Kaelyn was all right.

Arrow pulled out the transmitter she'd taken from the first soldier they'd encountered. Watch positions and assignments had stayed the same. So no one had found him in the tunnel they'd left him in. No one was on alert for any of them.

Arrow moved down the long tunnel as quickly and quietly as she could manage. When they reached the end, her mother moved to the other side. Arrow used her hands to indicate they would attack from each side. The reservoir was surrounded by a metal fence in a large circle. The room they needed to reach was on the opposite end of where they'd entered.

The loud rushing of the water being turned over to avoid algae and bacteria from accumulating drowned out anything else. It reminded Arrow of the video images she'd seen of Yosemite Valley before all the waterfalls had dried up because of climate change. The damp, cool air spraying her as she moved was a welcome relief for her heated body. The stress and intensity of the situation had been the culprit, and she was appreciative of both the relief and the cover it offered.

As she moved, she pulled her second gun from her waistband. The two soldiers on her end were both in sight now, and neither one of them seemed aware they were in any type of danger. Another few steps and she would have a perfect shot. But that opportunity didn't come. A loud siren started to pulse throughout the complex. Red lights started flashing, and the soldiers pulled their transmitters.

Arrow knew what the alarm was for; she felt it in every part of her body. She felt her heart start to crack with the realization. Even when she took her first shot at the soldier who was staring down at his transmitter, she felt it. The second shot hit the one trying to get his gun from the holster and dropped him. Kaelyn was in trouble.

She'd used the laser feature on both, and so did her mother. The soldiers would be out and paralyzed for at least an hour. She stepped over their bodies, and an image flashed of Kaelyn lying on the ground, helpless. She turned in the direction she thought Valor and Kaelyn would be in.

"It's just through here," her mother shouted over the rushing sounds of water.

Arrow hesitated. "They need our help."

Her mother grabbed her arm and shoved her toward the room. "We need to take care of this first."

Arrow pulled the door open. The mechanism controlling the reservoir was enormous. Large metal pumps moved up and down at a steady pace. The noise was so jarring, she had to cover her ears as she ran around to the other side of the room. She located the large basin of chemicals being intermittently delivered to the water supply. They'd had no way of knowing exactly how the chemicals were being delivered, but she wasn't expecting it to be so large.

They wouldn't be able to just stop the chemicals. They were going to have to destroy the whole thing. She pulled a small square of C4 from her pack and placed it on the control panel. She inserted the antenna in the top, along with a copper wire. She ran ten feet away and pushed the button.

The noise from the explosion was magnified in the large room. It bounced off the walls over and over. She touched her ears, surprised to find there was no blood on her fingertips from having her eardrums burst. She ran back over to make sure the panel had been destroyed. All that was left was a smoldering stump of metal. The large metal pumps that had been moving at a steady pace just moments before were now stationary.

"We have to go!" her mother yelled.

Arrow knew it was only a matter of a few seconds before soldiers were on top of them. She motioned for her mother to follow as she headed to the escape hatch, located at the back of the room. It would add a little bit of distance in making it back to their transport, but it was better than having to deal with a slew of armed soldiers.

She opened the hatch and started to climb down the ladder. If there were soldiers waiting for them at the bottom, she wanted to get there before her mother. Her mother closed the hatch, and they were left in almost complete darkness. Only the small amount of light seeping in from the bottom of the tube they were in offered them any assistance.

Arrow took several rungs at a time, wanting to get out and armed as soon as possible.

Her feet finally hit the ground, and she unholstered her gun. She could hear yelling echoing in from the adjoining tunnel as she slid along the side of the ragged mountain wall. They made use of the dark, ducking into the shadows and remaining still as a few soldiers ran past. She was keeping a mental count in her head. With a total of twenty-four people guarding the complex, and assuming at least five were unconscious, only nineteen remained. They were all heading in the same direction, toward the other reservoir.

They were sitting against the wall in the dark. Everything in Arrow told her to follow the passing soldiers. The very worst versions of what could be happening were racing through her mind.

"We have to get back to the transport," her mother said. She leaned against her, careful not to raise her voice too loud.

"They need our help." She couldn't fathom following their plan at this point.

"No. We don't know if they've even been caught. We have to head back. Do you want them waiting there for us, putting Kaelyn in even more danger? We stick to the plan." Her mother's voice was forceful and determined.

Arrow knew she was right. They should follow the plan. Deviating could put people in danger, but she couldn't shake the feeling that it wouldn't matter. She felt an overwhelming need to follow her gut.

Her mother must have seen it on her face because she grabbed Arrow's arm, forcing her to look at her. "It's not a request, it's an order. You do still take orders from me. I'm still the president."

"What if they have her?" Arrow didn't realize she'd asked the question out loud.

"One problem at a time. I know how you feel about her, but we don't know what's happened."

Her mother was right. Arrow choked down the fear that seemed to be caught in her throat and pushed herself toward the opening of the tunnel. She looked around the large hollow half-dome, but there was no one left.

She made a right, continuing down, staying hidden behind crates of food. When they finally reached their exit, she picked up her speed, hoping her reward would be Kaelyn on the other side of the hatch. She swung it open and ushered her mother through. She locked it behind her and hurried down the spiral metal staircase.

Valor leaned against the transport, tying a rag around his upper arm with his free hand and teeth.

"What happened?" she shouted at him.

"We have to get out of here." He winced as he climbed into the back seat.

Her mother ran around to the other side. "Get in, Arrow!"

Arrow climbed in and turned around, hoping she'd just overlooked Kaelyn. She wasn't there. "What the fuck happened?"

Valor's face was cut up and swelling. His mouth moved oddly when he spoke. "They took her."

She wanted to grab him and shake out all the answers at once. "What do you mean they took her?"

"I'm sorry, Major. We got to the reservoir building, we blew up the control panel, and then…" He winced again. "I don't know. There were gunshots, I got hit in the side of the face several times. I got several shots off, and they took off running, but they had Kaelyn."

Arrow sat back down in her seat. Adrenaline coursed through her body, and rage took over her senses. Thinking about what they could be doing to Kaelyn, about what this meant for the Resistance, crushed the air from her chest. The fury she felt rushing through her body made it so she could barely breathe and then it seemed to grab her heart and squeeze. If it was the last thing she did in this life, she'd get Kaelyn back.

CHAPTER THIRTY-ONE

Kaelyn sat in the empty, cold room. The walls were cement with poorly working lights. The table was made of metal, cold to the touch, and the chair was intentionally uncomfortable. She assumed they had her in the detention facility that had been about one hundred and fifty yards from the White House back in her time. *Is it still the White House? Or has the MacLeod family given it some new, abhorrent name to suit their egos?*

She knew they wouldn't keep her waiting long. From everything she knew about MacLeod, he was too impatient and far too arrogant to let her simmer. No, he would want to know as much as possible as soon as possible. She tried to ignore the shivers that ran through her body, not from fear but the temperature in the room. *Another tactic.*

She prayed that Arrow, Valor, and Macy had made it out alive. She knew the Hand of God had no intention of sparing them. They only wanted her. MacLeod would want to make an example out of her, a way to prove his power. She imagined what they'd do to Arrow and the others. Of course, only the worst came to mind. She felt her heart ache at the possibilities. Her stomach started to turn as she imagined a world without Arrow in it. It wasn't a world she wanted to be a part of, even under the circumstances they'd left things. The world needed people like Arrow. She needed her. She forced herself to believe that wasn't even a possibility. Arrow, Valor, and Macy were okay. They had to be, or she would never be able to continue.

She willed herself not to cry. She wouldn't let any of her captors see her anguish. It would be seen as a weakness, and weaknesses were used against you. If she had any chance of making it out of there, she needed to play their game. She needed to be smarter. She needed to pay attention. She needed to be Phoenix One.

The door opened, and an older looking, gray haired man took a seat across from her. He was ordinary looking, and he could've been anyone. But the pure hatred in his eyes told her that he was someone in particular.

He tossed his hat on the table. "System activate." A floating keyboard appeared in front of him, and he made several keystrokes before turning his attention back to her. "State your name."

Kaelyn knew they were already aware of who she was, so there was no reason to lie at this point. "Kaelyn Dorothy Trapp."

His jaw clenched. "When were you born?"

She didn't want to sit through a hundred individual questions. Plus, she wanted to assert a bit of power over this man. "Look, I'll save you some time. I'm the daughter of Daniel and Dorothy Trapp. I was cryogenically frozen in the year two thousand and twenty. My parents were trying to save me from the impending disaster our country faced. It was called the Phoenix Project." She wasn't sure what they knew or thought, and she didn't want to give too much information away about the Phoenix Project. She would try this small lie about her parents trying to spare her to see what they knew.

He cracked the knuckles on his left hand with his thumb. "Tell me more about the Phoenix Project."

She made sure to keep her voice steady and calm, wanting to be believable. "There's nothing more to tell. They wanted me to survive, so they made sure I did."

The door swung open again. One of the most beautiful women Kaelyn had ever seen sauntered in. Her eyes were a turquoise blue that reminded Kaelyn of the Caribbean Sea. Her blond hair was tied back in a simple ponytail. She seemed to exude power and dominance. Kaelyn wasn't sure what to make of her.

"Get out," the blonde told the man sitting across from her.

His mouth twitched. "Ms. MacLeod, this is my job."

"It was, General, but it's mine now," she said.

Kaelyn wasn't sure if she should be impressed or terrified.

He hesitated but stood up. "Your father—"

"My father sent me in here." She didn't even bother to look at him and kept her intense scrutiny on Kaelyn.

The man grabbed his hat and left the room, his annoyance apparent by his heavy footsteps and the eye roll he made sure she saw.

The woman sat on the corner of the table closest to Kaelyn, her green skirt sliding up as she sat. "As I'm sure you've put together by now, I'm Nora MacLeod, First Daughter. You can cut the crap about your parents trying to save you. It's bullshit. They wouldn't have kept you frozen just to be woken up here, alone, without any family. Now, where are the Resistance forces?"

Kaelyn sat farther back in her seat, wanting to put distance between them. "I don't know what you're talking about."

Nora seemed amused by her defiance, a slight smile creeping across her face. "I'm only going to ask you one more time."

"You're going to get the same answer. I can't tell you something I don't know."

Nora walked over the other side of the room and pushed a few buttons on a screen. A small door opened, and she pulled out two metal bands. She set them on the table. "Technology has come far since you were frozen. We have a multitude of options now when it comes to making people tell the truth." She traced her finger over the top of one of the bands. "Sure, I could inject you with something and the information would just start flowing. But I'm old-fashioned."

Kaelyn focused on keeping her breathing controlled and rhythmic. "It won't make a difference. My answers will be the same."

Nora picked up one of the bands and played with the wires that were attached. "If I put these around your arms, it will send an electric pulse through your body every time you lie to me."

Kaelyn wasn't sure what the right answer was at this point, so she said nothing.

Nora ran her fingertips over Kaelyn's arm. "Eventually, I'll grow bored and increase the electricity level. The pulses will, at a certain point, disrupt your sinus rhythm and your heart will stop."

"That would be unfortunate for you. Killing me won't garner you any favor with my people. And you need that, don't you? Their favor?" Kaelyn said with a calm she didn't feel.

Nora laughed. "Your people? Is that what they are now? Last I checked your people voted my grandfather into office. Your people have followed my family without question for almost seventy years.

Your people discarded the misguided ramblings of your father and put their faith in a real leader."

Kaelyn rolled her eyes and continued to egg her on. The longer she could keep her preoccupied with this, the longer she was giving the Resistance. "A real leader? Please." She laughed. "Your father runs an authoritarian society that keeps its people sedated and uneducated. Your family doesn't govern; it forces, manipulates, lies, and controls. You're too afraid to give people a choice because they wouldn't choose your father. Your family is an embarrassment to the history of this country."

Nora came across the table as if she were going to slap her. She pushed the tips of her fingers down against the table until they were white. "Tell me why I shouldn't kill you right now."

Kaelyn smiled at her. "Even if you killed me, it would be too late. Phoenix isn't a person; it's an idea. You can't kill an idea. The Resistance is a movement that was created long before my family. It has lived in people since the American Revolution, during the Civil Rights Movement, the Women's Rights Movement, and I could name thirty more. You might have won temporarily but not indefinitely. It's not how Americans are built. The fear you've built into your approach can't last. People are smarter than that, and they're ready to fight back."

"People crave protection. They handed over their rights, their privacy, even their identities in order to be protected. That hasn't changed." Nora slipped the bands over Kaelyn's arms, grabbing her more tightly when Kaelyn tried to pull away. "You overestimate people at their core. All of those things sound lovely on paper, but when it comes down to it, people will protect themselves before they give another thought to their neighbor."

"We'll see about that." Kaelyn glared at her. She had no plan, no idea what was happening, or if Arrow was even alive. All she could do was endure whatever was about to happen and hope her belief in her people was enough to keep her alive.

CHAPTER THIRTY-TWO

A rrow sent out a distress signal. It was a calculated decision that could make their situation even more dangerous. The signal would notify the Resistance that the war had begun, but it would also give away their location. It'd be an upward battle from there.

She flipped the three turbo switches on the console. They would be in what used to be Washington, DC, in less than an hour. She tightened the straps on her seat, holding her body in place.

She turned her head, and Valor and her mother were doing the same. Valor had the rejuvenation system in place, and his breathing had leveled, the bleeding stopped. The rejuvenation system wouldn't be complete by the time they got there, but there was no other option. They had to move now. Losing Kaelyn wasn't a reality she was willing to accept. She flipped the go button, and the transport slammed forward into turbo drive.

"Mom, when we get there, I'm going to drop you and Valor at the rally point. There should be several small platoons pushing their way through the streets now. You're going to have to speak for Kaelyn."

"Take some of the forces with you. You're going to need help," her mom yelled from the back.

Arrow pretended not to be able to hear her over the loud winds whipping over the transport. She had no intention of taking anyone with her. They were keeping Kaelyn somewhere, and getting her back would be easier on her own. She didn't want to risk spooking Kaelyn's jailers and having them kill her on impulse.

They were coming up to the farthest gated entry point to Eden. The protocol here was to stop, be inspected, and then be given access. That wasn't about to happen.

Arrow flipped on the barrier eliminator gun they had specially installed in this transport. CAM had said it worked, but she'd never tried it herself. She grabbed the joystick and pushed the red button. A large orange blast radiated from the front of the transport. It completely leveled the guard station and barrier. There was smoke, dust, and gunfire raining down on top of the transport as they shot through.

If the situation hadn't been what it was, she would've given herself a moment to be thoroughly impressed. But as the dust started to clear, she heard the small artillery craft overhead. There was one above and then one on each side.

She clicked the button for the protection barriers, but it wouldn't protect the transport for long. Their energy supply was running low, and every hit would deplete it further. She just needed to make it farther. Then she would be able to disappear into the streets, under the cover of the ultra violet personal protectors.

The low energy alert was blaring, and they only had a minute or two left before they'd be left completely vulnerable. They came upon a small building, and Arrow turned the steering wheel, forcing the transport to head directly into it, taking down the wall as they slammed through it.

She grabbed the two bags from the front seat and jumped out of the transport. She pulled open the back door. "Go."

Macy and Valor climbed out as they were told, as quickly as possible. She reached back into the driver's seat and set the transport to autopilot. She flipped the button for turbo speed and then closed the door. The transport pushed out the other side of the wall and only made it about sixty feet before the artillery craft blew it up.

They waited, listening for the crafts to leave the area. When the humming sounds finally stopped, she checked her weapons. She grabbed a few magazines out of the bag and put a charging mount on the laser portion of her rifle.

"Take the rest and get to the rally point. I'm going to go get Kaelyn." Arrow handed the bags to her mother and Valor.

"You can't go by yourself. You don't even know where to start." Valor looked at her as if he didn't recognize her.

"I synced Kaelyn's bracelet to our transmitters before we left headquarters. There's still a signal. They might have taken it off her, but it's a good place to start. You two have to meet up with the platoons.

This whole thing is about to blow up. People are going to be scared. They're going to be confused. They'll need a leader to let them know we're still here and we're still going ahead." She grabbed her mom and hugged her as hard as she could without seeming scared.

Her mom put her hands on the sides of Arrow's face. She looked like she wanted to say a million different things, but all she could manage were two sentences. "I love you. Be careful." She kissed Arrow's forehead.

"This is foolish." Valor wasn't going to give up as easily. "Let me go with you."

Arrow grabbed Valor's transmitter and held her metal bracelet up to it, allowing the devices to sync. "No. If I can't get Kaelyn back, they'll need to know their president is still there. The other three Phoenixes should be in place soon."

He did the same with his bracelet. "At least we'll be able to find each other now."

She stuck the transmitter in her pocket. "Yeah, but so will other people. I need you to cloak your location until you make it to the center of the capital."

He nodded. "Hey, Arrow…" He put his hands on his hips and looked down at the ground. "I'm not good at this kind of thing. But I need you to come back."

She hugged him, smiling into his neck. "I love you too, Valor." She smacked his arm. "I'll see you soon."

She turned and went in the other direction before they had a chance to see her eyes filling with tears. They had enough to worry about without her laying her fear at their feet. She knew this could possibly be the last time she would see either of them. The thought should've scared her, but what scared her more was the possibility of something happening to Kaelyn and her doing nothing to stop it. She could live with her own demise if it meant she was able to get Kaelyn to safety. Nothing else mattered more than that.

She ducked behind the corner of the building she'd just allowed the transport to demolish. She needed to get her bearings and figure out where she was in relation to the complex she assumed they were keeping Kaelyn. She'd studied rudimentary maps of Eden, based on defectors' recollections and how the area used to look before the Resistance had left. But she wasn't quite prepared for the actual beauty of it all.

The buildings seem to reach all the way up to the clouds. Some held their timeless and classic architecture while others had been updated over the years. The glass windows that reflected in the sun looked like diamonds that remained just out of reach. The streets were incredibly clean. As a matter of fact, she didn't see a single piece of trash anywhere.

Come to think of it, no one had shown up where she'd crashed their transport. There were no people crowding around wanting to know what happened. People walked past her without even looking in her direction. The crash should've alerted someone to the location, but there were no sirens, no soldiers. There was nothing.

Here she stood in the middle of a street in broad daylight with a gun strapped to her back, blood on her clothes, and a uniform that didn't match anyone's in the vicinity, and no one was alarmed. They moved at a steady and controlled pace. Their faces were blank, void of any emotions. Their eyes seemed to be glassy, probably the ramifications of the sedatives they'd been ingesting their whole lives. Then she realized everyone was heading in the same direction, toward the center of Eden.

Arrow didn't know why everyone was heading to one location, but she could guess. MacLeod was going to impress his people with a public display of dominance. And there was nothing that would broadcast that more than Kaelyn Trapp. Everything she knew about MacLeod led her to believe that this display would involve humiliation, blood, and pain. He was going to try to use Kaelyn to discredit the Resistance and incite violence.

What he didn't bother to realize was that his ego would end up being his downfall. He was gathering all his people in one place. He would transmit the event to everyone and anyone in the country. He believed the whole movement was tied to one person, and if he could get rid of that person, the Resistance would fall apart. His mistake was not only underestimating the Resistance, but Kaelyn as well.

Arrow felt the first tingle of relief since Kaelyn had been taken. If he was going to bring her out into public, it would be her one opportunity to get her back. She felt the swell of anticipation rise low in her chest. She could and would save Kaelyn.

CHAPTER THIRTY-THREE

Adon glared at his daughter. She was wasting time trying to get information out of Kaelyn Trapp for no reason. They didn't need to know their plans at this point. The forces were already within the city limits. They needed a sign of strength, one that only Kaelyn could give.

He pushed the microphone on the desk that was linked to Nora's ear. "Get in here."

He watched as she turned toward the mirror, irritation washing over her face. She stomped into the room he was waiting in.

"What is it?" She motioned to the glass where Kaelyn sat slumped on the other side. "I just had her hooked up and we were going to get somewhere. Now she's going to think we're weak."

"Why waste our time doing this where no one can see it? Let's get her out in the square. Her people need to see they've placed their hopes and dreams in the wrong person." He looked over to the two soldiers. "Get her ready for transport."

Nora looked as if she was going to argue for a second but changed her mind. "Whatever you think is best, Daddy."

He waited for her to continue, sure an argument about his decision was next, but it didn't come. "Okay, good. Go get changed. We'll leave in fifteen minutes."

Nora left and he watched as the soldiers unhooked Kaelyn from the electric bands around her arms. She was much prettier than he had expected. He'd seen pictures of her, but they didn't do her justice. Maybe if she made it through this without dying, he would make a wife out of her. She would look lovely on his arm, and that would be the final nail in the coffin for the traitors she aligned herself with. Nora wouldn't like it, but she'd get over it.

The soldiers dragged Kaelyn into the hallway, and Adon couldn't pass up the opportunity to speak with her. He stepped out in front of them before they made it past the door.

"Hello, Ms. Trapp." Adon tried to touch her face, but she pulled away. "Oh, come now. There's no reason to make this more difficult than necessary. I think if you give me a chance, you'll see I'm not the monster you've made me out to be in your mind." He touched her face again, and she pushed her chin out. Defiant. That wasn't anything he couldn't train out of her.

"You can throw me into the deepest, darkest hole you have. I'm not going to tell you anything." She pulled her face away again, and one of the soldiers shoved her, causing her to have to step toward him.

"A hole? I'm not going to throw you into a hole. I know it's been quite some time since you were part of this world, but that's not how we do things anymore." He started walking and the soldiers forced her to fall into step alongside him. "I want us to be friends. I have much bigger plans for you than dropping you out of sight, but we can start there if you prefer."

They reached the end of the hallway and stopped, waiting for the transport. "Tell me, what would your father think of his only offspring bearing a MacLeod child?" He looked her over, interested in what she might have to offer.

Kaelyn pulled against her restraints. She clenched her teeth and practically spit out her words. "I'd never touch you."

No woman had ever refused him, which made this exchange that much more fascinating. "You're speaking as if I need your acquiescence. Many things have changed since your time here, not just technology. I don't need your permission to have my way with you."

He finally received the reaction he had been searching for. He had rendered her speechless, and he could tell by looking at her face that she was terrified. Exhilarated, he thought maybe this whole situation might be exactly what he needed to rejuvenate him. He'd be able to renew the faith of the people and gain a little trophy at the same time. Killing her would be easy, but keeping her for himself would be the greatest triumph of all. Yes, she was going to look perfect lying in his bed, tied up and waiting for him.

❖

Kaelyn fell into the transport, courtesy of the soldiers who seemed to not care one way or another what happened to her. She knew what MacLeod intended to do with her, and it was enough to make her feel nauseous. Nora, on the other hand, was a different story. She couldn't quite pin down her angle. She understood that Nora was MacLeod's daughter, but there was more to her than she could figure out without more information.

She only briefly allowed the thought of what would happen if the Resistance wasn't successful. She could only handle one problem at a time, and right now, she needed as much information as possible to help push the mission forward. She thought of Arrow and what she'd want her to do in this situation. She knew MacLeod was an arrogant man, and the best avenue would be to pursue information

"The weather bubbles were a genius idea," Kaelyn said, staring out the window as though she was really sharing her thoughts.

MacLeod smiled at her. "Yes, they're imperative to our survival. Other countries haven't quite mastered the technology yet."

Kaelyn kept herself from bristling at his remarks. "You haven't shared the technology then?"

"The survival of other countries isn't really our problem." MacLeod touched the window, the behavior of a child who only reacted to whims.

"And if they don't survive because of it?" Kaelyn asked.

MacLeod smiled, a light flickered in his eyes. "Once they're all dead, the whole world will be ours. No more sharing resources."

Kaelyn felt the bile rise in the back of her throat. "Interesting."

Nora crossed her arms. "She wants to know why you'd allow millions of people to die if you had the ability to save them. She's only pretending to be interested and impressed to fall into your good graces."

MacLeod put his hands on Kaelyn's knees and started to rub them. Her involuntary response was to pull away, but she forced herself to remain still.

"It's God's will. We're the chosen people. While the Muslims, Buddhists, and Jews all die because of a failing earth, we prevail. That's not coincidence."

"So, Christianity has turned into watching as people suffer and die? Besides your perverted interpretation of religion, what about the Constitution? The Founding Fathers didn't want there to be a single religion. They wanted people to be free to worship however they saw fit." Kaelyn knew she was treading on thin ice, but she couldn't help herself and she really needed to know.

"The Constitution?" He shook his head. "Please, we tried that and it failed. People can't be trusted with that much decision-making power. They need to be told what to do and who to follow. When my father came to power, the whole country was falling apart. People from all over the world were flooding across the border, sucking up our natural resources, spending our tax dollars, and taking jobs from hardworking people. American people. Mothers were killing their babies right before they could be born, men thought they were women, and young men thought it was okay to have sex with other young men. It was complete depravity." He sat back in his seat and rubbed his face. "Before my father saved America from itself, there was a war on men. Women thought they were capable of doing the same jobs as men. They didn't want to raise children; they wanted men to stay home while they went out and pretended to be men. It was disgusting. Who knows what would've happened if my father hadn't been elected."

Kaelyn tried to swallow her words, but they were too big. "There was no war on men. Women just wanted to be treated equally. They wanted control over their bodies, over who they loved, and what they did with their lives. They didn't need saving from anyone but men like your father and you."

Rage filled MacLeod's eyes, and his upper lip twitched as the transport rolled to a stop. "And yet, here you are, no power, no voice, and no ability to change your fate." He pushed the door open. "Now get out and do as you're told before I put a bullet in your head."

Kaelyn pulled against her steel restraints. She wanted to throw herself across the transport and hit him. Not just to extinguish the anger she felt pulse through every nerve ending, but for the thousands of women and minorities who had been impacted by this mindset. She couldn't begin to imagine the vile behavior and agony they'd all endured while nothing was done. Well, that would end today. Even if she wasn't successful she'd at least do her part, even if it killed her.

Chapter Thirty-four

Arrow was only a few blocks from the center of the city where the large group of people had congregated. She ducked into one of the alleyways and opened her transmitter. She programmed in the code to reach the leaders of the Resistance forces. There were several small scuffles taking place along the outermost part of the city limits, but they'd otherwise gone unchecked.

Arrow instructed them to keep their heads on a swivel. Overthrowing an entire government wasn't going to start or end with a few minor skirmishes. Plus, it would take several days for the sedation drugs to work their way out of the systems of the people of Eden. During that time, no one was entirely sure what to expect from the masses.

She realized that most of the citizens of Eden probably believed the Resistance forces in the streets were there because MacLeod was bringing them into the fold. He had said as much on his emergency transmissions. Even though they were armed, they might not have any reason to think they were anyone but a new soldier force. This group of people had been bred to be complacent. She wasn't sure if that would benefit them or work against them. But it was too late to weigh the pros and cons of that now. Fortunately, no one gave her a second glance, and when they did, their eyes were so dull it was surprising they'd register anything at all.

She was able to get in contact with her mother and Valor. They were working with one of the platoons to overrun the broadcasting system. Her mother was ready to make an announcement that would be shared not only with the Resistance but all of Eden as well.

Arrow found a reasonably secluded place, pulled the rifle from her back, and fastened the grappling attachment to the end. She took aim at the rooftop and pulled the trigger. Once the hook was anchored at the rooftop, she attached it to her belt loop and pushed the button. She was pulled to the top of the building a moment later, and though she listened for shouts of warning, none came. She removed the drone cloak from her backpack and set it up over the top of her. It would give her a three-foot-by-three-foot space to work in, which was more than manageable. She removed the binoculars from her backpack and scanned the area. The images behind the stage announced that a message from the president was coming soon, with images of MacLeod rotating beside it. She turned her binoculars in the direction the Resistance forces should be heading in from. There they were, a sea of blue uniforms at the edge of the crowd. She felt several things at once—pride, determination, and fear. She worried about all the ways this situation could go and how many people would be in danger. *Focus. Get to Kaelyn. Deal with the rest later.*

She set her transmitter to the broadcast frequency to be able to hear anything that happened, and then set up her long-range rifle and adjusted the scope. She had a perfect sightline from this vantage point. She'd thought about hiding out near the stage and attacking from there but changed her mind when she saw the soldiers congregating at each end. Even if she was able to get near MacLeod, she would likely get herself and Kaelyn killed. This would buy her a couple of crucial moments while everyone tried to figure out what to do next. She knew the army of the Hand of God would find her within a few minutes, but she hoped it would be a big enough distraction for Kaelyn to escape.

Arrow set up the rifle's targeting system on the podium where she assumed MacLeod would make his announcement. She tucked the remote activation button into her pocket and went back down the side of the building. She wasn't sure she knew what the exact right moment would be; she just hoped she would know the opportunity when it happened.

❖

Kaelyn listened from behind a black curtain where she was waiting with MacLeod, Nora, and several soldiers. There was a prerecorded message playing on several screens. It was clearly intended to invigorate the crowd. The recordings were of people from Eden speaking about their great fortune to live in such an incredible place, free from the dangers and issues of the rest of the world. Then there was a segment regarding genetic modification. The geneticist was offering to help people rid their potential offspring of any issues that were of concern— brown eyes, homosexuality, red hair, and so on. Kaelyn knew more traits had been listed, but she couldn't bring herself to log them into her memory.

She looked over at MacLeod and Nora, who stood there so smug and proud of the society they were helping to create by eliminating traits they deemed less worthy. She thought of all the different personalities they wanted to wipe out and how much dimmer the world would be because of it. She wondered if this world was even worth saving. If this is what they were striving toward, maybe they had found a way to eliminate human decency as well. Then she thought of the people she had met since she started her journey here. They were decent, special, and wonderfully unique. They were worth saving. They deserved better than the MacLeods. That's who this was all for.

She wanted to see Arrow and disappear into her arms for several years, possibly forever. She thought about her devotion to these people and the belief that they were worth saving. She wished she was here with her now. She wanted some of that adoration to seep into her skin, to make her believe. But that wasn't reality. This was where she was, and these were the circumstances she needed to deal with.

MacLeod grabbed her by the arm and squeezed. "If you fuck this up, I'll find every one of your little friends and see that they pay for your poor decision-making."

She tugged her arm away from him. She knew it wasn't much, but it was all she had. Nora pushed her from behind, and she practically fell onto the stage. The crowd started cheering for MacLeod and Nora, who stood on either side of her, waving back. The square was filled with people. She scanned their faces, hoping to find a few familiar ones, but there were none. What did occur to her was that these people were clapping and cheering, but not a single one of them was smiling. They were giving the MacLeods what they wanted, but it wasn't because of loyalty; it was because of fear and conditioning. She had been in crowds of people with her parents who cried when they walked out on stage, who wanted her parents to hold their babies, and to take pictures. These weren't the faces of people in awe. This was a group of people who had never experienced real leadership.

MacLeod was presented with a small tray with three small dots that looked like buttons. He grabbed one and put it on his throat. Nora grabbed the other and then she placed the last on Kaelyn's neck. It wasn't until MacLeod started speaking that she realized the buttons were microphones.

He spread his arms like he was embracing the crowd. "Thank you all for coming out today. I have such a wonderful surprise for you." He motioned over to Kaelyn. "I know many of you don't recognize her, but this is Kaelyn Trapp. Her father was defeated by my father to give you Eden." He slid his arm around her waist and held her hard when she tried to pull away. "But God saved her for us. He has brought her through the decades, a true miracle. God's intention, I'm sure, was to prove to you that you are his true believers, his real followers, his chosen people." He kissed her cheek. "Kaelyn, please tell everyone how impressed you are with their new country."

Kaelyn studied the faces of the people again. Some looked confused, others scared, but some seemed blissful. She tried to calculate those reactions to figure out who would remain loyal to MacLeod. "It's very beautiful."

He rubbed her back, his fingertips pressing cruelly into her skin. "Why don't you tell everyone a little bit about the newcomers who have been coming through the city gates? Tell them how they're here to help. How they've been long forgotten, but now that they've returned we'll welcome them with open arms and place them into the worker force."

Kaelyn saw Arrow duck behind one of the dozen statues of MacLeod that lined the square. Her pulse raced and she scanned the crowd again to see the spread of the blue uniforms that signaled hope. Arrow was getting closer, but she needed to buy her a little more time and not alarm any of the people who surrounded her.

Kaelyn smiled and folded her hands in front of her. "The people you see behind you are known as the Resistance. They are here to help you."

MacLeod's eyes bored into her and his grip around her arm tightened. "Surely, the Resistance is no longer the name they'd like to go by. I'm sure we can think of something better." He smiled into the crowd.

Arrow was only about thirty feet from her now. She didn't want to keep staring at her and give away her location, but it was hard to look away. She was sure Arrow had a plan of some kind or she wouldn't have put herself in this position. Kaelyn tried desperately to think of what it might be so she could be prepared to help.

Kaelyn yanked her arm loose of MacLeod's grip. "There is a better way to live. MacLeod wants to be your king, but that's not who we are. That's not who any of you are. You're not servants or peasants. You're Americans. The Resistance is here to help take the government back from this treacherous family. They're here to help you—"

MacLeod grabbed her by the throat and shoved her backward. She heard Nora begin to speak, but she couldn't make out what she was saying. Her only focus were the white dots that were beginning to take over her vision from the lack of oxygen as she pulled at MacLeod's hand.

A round of gunshots filled the air. People screamed, and a heavy weight fell on top of her. The last thing she saw before everything went completely black was Arrow running up to the stage. Somehow, she knew everything would be all right.

CHAPTER THIRTY-FIVE

Arrow wasn't sure if she had chosen the right time to pull the trigger. She knew the rifle would have a difficult time hitting MacLeod from the position he was in, but she couldn't stop herself when she saw him grab Kaelyn. Now there were people running in every direction, slowing her progress to the stage but also providing cover so she could get there.

Soldiers had surrounded MacLeod and Kaelyn, which meant Arrow couldn't tell if Kaelyn was okay. But even from a distance she could see a pool of blood forming on the stage. *Please don't let me have shot Kaelyn.* She felt someone try to grab her, and she pulled her arm away, needing to keep moving forward. They grabbed her again, more forcefully. She grabbed the hand and turned it over, effectively wrenching the soldier's arm behind his back. She shoved him away, pushing him into the crowd of scurrying people.

She was almost to the stage when another soldier stepped out in front of her, gun drawn. She grabbed the gun, turning it over in his hand. When he loosened his grip, she took the gun from him and used the butt to smack him in the side of the head, and he fell to the ground unconscious.

There were four more running toward her, and she pulled her breathing apparatus from her pocket and pushed it into place in her mouth and nose. She pushed the activation button, allowing her to breathe as she rolled a smoke sphere toward the approaching men. It hit the ground, and smoke started pouring out of it, blinding the soldiers and causing them to double over in a coughing fit.

She finally reached the stage. There were several people surrounding MacLeod, who was lying facedown on top of Kaelyn. She had assumed this was their position, but the idea hadn't prepared her for the rage and fear that flowed through her body. As she moved toward them, she assured herself that Kaelyn was simply unconscious and the blood belonged to MacLeod. There was chaos all over and around the stage. Several soldiers hurried Nora MacLeod off the stage while others were making a path for the emergency transport to get close enough to assist the fallen dictator. People were yelling and crying; there were shots being fired in the distance. The uprising was beginning, and MacLeod was going to be helpless to stop it.

She wasn't going to get Kaelyn out of here with any fancy maneuvers. She pulled her gun from its holster. There were six soldiers and one of her, not great odds. But she was going to get Kaelyn out of here or she was going to die trying. She took a deep breath and was about to charge forward when she felt someone next to her. Valor.

"I wasn't going to let you have all the fun by yourself." He activated the electricity in his baton.

Now that the odds were better, she put her gun away and pulled her baton from the sling on her back. She hit the button on the bottom of the rod, and it started to buzz with electricity.

The city soldiers who stared at them appeared confused. They weren't sure what to make of the two of them. Unlike the Resistance, these poor men hadn't spent a lifetime training for this day. They had probably been forced into service, an unfortunate consequence of being born into the wrong class, and the ones facing them were marked as city soldiers, the kind who never left to patrol the outside. Up until today, they probably hadn't had to face anyone fighting back, questioning their position. They'd always been the takers, and now that they were forced to deal with opposition, they were freezing.

Arrow noticed a few trembling hands wrapped around their guns. It only gave her pause for a second. Then one of them fired off a shot and she and Valor went in different directions with an unspoken understanding they would attack from the sides.

Arrow rolled on the ground and came up alongside one, pushing her baton into his kidney. He went down as the next fired another shot. She flipped over on her stomach and used her legs to sweep around, taking him out at the knees. When he hit the ground, she shoved the baton into his stomach, causing him to start convulsing.

The final soldier in her path was backing up toward MacLeod. The panic in his eyes was real as he fumbled with his gun, which ultimately fell to the ground.

"We're aren't your enemy." She motioned at him with her baton. "We want to free you from all of this."

He glanced down at his gun like he was going to try to go for it.

"You don't want to do that and I don't want to hurt an unarmed man," Arrow said.

He stared at her for what seemed like several seconds, then he turned and ran in the other direction.

A very large, daunting man with a general's stars was standing in front of MacLeod. With a gun in each hand and his legs planted firmly, he pointed the weapons at Arrow and Valor, and he made no move to leave. "You will let emergency services through."

"I'm not letting you take Kaelyn Trapp," Arrow said.

"I don't give a shit about the girl. I just want to get him out of here." He nodded to the emergency responders who waited at the side of the stage.

Other soldiers were running toward the stage now, and they'd run out of options and time. "Okay. I have explosive devices set all around the stage. Tell the approaching soldiers to stop. You take MacLeod, we'll take Trapp, and no one else has to get hurt."

The general looked like he didn't believe her, and with good reason. There were no explosives anywhere near the stage. She would have never risked Kaelyn like that, but he didn't know that. He pushed his transmitter button all the same and told the soldiers to stand down. The emergency responders put MacLeod on a gurney, and Arrow was disappointed to realize that he was simply unconscious and not dead. The shot had hit him in the leg. *Hopefully, it hit an artery.*

The general walked backward off the stage, following MacLeod while keeping his guns pointed on Valor and Arrow. As soon as the emergency group left the stage, Arrow knew they only had about twenty seconds to get Kaelyn out of the vicinity. She was no fool. The only reason the general had told the soldiers to stand down was to protect MacLeod. He'd give them all the go-ahead as soon as the emergency transport was out of the blast zone.

JACKIE D

Arrow hurried over to where the responders had rolled Kaelyn over. Arrow didn't bother checking her vitals. She picked her up and put her over her shoulder. Valor tipped over the podium and trained the heavy artillery blast gun in the direction the soldiers were approaching.

He pushed the button on the side of the gun and it started to hum. "Get out of here. I'll lay down cover. Go to the basement of the bakery on Second Street. I'll be there as soon as I can."

Arrow didn't like the idea of leaving Valor behind, but there was no other option now. She made it down the stairs of the stage and did her best to calculate the distance to Second Street, about a quarter of a mile. She should be able to make it there in three minutes with Kaelyn on her back.

The chaos in the streets added good cover for her movements. There were people running in all directions, unaware how to handle the gravity of what just unfolded. Most of these people had lived a very structured, scheduled, and methodical life. They ate, exercised, worked, and even had sex at prescribed times. Everything was dictated by MacLeod, and now they weren't sure if he was dead or alive. This uncertainty would fuel an untapped source of independence and hope, both of which were essential to the success of the Resistance. There would be those who would cling more fiercely to the structure they knew, but Phoenix would've never changed those people's minds anyway.

Arrow ran past several stores on Second Street, looking for a bakery. She finally saw a sign in the shape of a cupcake that read Old Time Bakery. She went behind the store and found the staircase. She pushed on the door and nothing happened. She carefully brought Kaelyn down off her shoulder and rested her against the wall. She was about to kick the door in when it opened.

A rather short, angry looking woman with red hair glared at her. "Were you seriously going to kick down my door? You could've just knocked."

Arrow wasn't sure what she had been expecting, but she wasn't it. "Valor sent me."

The woman looked down at Kaelyn and her eyes grew large. She waved them in. "Why is the Phoenix unconscious?"

Arrow picked Kaelyn up and cradled her in her arms as she carried her into the bakery's basement. She didn't want to answer questions;

she just wanted to make sure Kaelyn was okay. Her mother was talking to someone on a transmitter when she saw Arrow. She ended the call, quickly cleared off the table in the center of the room, and grabbed a medical bag.

❖

Kaelyn heard the voices before she could open her eyes. A sense of relief overcame her when she realized one of them belonged to Arrow. She wanted desperately to see her, to touch her, to know she was okay, but she couldn't move. In her mind, she was screaming, telling everyone she was all right, that she had made it, but nothing came out. She focused on moving her fingers. She could feel them. She knew they were there, but they weren't connecting to her brain.

She knew Arrow was leaning over her because she could smell her. Hints of vanilla with a bit of sweat. Arrow placed something small and round on the side of her head. She only had a second to wonder what it was before she was able to open her eyes and move her body. It felt like electricity, and a welcome jolt back into the world allowed her to open her eyes.

Arrow smiled down at her. "We had to temporarily paralyze your body while we did a scan to make sure you hadn't suffered any major injuries."

Kaelyn just stared at her. She wanted to thank her. She wanted to tell her how much she missed her, but all she could do was smile.

"You took a pretty mean hit on the head, but you're okay overall. The regen machine has taken care of the damage MacLeod did to your throat." Arrow handed her a cup of water.

Kaelyn sat up. "You saved me." She managed after a sip of water.

Arrow's face softened. "I'll always save you."

"Are you two always so obnoxious?" a voice Kaelyn didn't recognize teased her from somewhere behind Arrow.

Arrow rolled her eyes and nodded toward the woman behind her. "That's Sloan. She's a loyalist to the Resistance who lives here in Eden. We're in the basement of her family's bakery. She seems to say whatever pops into her head."

Sloan had short hair much like Arrow's, but she seemed to only be about twenty years old. Her angular face was dotted with small freckles. She wore a black tank top, and her lanky arm stretched out in front of her to shake Kaelyn's hand. She was rather adorable.

"Nice to meet you, Sloan." Kaelyn shook her hand.

"Believe me, the pleasure is mine. I've been hearing about you and your family for like, my whole life." She pointed to a picture on the wall. "You probably can't tell from here, but it's a picture of your family. My parents and grandparents thought you guys were the best. Seriously, the best."

"That's very kind. How old are you?" Kaelyn stood and got dizzy. Arrow steadied her right away.

"I'm twenty-one," Sloan said proudly, the way all people do before the age of twenty-five.

Kaelyn moved closer to the photo and remembered the day the picture had been taken. It was a stock photo that hung in many locations, but she loved it all the same. Her family had been preparing for the Veteran's Day celebration. It was taken two full years before things had taken a turn for the worst. A simpler and happier time.

"Why did your family stay in Eden? Why didn't they go to the Resistance colonies?"

Sloan pointed to another wall where there were different pictures, family pictures. "My grandpa always said the Resistance would come to take the country back, and when they did, they would need help. He thought it best to be that help. There's more than just my family. There are a bunch of us actually, at least fifty."

Kaelyn knew in the scheme of things, fifty wasn't a significant number, but it could make the difference when needing friendly aid within the city.

"Well, thank you for everything you and your family have done. Are your parents here? I'd love to meet them," Kaelyn said.

Sloan picked at the bottom of her shirt. "They died about six years ago. See, this isn't really our bakery. I mean, it used to be, when my grandparents were alive. But MacLeod confiscated all personal property and land. He owns everything. We just run it for him. We don't make any real money; my family was allowed to live in the apartment above the bakery, and everyone in my class receives a food and clothing ration. Anyway, MacLeod took an interest in my mom after meeting her once and wanted her to go live with him. When she refused, he had her killed. When my dad tried to stop it from happening, they killed him too."

Kaelyn felt her heart cry out in pain for this young woman and all the people who lived under MacLeod's rule. She wanted to say something to make it better for Sloan, but words with that kind of power had yet to be conceived. She watched Sloan make an obviously practiced maneuver of taking a deep breath and wiping tears from her eyes before she revealed a smile.

"So, I'm at your service full-time." She clapped her hands together.

Kaelyn knew what Sloan was doing, and she also understood that pushing those types of feelings down would only take you so far. Eventually, they'd explode in one form or another. She was about to voice her concern when Macy called her name.

"Kaelyn, Arrow, I need you to come over here and look at this."

Valor used his hand to push an image up onto the wall. It was the outline of Eden.

"Right now, we have platoons moving in from all directions. One, as you know, is already within the city limits. The Hand of God showed a small amount of force during MacLeod's rally but nothing since then." Macy pointed to various points on the map as she spoke.

Arrow was laser focused on the map in front of her. "No, they haven't, which doesn't make a lot of sense. It's like they let us walk in here."

Sloan, who was clearly anxious to contribute, spoke. "They're hoping the Resistance becomes part of Eden. The government wants to make a secondary working class to keep everyone else in line. If there's someone below you, they think it'll keep people happy and dormant."

Arrow rubbed the back of her neck. "They can't really think that. They think the Resistance will just put down their weapons and agree to come under the command of MacLeod?"

Macy pushed another image up onto the wall. "It makes sense. He has kept people under his control for decades by keeping life bearable, and he's had plenty of time to grow complacent. He probably expected some pushback, but I bet he didn't expect and all-out assault. I'm never surprised what people will trade for easy comfort, but this might be what they needed to be forced out of their stupors."

Sloan took a step toward the map. "If you already took out the water supply, it should only take twenty-four hours for people to start feeling the effects of the drugs leaving their systems. We'll be able to get more people on our side, but the Resistance will have detractors." She pointed to an elaborate mechanical system over in the corner. "We've been making our own water here my whole life. Those of us who were aware what MacLeod was doing to the water have all been doing it."

Valor looked at the machine but was clearly thinking of something else. "I don't know if we have twenty-four hours."

Arrow put a hand on Kaelyn's back, and she felt it tingle where they touched. "Tell us what you learned while they had you."

Kaelyn thought back to the brief period of time she had spent in the custody of the MacLeods. "The daughter, Nora, she's much smarter than her father, which could actually make her more dangerous. She doesn't call the shots, but she has a much bigger view of what's happening than he does. I think she's the key."

"They key to what?" Valor asked.

"Everything," Kaelyn said. "MacLeod seems to only care about his image, sex, and power. But if he has one weakness, I think it's her."

"So, we what? Kill her?" Valor seemed irritated. "After today they'll be more protected than ever."

"We don't need to find her. She'll come to us. We just need to give her a reason." Kaelyn paced back and forth in the small room.

The relief of being saved and back with Arrow was quickly being replaced by the need to take this family down. She wanted them to only exist in history books, a story told in civics classes about how bad things could get when you allow fear to take over your life. And she wanted to smack that smug smile right off Nora MacLeod's face.

CHAPTER THIRTY-SIX

Adon winced in pain as the nurse attached the reanimation machine to his leg. Partially because it hurt but also because the fury he felt needed to be directed somewhere, and this unsuspecting nurse would bear the brunt of his anger. "Watch what you're doing, idiot."

The nurse kept her head down. "I'm sorry, sir."

He was ready to hit her when Nora walked through the door.

She hurried over to him. "Daddy, are you okay?"

"Just a little leg wound. Nothing to worry about," he said.

She looked like she wanted to tell him something but changed her mind.

"What is it, sweetheart?" He rubbed her hand.

"Can you excuse us for a moment please, Nurse?" She politely smiled at the retreating woman. "I think Eden needs an idea that will bring it all together. Something for them to rally behind. I believe we've underestimated the Resistance, and now drastic measures will need to be taken."

Nora was so intelligent, so driven. It was a shame that she hadn't been born a male and thus able to contribute to society in a more meaningful way. No matter, her insight had always been beneficial and influential in his decisions.

"What were you thinking, honey?"

She walked to the window. "The reason Grandfather was so successful was because he had a martyr, well, several actually. We need to give the people the same. Fear and rage are the best motivating factors. They also foster the most blind loyalty." She walked back over to him and kissed his forehead. "You know I love you, right, Daddy?"

He grabbed her hand and kissed her palm. "Yes, sweetheart. Of course."

But something changed in that instant. Nora's beautiful blue eyes went cold. A flash of something he had never seen within her appeared, and he felt a sense of primal fear rush through his body. He went to grab her hand, but it was too late. She attached a vial to his IV and pushed the stopper. He wanted to grab the IV lines from his arm, but he couldn't move. His limbs all felt heavy, like they were stuck in cement. He wanted to yell, to say something, but he couldn't move his mouth. Adon wanted to panic, he wanted to feel anything, but there was nothing left. He looked at her calm and thoughtful face in his last moments, hoping to see a bit of love or admiration.

But there was nothing in the familiar smile except triumph. But in his own way he knew he'd succeeded far more than he could've ever anticipated. Nora had his desire for power and control. It was just cleverly disguised in artificial empathy, and he'd never had a clue. He had raised someone far worse than he had ever been, and that thought brought him his only solace as his breathing slowed from quick gasps to nothing and the world faded away.

CHAPTER THIRTY-SEVEN

Arrow stared at the other three Phoenixes on the videoconference. She knew them by name only up until this point. But listening to them talk, she fully understood why they'd been chosen. They were smart, articulate, and eager. They listened to each other speak and offered thoughtful feedback. They'd been yanked out of history and dropped into a new world, and yet it was apparent that they truly cared about the outcome. They were as devoted to the cause as anyone else in the room. It was inspiring.

They were exchanging ideas with her mother and the other Platoon leaders about the best way to isolate and apprehend MacLeod. She was in awe of the magnitude of what it all meant. She watched as Kaelyn jotted down several notes and interjected her opinions where necessary. Arrow knew in that moment that she loved her. The empathy for people she'd never meet threaded its way through her. The way Kaelyn was concerned about the fallout for the people of Eden as well as her own was the emblem of true leadership. The way she chewed on the top of her pen when she was in deep thought and the way she tucked her hair behind her ear before she was going to make a point. Each of these unconscious movements were little glimpses into Kaelyn's psyche, and Arrow wanted to memorize every detail. She needed to save them, keep them for the time when they were no longer together.

The door to the basement flew off the hinges with a loud bang, and smoke filled the small room. Arrow slipped her breathing apparatus on and pushed through the pain she felt in her eyes. She grabbed both weapons from her back and turned to face the intruders. She heard a door from behind her open and then close, and she knew Sloan had taken Kaelyn and her mother out, just as they had discussed if something like this came to pass. Unable to see, she relied on her senses to guide her. She knew Valor was nearby, and she heard him switch his weapon's electrical baton on.

She swung her baton out in front of her, knowing someone was approaching, but it hit nothing. The smoke was becoming denser and burning more profusely. This wasn't like the smoke the Resistance used. This was heavy, disorienting, and unbearable. She was becoming more disoriented by the second. Whatever this was seeping into her eyes and entering her bloodstream, the breathing apparatus wasn't helping. She tried to force her body to engage, but she couldn't send accurate signals to her brain. She felt the hands grab her and pull her to her feet and then toss her back to the ground. She saw the boot connect to her ribs and knew someone was taking advantage of her inability to fight back, but she didn't feel it. They were either going to kill her or take her. Since she served no purpose to them alive, she knew it would be the former. She resigned herself to never seeing Kaelyn again. Death didn't scare her, it never had. What scared her was what would happen to Kaelyn.

The types of loss a person had to experience throughout their lives were countless. People lost their transmitters, their boots, even their place in line. But the loss of a person wasn't like the others, and it needed a different name altogether for the devastation it brought with it. It didn't seem fair to lump it into the same category as those other mundane objects. There needed to be a word to encompass that type of grief. The kind of grief that became so consuming, it crept into every corner of your life, forever casting a shadow you never seemed to escape. Arrow's last lucid thought was that she hoped her feelings for Kaelyn weren't reciprocated so she wouldn't have to feel this kind of pain, but even as her mind slipped away, she knew it wasn't true.

❖

Kaelyn tried to push past Sloan. "The soldiers are taking them! We have to stop them!" This small room she had them hidden in was becoming smaller by the second, her fear taking up more space than what was available.

Macy, who seemed to slip easily in and out of being Arrow's mother and president, pushed her back. "Valor and Arrow will be fine. No matter what happens, they'll figure it out. You getting captured again isn't helpful."

Kaelyn wanted to argue, but soldiers had come through the door just on the other side of the wall. She sat still, watching the screens from inside the room Sloan had ushered them into. She watched the soldiers walk directly past the bookcase that hid the room they were in.

Sloan turned on several monitors and pushed a variety of buttons. "Believe it or not, my grandfather built this room, with this very day in mind. I'm not sure if it was wishful thinking or fear, but I'm glad he did." She glanced at the soldiers on the screen. "Don't worry, they can't hear you. This room is enclosed in concrete."

Macy sat in front of the screen and pulled out the old keyboard. "What are your orders, Phoenix?"

Kaelyn rubbed her stomach to push away the emotion boring a hole there. There was enough adrenaline pumping through her body to power a small car, if someone knew a way to convert that kind of energy. She thought about the other three Phoenixes. Each had their own area of expertise: technology, military, and education. They were picked carefully in the event a new nation would need to be rebuilt, so they would have, at the very least, the basic knowledge. But she was to lead based on the knowledge she had of history and what had worked and not worked in the past. She was their strategist. She flashed back on the research she had done, the theories she had helped to create, the people she had interviewed. Everything at the time had been theoretical, a tool upper levels of leadership could use to help assist in their decision-making process. She helped develop ideas that would produce the most successful results for people and governments. She had taken on the daunting task of proving that through strategy and leadership, everyone could benefit equally. Now, those theories were being put to the test, and she was being asked to prove their faith in her had been well placed. She could ask their opinions, but ultimately, this was on her. The burden was a heavy one, and she felt the weight of it now more than ever before.

She thought of Arrow. She wanted to send all available platoons to her rescue. She wanted her brought back to her. She wanted to build a world around the two of them where the outside couldn't interfere and they could simply spend time together. Maybe she could have, if Arrow had been born into Kaelyn's time and a tyrannical force hadn't held the country she loved hostage. But that wasn't the world they lived in, and they weren't normal people. They had both been born into a life of service. They both lived with the understanding that their lives would never really be their own. Their devotion to country was a fundamental piece of who they were as people. There had been thousands like them before. People who had dedicated both their personal and professional lives to an ideal that might never be obtained in its purest form. But those other people weren't there. It was them, and this was their responsibility. So she did the only thing she could do, the only thing that would let her sleep at night, and what Arrow would want of her.

Kaelyn turned toward Macy. "Send the westward platoons to the Soldier Reserve Base, the southern platoons to the Hand of God Officer Base, and the northern platoon will take the capital with us. Follow the protocol. Anyone who surrenders needs to stay in their homes until the situation is under control. Everyone else should be considered hostile and potentially armed."

The last order stuck in her throat like a marble. She wasn't sure if she'd been better off spitting it out or if she should just swallow it. But it was too late for that now. The decision had been made, and whatever Arrow's fate turned out to be would live in the depths of Kaelyn's heart for the rest of her life.

CHAPTER THIRTY-EIGHT

There was a dull and painful thrum that reached from the back of Arrow's head to her eyes. She could taste blood in her mouth, and there was a throbbing in her ribs. She knew her hands were restrained, but she did her best to pull them apart. Unfortunately, she discovered each pull only made the restraints grow tighter.

"Valor?" The room was dark and she couldn't see anything but knew she'd feel better if he was there with her.

"Yeah, Major?" His voice was dampened, a little disoriented.

"We're going to be okay."

The door swung open and light flooded the room. A tall woman cast a shadow in front of her.

"How very sweet of you to reassure him, Major Steele. But I'm afraid you might not be able to keep your promise. It's been almost six hours since we've had you here, and no one has come for you."

Arrow forced her body to sit up, ignored the spinning room, and did her best to focus on the woman in front of her. Once her eyes had adjusted, she was able to place the voice. Nora MacLeod.

"I always keep my promises." Arrow spit on the floor, the familiar taste of copper coating her teeth. "I'm not a MacLeod."

Nora waved to the soldiers who stood on either side of the door. They promptly walked in and hoisted both Arrow and Valor into a set of chairs. Nora turned on the light inside the room, smiling when they both flinched at the sudden change of surrounding.

"Unfortunately for you, that's true." She sat on the table, intentionally close to Arrow. "If you were, you wouldn't be in the position you're in now." She ran the back of her finger down the side of Arrow's jaw.

"I would rather die." Arrow pushed her chin forward.

Nora smiled at her. "We're going to do better than that, Major. You killed Adon MacLeod, and you'll be publicly executed."

Arrow replayed what she'd seen at the stage. There was no possible way that leg wound would have killed MacLeod. Granted, her intention was to kill him, but the shot had missed.

"I don't believe you," Arrow said.

Nora waved her hand at the wall, and a news story that was halfway through its broadcast appeared. There was video footage of what had happened at the stage, MacLeod falling, images of both Arrow and Valor hitting and shooting at the soldiers. Next, the doctor explained the loss of blood had been too much and his heart had given out. Eden was without a MacLeod in the president's office for the first time in almost seventy years. There were people flooding the streets. Some were screaming for revenge against the Resistance; others remained silent, seemingly stunned.

An uprising had always been the plan, but now the Hand of God had found itself a martyr rather than a villain. They were now in control of the story and able to spin it however they saw fit. If she'd known MacLeod was dead, she would've had Kaelyn on every airwave available, explaining their position and the rights of the people. Now they were nothing but cold-blooded extremists in the eyes of the very people they were hoping to join forces with.

"The people will cheer when I put you up on that stage for your execution. Think of it this way, you'll be bringing peace and order to a devastated society." Nora picked at a loose thread on her clothes.

"Killing me won't solve your problem. Deep down, people don't want to be controlled. It's not in our nature. And you know that, or you wouldn't have been poisoning the water all these years." Arrow's headache was growing stronger, and her head throbbed at twice the speed.

Nora stood, waving her hand around the room in a circular motion. "Oh, Arrow, how I wish things were different between us. I completely agree with you. My father's ideas were old and outdated. He might not have lost power in his lifetime, but it would've happened. He's been pushing away the outside countries. Refusing to help them, not wanting to let in people who are dying because of climate destruction, plagues, and rogue military forces. He forced people into servitude, taking away their identities, money, and whatever else he could pry from them in a show of force. That's not what I want." She pulled a long pin from her hair, letting the curls fall to her shoulders. "The world is so desperate now, everything is different. If we open our borders, with our advanced technology, sustained infrastructure, and resources, we could control the world. It's a win for everyone. They'll have the resources they need to stay alive, for a fee, of course, and we'll be in charge of those resources, keeping us at the top of the food chain. I have no interest in controlling or dictating their comings and goings. That's far too much work."

Arrow's neck flushed with anger. "You don't want to help people. You want them to believe you're here to protect them when really you just want all the power."

Nora leaned down on the table, bringing her face within inches of Arrow's. "Your idealism is adorable. Of course I want the power. That is fundamentally who people are. But it *is* mutually beneficial. People will be happier because they finally have *some* say in things, and I will be richer than any other person who has ever lived. Entire societies will finally bow to a woman. Isn't that what you want too?"

Arrow shook her head. "No. I want people to have the opportunity to live their best lives. I want them to be able to decide they want to be an engineer, even though their parents were farmers, and be able to obtain that. I want them to decide who the best leader is for them, based on their needs and not on what the leader wants. I want people to be able to decide they want to make a difference and be able to succeed. You want to rig the system against them. I want to give them the codes to the system. What makes you better than anyone else? Because you were born with the last name of MacLeod? Keeping ninety percent of the power and wealth with the same people and handing out the other ten percent as you see fit, just to give the illusion that people have a chance, isn't right."

Nora straightened her jacket and used her fingers to bounce her hair. "Those are strong words coming from someone with the last name of Steele. You didn't end up where you are without the assistance of your parents and their heritage. You think I'm duping everyone, but I'm creating the balance. If it weren't me, it would be someone else. For all your idealism, you're failing to recognize that by nature people are greedy, power hungry, and selfish. You believe that other ten percent you speak so highly of wouldn't trade places with me in an instant, given the chance? You've fooled yourself into believing that people are good by nature and they aren't. Your precious notions were tried for several hundred years, and they failed. But under me, I'll restore enough balance that people will follow out of true loyalty rather than forced loyalty because they'll believe the choice was theirs."

Arrow closed her eyes, partially to keep from crying and partially because she couldn't look at her. Was there truth to what she was saying? Were people truly so lost? Her heart railed against it even as her mind wondered. "You're wrong."

Nora pulled the door open. "Too bad you won't be alive to see how right I am. But think of it this way, you'll be able to die with all your childish ideals intact. They might even hang a picture of you somewhere with a nice little plaque. Ooh, maybe you'll even get a park bench." She motioned toward Arrow and Valor. "Bring them to the stage area in three hours. Don't bother with the blindfolds. I want them to see the people in the crowd cheering for their deaths."

"You're forgetting about the Phoenix," Arrow called out to her. She wanted to instill at least a little doubt in this suffocatingly arrogant woman.

Nora stopped and turned around. "No, I'm not. She just won't matter. People will gladly abandon their ideals when an easier solution is placed in front of them. People are fickle creatures, prone to selfish whims. Your faith is misplaced."

Arrow let her body fall limp. The success of this movement was always based on her fundamental belief that people wanted equality. But what if people were okay with just the illusion of equality if it was the path of least resistance? What if everything she believed in truly was an outdated ideal?

CHAPTER THIRTY-NINE

Kaelyn paced back and forth in the small room. "We can't stay in here."

Macy had just finished adjusting the camera on the stool where Kaelyn would speak in a moment. "We need to get our message out right away. We can't expect people to be on our side if they don't know what we stand for."

Kaelyn had just seen the announcement that Arrow and Valor would be publicly executed in an hour for causing the death of Adon MacLeod. Since that moment, she had felt like a stranger in her own skin. Her thoughts were jumbled together, and she hadn't been able to find a stable breathing pattern.

She turned on Macy. "How can you be so calm? She's your *daughter*."

Macy put her hands on Kaelyn's arms. "I'm not, so I'm doing the things within my control. You need to get it together. We won't be able to help Arrow, Valor, or anyone else unless you focus and be what we all need you to be. It's not fair and I get that, but it doesn't matter."

Kaelyn sat on the stool, letting Macy's much needed words sink in. "If we can pull this off, will you stay with me? I don't think I could manage any of this without your input and guidance."

Macy smiled. "Whatever you need, Kaelyn."

"And Arrow, can Arrow stay?"

Macy looked as if she might cry at the thought of either her daughter surviving or not surviving, Kaelyn wasn't sure which. "Let's just get through this."

Sloan handed her a glass of water. "You doing okay?"

"Yes," Kaelyn lied. "Let's get this started. We have a lot to do, and we need to get out of this room and get to work."

This seemed to resonate with Sloan, who did a slight hop back to the other side of the room where Macy sat, her finger hovered over the button, ready to send out the broadcast.

"I've encrypted the feed as much as I could manage, but you'll probably only have about thirty-five seconds before they cut you off," Sloan said.

Kaelyn nodded, indicating she was ready to begin. "People of Eden, you've been lied to, robbed, and manipulated. The people of this once great nation were promised something several hundred years ago, and that has been kept from you. You were promised an existence where you could achieve life, liberty, and the pursuit of happiness. At first, the MacLeods used fear to keep the people in their control. Fear of outsiders, fear of people who thought differently, looked differently, and wanted different things. Once they were able to fill people with fear, they said they were the only ones with a solution. They told us it was okay to turn on each other, to ignore people who valued different things, to harm people who threatened your beliefs. Once they were able to do that, they made their own propaganda machine. They told us all other information was false and they were the only ones who could be trusted. In fact, people began to believe the MacLeods instead of their own eyes and ears. Neighbors, family members, and congregations started to see each other as the enemy. They bought into the tagline that we were a failing society and there was only one antidote. I'm here today to tell you that we had the antidote all along. That need to stand up and cry out for change that you feel bubbling inside you needs to be heard. This country was built by people who were brave enough to seek out a better life for their families. They had the courage to challenge a system that was built to keep them oppressed and then create their own. We were never perfect. We hurt millions of people along the way. We treated entire races and minorities as less than. Our leaders made mistakes. They waged war against lesser countries. They killed indiscriminately in many cases, and at times forced people into servitude. I'm not here to make excuses for any of that." She leaned forward, closer to the camera, wanting the people to see the truth in her eyes.

"I'm here to tell you that we can do better. We've always been able to do better. Our united force is greater than any dictator, any king, and any president. The will of the American people lives inside every one of you. The MacLeods have kept you in a sleep state for almost seventy years. They've literally drugged your water to keep you from fighting back. Today is the day we wake up and take our government and our country back. The other three Phoenixes and I don't want to rule over you. We want to help you rebuild. We want to work with you to create the society we always had the potential to become. The Resistance forces are here *not* to harm you but to help you. They will only return attack; they will not initiate. For us to succeed, it must be the will of the people. *All* the people. Stand with us now and we will stand with you always."

Sloan wiped a tear from her face. "That was incredible."

The air was full of emotion, but Kaelyn ignored it. "We need to get to the center of town. The Resistance forces are waiting on us there."

Sloan pushed a button under the desk and the door slid open. "Do you think it worked?"

"I don't know, but we'll find out soon enough," Kaelyn said. She knew full well Arrow wasn't there, but she couldn't help looking around, just in case, before they left the building.

There were thousands of people in the streets, yelling and marching. As Kaelyn walked through, a few reached to touch her. At first, the contact scared her, then she noticed the emotion on their faces. This was the first time these people were awake, engaged, and present. It had been almost thirty hours since they had blown the reservoirs, and just as Arrow had said, people were coming out of their long sleep. They had lived a life moving from one day to the next, accepting their places, because they didn't know any different. Now, they had just been offered a different possibility. While there were definitely angry shouts cast their way, those were far fewer than the people who gathered around her, defiant and looking forward. It was a heady feeling.

The square of the capital was flooded with people. Some people were scurrying behind the wall the Resistance soldiers had created with their bodies while others were yelling their disapproval at those same soldiers. The Hand of God's soldiers made a large wall around the stage where Nora MacLeod would soon emerge with Arrow and Valor. But it didn't slip past Kaelyn that the Hand of God forces seemed to be diminishing.

Macy stayed next to her but had her hand on her weapon. "I don't like being out in the open like this. They could have snipers in position. We're sitting ducks."

Kaelyn glanced around at the rooftops. "Of course, they have snipers in position, but it won't do them any good to take us out like this. She needs to keep some semblance of law and order now that MacLeod is dead. And we need to be here with the people. Killing us now would be terrible publicity for them. It could cause more harm than good, and I think Nora is too calculated to take that chance."

As if she had summoned her, Nora MacLeod came out on the stage. Arrow and Valor were in tow behind. They had been stripped of their uniform tops, and Kaelyn's heart hurt at the sight. That clothing was more than a uniform for Valor and Arrow. It was part of their identities. Which, she assumed, was the affect Nora was trying to accomplish. She wasn't satisfied with simply having captured them. She wanted to strip them down to nothing. She wouldn't be happy until there was nothing left but a pale shadow of the people they used to be. What Nora didn't understand was that it would take much more than that to break Arrow. Yes, the uniform was important to her, but it didn't define her. Arrow embodied bravery, loyalty, and dedication in everything she did. A uniform signified who she was to the rest of the world, but Kaelyn knew Arrow's heart and always would, even if she never donned that clothing ever again.

Nora scanned the crowd, and there wasn't a single inclination of fear or worry on her face. She seemed almost amused. When her gaze fell onto Kaelyn, she smiled at her. The audacity of this woman was impressive. It would make watching her fall that much more enjoyable. Nora had been in the perfect position to really make a difference, but instead she fed into her father's rhetoric and the toxic world he had helped to create. She deserved far worse than what Kaelyn had planned.

"People of Eden," Nora began. "We're here today to witness true justice. The two criminals you see in front of you are responsible for the death of our leader, Adon MacLeod."

There were mixed reactions throughout the crowd. Some booed, but many more cheered. Nora's look of confidence only faltered for a moment, and unless you were paying close attention, it would've been missed.

Kaelyn glanced over, and Sloan was furiously typing on a small transmitter. Out of the corner of her eye, she caught a glimpse of the two soldiers moving toward them.

"Although he will live on in our hearts forever," Nora said, "he was taken from us far too soon. In the name of Eden and its faithful people, these traitors, these resisters, will now pay for their sins in blood."

The soldiers grabbed for Sloan and Kaelyn, but not before Sloan managed to finish what she had started. On every screen in the square, Kaelyn's face appeared. The short speech she had given earlier started to broadcast again. Kaelyn's voice drowned out Nora's next words, and the look on Nora's face made it clear just how she felt about that. Kaelyn tried to push the one soldier away, only to be stopped by the one next to him.

She watched as Macy raised her weapon and pointed it at the soldier, then she felt his arm move to retrieve his gun. Time seemed to slow as he pulled it out and brought it to her temple. Kaelyn glanced up at the stage one last time, wanting to see Arrow's face. Arrow's eyes were filled with horror and disbelief. Kaelyn watched Arrow's mouth form around the word "no," even though she couldn't hear her. Arrow struggled in her restraints to come to her rescue. Kaelyn hated that this would be the last thing Arrow would remember of her.

She heard the gun go off, a loud explosion next to her. She felt the soldier's body rock slightly backward. She waited for the pain and the darkness. She waited for eternity to finally come to claim her and drag her down into the depths of worlds unknown, but it didn't come. She touched her head, but there was no wetness, no entry wound. Everything was how it should be. She looked at the soldier, who continued to fire shots, but they weren't at her, or Macy, or Sloan. He was firing at the other soldiers.

Her own voice still played in the background. Sloan must have put her on a loop. The whole thing was surreal. Maybe she had been shot and now she was trapped in some kind of limbo, stuck between worlds because everything had happened so fast. Maybe God hadn't had time to collect her or damn her just yet. She looked down at her hands, and there was blood splatter on the back. Then she realized it wasn't her blood. She took another look around. In her brief moments of confusion, chaos had overwhelmed the square. This wasn't the end; it was the beginning. The Resistance was rising up against the tyranny that had plagued their country for so long. People were fighting back.

Kaelyn pulled the weapon from its holster and ran directly toward her destiny.

CHAPTER FORTY

A rrow watched as Nora moved around the stage, looking for an escape route. Unfortunately for her, they were clogged with her own people and soldiers, but it was impossible to tell which were on her side. Soldiers were fighting soldiers, people from the old government fighting back to back with Resistance fighters. It was a beautiful sight.

Arrow sat on the ground and pulled the scanner from the back of her boot. She put it over the restraints, and the number key searched through hundreds of combinations before it fell on the correct sequence. The restraints popped opened, and she moved to Valor.

Arrow kept her eye on Nora, who had just found an escape route and disappeared behind the stage. "I'm going after Nora."

"I'm coming with you," Valor said.

Arrow was already two steps past him. "They need your help. I have this." She'd seen Kaelyn with a gun, heading into chaos, and in her soul she knew she'd be okay.

Arrow hopped off the stage in the same place she had seen Nora disappear. She didn't have much of a head start on her, and Arrow would be able to catch up quickly if she knew which direction she'd headed. Arrow looked around and headed toward what looked to be a large warehouse about six hundred feet away.

She approached the warehouse with caution. Nora was smart, and this could very well be a trap. Arrow decided to go in anyway. She knew Nora was smart, but she had also gravely underestimated the people of Eden. She probably never formulated a backup plan for today, and like an animal backed into a corner, she could be unpredictable.

She found a door in the side of the building and pulled it open. There were old shipping containers and pallets arranged throughout the room. The air was damp with old air that smelled of mildew and rotting wood. The space was poorly lit, perfect for an ambush, but it was eerily quiet. She heard a few footsteps and stopped to listen, wanting to gauge their location.

"I'm not just going to surrender. You'll have to kill me." Nora's voice echoed throughout the building. It bounced off the walls, giving off the illusion that she was everywhere.

"I have no intention of killing you, Nora," Arrow yelled back, their anonymity now abandoned. "This was your father and your grandfather. The only thing you're guilty of is being born into the wrong family."

"You have no idea what it's like to be me." Nora's voice held a bit of sorrow.

"Why don't you come out here and talk to me about it." Arrow continued to turn in circles, looking for the source.

"I am smarter, more calculating, and better equipped than any of those stupid generals, but I was never given an official position. Those men, they mocked me my whole life. Ridiculed my ideas and openly berated me in front of anyone they could. And all for what? If they had just listened to me, we wouldn't be here. I wanted to do things differently. I wanted a chance. I wanted to be heard."

"I'm willing to listen. If you just come down here and talk to me, I can help. I know that if our leaders know your story, they'll show mercy." She placed her gun on the ground. "Look, I put the weapon away. Just come on out and talk to me."

"You're all so weak," Nora said as she came up behind her, her tone acidic. "Did you ever think the world doesn't need saving? The people of Eden didn't ask for your heroic bullshit. Do you really believe that positive talk and a pat on the back is going to restore Eden to the garbage fire that was here before my family? They were the real heroes. The country was on the verge of civil war when my grandfather finally stepped in. The people were sick. Shooting children in their own schools, at concerts, and even shooting themselves. Everyone was addicted to something. Drugs, sex, money—they're all the same. Your people demonize my family for shutting our borders, while the time you so long for was a world plagued with war and horror. How many innocent people died because we thought we had to step in and save everyone? But the truth is, we weren't saving anyone but our own reputation and our own bottom line. So, what are you mad about? Our honesty or our patriotism?" She flipped her gun to rapid-fire.

Arrow held up her hands. "Everything you said was true." Arrow waited for the shocked look on Nora's face to return to the one of perpetual disgust she'd grown accustomed to. "But there was a lot of good too. There were people who dedicated their lives to helping others, to helping the planet, to helping the animals. There were people who protested, shouting in the streets for gun control to be taken seriously, to put more money into education, and to stop the wars. There were people so full of passion it spilled out onto canvases, creating beautiful art. Musicians wrote music about pain, anger, love, and wonder. The discourse ended because people stopped communicating and only cared about being right. They ignored how their actions and words affected others."

Nora took a step closer. "And we fixed it. People here don't argue, fight, or disagree. People are happy with their station in life. We protect them from the outside world."

Arrow realized then that Nora truly believed they'd been doing the right thing, that she was a victim of the propaganda too. "If all that's true, then why did you keep them drugged? Why were you trying to bring in a lower working class to appease the people here in Eden? The truth is, humans are messy and complex creatures. We're designed to search, discover, and create. You took that from them. Even if the Resistance had never existed, this would've eventually happened. You can't fix the human condition."

"We're also designed to destroy, consume, and kill. You can try to pretty it up all you want, but we're evil beings. And killing you would simply keep me true to my nature." Nora was within a foot of her, her hand trembling.

Arrow took a chance and put her hand on top of the gun. "There is good and bad in all of us. You decide which one you'll become. Your hand is trembling because you don't want to kill me. Because as hard as it is for you to hear, you know at least a part of it is true."

"That's where you're wrong. I know killing you won't stop what I'm going to have to go up against, but it will show the people of Eden that I'm here to protect them. My family was appointed by God to protect them, and killing you will prove that." Nora pulled the trigger.

Nora's face grew red as she pulled the trigger again and again. Nothing happened.

Arrow pointed to her bracelet. "It's programmed to disarm guns in close proximity that aren't being held with my palm." She pulled the gun from Nora's hand. "Looks like God has different plans for me."

Nora dropped to her knees, tears rolling down her cheeks. "Please, just kill me. No one will ever know. You can tell them that I shot first."

Arrow pulled the restraints she'd removed from her wrists earlier and put them around Nora. "I'd know, and that's what matters to me." She pulled her up to her feet. "You'll stand trial; the outcome isn't up to me. It's up to those people out there you think were so happy living under your regime. Wonder how that will turn out?"

CHAPTER FORTY-ONE

Kaelyn ran her hand through her hair as she paced back and forth. "Has sector one been secured?"

Sloan pulled up the video image on the screen. "Yes, we received the field report from the platoon leader ten minutes ago, and all looks well."

The battle hadn't lasted long. The Hand of God's soldiers had fought at first and then either surrendered or retreated to a location they'd yet been able to determine. With Nora MacLeod in custody, for the first time in seventy years, there wasn't a MacLeod to direct the military forces or the people. The drugs people had been ingesting had worn off, and now they were forced to make choices they'd never considered before today.

Even though the battle hadn't lasted all that long, the road forward was going to be long and daunting. There were still Hand of God military officers and soldiers hiding in different locations, undoubtedly biding their time and trying to get organized. The Resistance might have been able to assume the role of leadership for the time being, but nothing was guaranteed. Some of the damage that had been done would be irreversible. Women's rights had been shoved back into the early nineteen hundreds. People of color and the LGBTQ community had been systematically removed from Eden. Introducing the population of Eden to their long-lost countrymen who looked different and loved different types of people would be a process, to say the least.

There was also the discussion of the government and America's place with the rest of the world. The country had been long shut off to the rest of the planet, and finding its footing again wouldn't be easy. Bridges had been burned because of bigotry and arrogance. Convincing the rest of the world that they'd now be acting in good faith was going to be an uphill battle.

Kaelyn had started to make a list of all these issues and then had to stop. The enormity of it was overwhelming and seemed to make her less productive. No, they needed to take it one day at a time. And these first few months would be dedicated to finding and isolating the remaining regime of the Hand of God, and then putting in place an impartial, well-rounded board of directors who could help oversee the new changes. They would be made up of people from both Eden and the Resistance. There had to be room for everyone at the table.

Arrow walked into the room, and Kaelyn's heart rate increased. They hadn't been able to spend any significant amount of time together in the last three weeks, and the separation was making her anxious. For all her grand thoughts of spilling her heart out into her hands and handing it to Arrow, she hadn't been able to find the words.

"Hey," Arrow said, standing next to her and looking at the screens. "Looks like everything is going as planned."

Kaelyn wanted so desperately to touch her face. She needed contact with Arrow to recharge. "Yes, the rest of the Phoenixes and I are meeting in a bit to go over the next steps." She put her hands in her pockets.

Arrow shifted back and forth. She seemed nervous, which was out of character for her. "We just received our orders from Phoenix Two. Valor and I are being sent back to headquarters. There's work to be done everywhere, and you don't need my protection anymore. My father will be coming to Eden once we return, should you need anything."

Kaelyn felt her heart freefall into her stomach. "Are you coming back?"

"I'll be visiting. After all, my parents will be here." She rubbed the back of her neck, which Kaelyn had learned was a nervous habit.

"Stay. Don't go back. You can stay here with me and we can be together. There's nothing stopping us now. You got me here. I'm alive and well and want you here with me." Kaelyn held her breath, waiting for Arrow's answer.

"But the people back at headquarters, they need me too, and they're counting on me." Arrow took a small step backward, putting distance between them.

"I need you, Arrow. Can you honestly say you don't love me and don't want to be with me?" Kaelyn's blood pressure was rising. She couldn't believe the chance was finally right here in front of them and Arrow was backing away.

"Headquarters, those people, it's what I know."

"Yes, but you know me too. Please don't throw us away." Kaelyn took a careful step toward her.

"I'm sorry. I have to go."

Kaelyn covered her mouth, trying to hold in the tears she knew were coming.

"Kaelyn, I—"

Valor came into the room and tossed a large duffel bag in front of her. "I secured the transport. You ready?"

Arrow grabbed Kaelyn and pulled her into an embrace. Kaelyn buried her face into Arrow's neck, wanting to memorize every curve, every smell, every muscle. The hug was too short by about forty years, and when Arrow pulled away, Kaelyn felt like a piece of her had been taken.

Arrow kissed her cheek and let her lips linger over her jawbone. "Take care of yourself, Kaelyn. This is exactly where you're supposed to be."

Kaelyn didn't know if that was true. She'd thought when the dust settled, she'd be with Arrow. She knew Arrow loved her by the way she touched her and looked at her. But she'd just given Arrow the chance, and she'd thrown it away. The realization weighed her down, forcing her to sit. She put her face in her hands and cried. She'd won a battle but lost her chance at love.

CHAPTER FORTY-TWO

A rrow sat in the control center at her headquarters. Now that her father was in Eden, she was left in command. The officers and citizens still loyal to the Hand of God had managed to avoid their efforts of peace talks for the last seven months. They'd move their bases from one location to the next to avoid the Resistance scouts. They'd also managed to take with them dozens of drones, an expensive arsenal, and quite a few land cruisers. Arrow couldn't say if they were planning on a war, but it seemed like it.

She listened as Phoenix Two, Hadlee Price, discussed current military operations. Hadlee was smart, efficient, and rational. Arrow liked her immediately.

Arrow informed Hadlee of the current happenings at her base. They were in the process of expanding the schools and farms and were building a new hospital. Now, with the resources of Eden, they had started building a refugee center that they hoped to have open within a year. There were still thousands of people all over the globe with no place to call home, and she hoped the new center could be just that when it was ready. They'd managed to take a few thousand in already, placing them in different villages and even some in Eden. The weather bubbles were being expanded so people could spread out a little more, and communities were already taking on their own distinctive personalities.

This work kept Arrow busy and she was proud of it, but she always felt like there was something missing. She knew this center would make a difference in people's lives for generations. But it was never enough to extinguish the loneliness she felt due to Kaelyn's absence. She not only longed for her, she craved her. There wasn't a single night that went by where Arrow didn't lie in bed, clutching her pillow, fighting back the tears. She missed her in a way that didn't seem possible. It consumed her every free moment. And even in her busy moments, Arrow longed to share each triumph and setback with Kaelyn.

When Kaelyn had asked her to stay, it was exactly what she wanted to hear. She jumped for joy on the inside, but then doubt and fear had ambushed her. She'd spent her whole life studying and learning about Kaelyn. When she had the opportunity to actually know her, it was even more overwhelming. She'd been all in until she realized that wasn't what was best for Kaelyn. At first, it had just been about the mission and getting her to Eden. Valor had been right to warn her off, in order to keep her safe.

Arrow had witnessed firsthand Kaelyn putting herself in harm's way for her. She would risk herself in order to protect Arrow, and it was impossible to know the dangers that were still out there. Not all the Hand of God forces had been isolated, leaving the new country they were trying to create vulnerable. If Arrow could be used to manipulate Kaelyn for their gain, she couldn't take the chance. No, it was better for her to stay as far away from Kaelyn as possible. She wouldn't be a point of weakness for her, not when they'd come so far and with so much still at stake.

"Major Steele?" Hadlee said. "Arrow?"

Arrow sat up in her seat and focused on the screen, pushing Kaelyn from her mind. "Yes, sorry about that. I'm not sure where my mind went."

"That's okay. I'll see you in two weeks," Hadlee said.

Arrow was confused for a moment, and then she remembered. *Refugee meeting.* "Yes, I'll be there."

The screen went black, and Arrow fell back into her seat.

"You okay?"

Shit. Arrow had forgotten Valor was in the room. She wondered if these were the beginning stages of dementia. Was she starting to lose it?

"Yes, I'm fine." She pretended that she remembered he was in the room.

"You're a terrible liar. Even when we were kids, you couldn't do it. Good thing we never went into a life of crime. You'd be a terrible accomplice." Valor smiled at her, and his expression was kind.

"I just have a lot on my mind." She checked her transmitter, trying to keep herself busy.

"No, you have *someone* on your mind. You haven't been right since we left."

She took a deep breath, not wanting to lash out at him. "We've been getting along just fine."

Valor slid his chair closer. "Yes, what we've been doing here is incredible. Your work is always perfect, but we both know that's not what I'm talking about."

Arrow stood to walk out of the room. "Then I'd rather you not talk at all."

Valor mimicked her movement. "Arrow, you're my best friend. I love you. But for your own sake, you need to find a better way to deal with this. You know you deserve to be happy, right?"

"I'm not going to put her or the country in danger, Valor. You saw what she did when those soldiers captured us. She walked right out into the square and almost got herself shot. If she has a weakness, they'll exploit it, and I'm not going to let that happen." She pulled her hat down tighter over her head, feeling like it helped make her point.

He put his hands on his waist, the same way he did every time he was going to make a point. "You made this decision all on your own, without even giving her a say-so. Have you ever thought you might be worth it?"

She turned and looked at him. "I'm not worth jeopardizing everything we've done."

"That's bullshit and you know it. You got scared. You've never been in love before, and you didn't know how to handle it. It was easy in theory when everyone told you that you couldn't be together, but then when the time came, you chickened out. And you know what, you're better than that. I've never seen you run away from a single thing in your whole life. But you choose now? When there's something right in front of you that can make you happy? Get your shit together before it's too late and you lose her for good."

He walked out the door before she had a chance to leave or say anything else. Arrow wanted to yell after him, to tell him he was wrong, but she didn't know if that was true. In fact, she wasn't really sure of anything anymore, except work. In the last several months, she'd become a version of herself that she didn't recognize. There was no joy, no fun, nothing. But the truth was, it was because she was heartbroken. She missed Kaelyn and she missed who she felt like she could be because of Kaelyn. There was no way around that truth, and no amount of extra hours in the control center was going to fix that.

❖

"You need to attend this meeting," Macy said from somewhere behind her.

Kaelyn was watching several children play in the grass in the park across from her office. "Is it the strategy meeting for the Hand of God loyalists?"

"No, it's the constitutional congress planning meeting." She sounded mildly exasperated.

Kaelyn couldn't help but smile at the disregard the children had for everything else going on around them. It was the kind of naivety that only children could experience. "Okay. When is it?"

"Now." Macy pushed the door open.

Kaelyn took a deep breath and headed for the door. She would go to this meeting and she would give her input. She would smile and tell everyone what a great job they were doing. She would do all this to try to hide the fact that even after seven months, her heart still felt like it had been ripped wide open.

At first, she had kept up with all the progress Arrow had been making. But eventually, she had to stop listening to the updates. It was too hard to know what she was up to and not talk to her or be near her. She had wanted to call her at least a thousand times but stopped herself, knowing that even hearing her voice for one second would force her backward. No, she'd made a plan. She'd keep pushing forward until one day, maybe she would wake up and not feel the aching in her chest. Maybe one day she would stop looking for Arrow's face in a crowd. Maybe.

Macy pushed open the door, and the people around the table stood. Kaelyn's mouth went dry and her palms grew sweaty. She felt her neck tingle, and there were goose bumps on her arms, just as there always were when she saw Arrow. Kaelyn glanced over at Macy, partly because she didn't believe Arrow was really there, but also because she felt like Macy had set her up, somehow.

"This is the constitutional congress meeting?" Kaelyn asked anyone who would answer, but her eyes never left Arrow, who stared back at her looking equally surprised.

"No," Hadlee Price said. "It's the refugee meeting."

Macy had lied to her because she knew she wouldn't have come. Kaelyn took her seat at the head of the table, which happened to be next to Arrow. Arrow's cheeks were flushed. Her hair had grown out a little bit, and she looked like she had lost weight, but she was still undeniably beautiful. She was in her military uniform and looked as dashing as ever. Kaelyn fought against every instinct she had in her body to touch her. The hurt and anger were still there, but it paled in comparison to her need to feel Arrow's ever-solid presence.

Kaelyn wasn't sure what to do with her hands. She wanted them on Arrow, so she put them on the table and folded them. She managed a glance at Macy, who was proudly beaming at her apparent white lie. Arrow began to speak, and Kaelyn was sure there had never been a better sound than her voice. She could listen to it for hours.

Images from the progress in Arrow's assigned area flashed on the screen, and Kaelyn forced herself to pull her eyes from Arrow to witness all that she had accomplished. It was impressive, and not just because it had been Arrow's work. The strides she'd made in a short period of time were inspiring.

After several minutes, Arrow took her seat again, and the other refugee director began his presentation.

"You've done an amazing job," Kaelyn whispered.

"Thank you." Arrow blushed and looked away.

Both turned their attention to the man speaking. He went on with his work, which was also great. Kaelyn wanted to focus on him and what he was saying, but she could hear her heart beating in her head. The proximity to Arrow was making her dizzy, and she worried it was written all over her face.

Kaelyn wasn't sure if the man had been speaking for twenty seconds, minutes, or hours. All time came to a crashing halt when she felt Arrow's fingertips touch her leg. She thought about reaching down and grabbing her hand, but she worried she wouldn't be able to stop there.

The meeting finally came to a conclusion, and plans were made for the directors and the military leaders to meet again tomorrow and discuss their future priorities. Kaelyn wanted desperately to talk to Arrow, but she didn't want to embarrass either of them.

"Please come see me when you're done," Kaelyn said to her, not caring that she had interrupted a conversation Arrow was having with someone else.

Kaelyn practically stumbled back to her office. She felt a little drunk, a little nervous, and very excited. When the door opened a few minutes later, she thought she might jump over her desk.

"Do you have a minute?" Hadlee Price asked.

Kaelyn did her best to hide her disappointment and waved her in. "Sure, what can I help you with?"

To Kaelyn's surprise, Arrow followed Hadlee inside.

"Normally, I wouldn't bother you with personnel matters, but since you know Major Steele personally, I thought I should tell you that she's being reassigned."

Kaelyn's immediate reaction was to object. The one saving grace of having Arrow where she was that Kaelyn knew she was safe. She didn't want her put back into the field. No, if she couldn't be with her, she needed to know she was okay. "I don't think that's a good idea, Hadlee. Major Steele has done a fantastic job with her assignment. Moving her now could force the progress backward."

Arrow looked hurt by her words, and Kaelyn wanted to take them back.

"She has done a great job, but Captain Markinson will be able to handle things. He's a very quick study and will still be under the supervision of Major Steele." Hadlee tilted her head, her eyes narrowed thoughtfully.

How could Arrow still supervise Valor if she was being placed in the field? "I don't understand."

"I've decided to move Major Steele to Eden. We'll be promoting her and making her head of refugee relations. I think she's the perfect person for the job." Hadlee smiled at Arrow.

Kaelyn couldn't be sure, but she thought the blood stopped pumping to her head. Her stomach flipped and tried to reach up and grab her heart. "Well, then…I think that's an excellent decision. She'll be perfect for it."

"I agree." Hadlee opened the door again. "I'll let you two catch up. Arrow, we'll get your living arrangements taken care of after dinner tonight."

Months had passed since they had seen or spoken to each other. Arrow had made it pretty clear that she didn't want to be with her. She had no reason to think anything had changed.

"I'm sorry," Arrow said after Hadlee had left the office. "I thought I was protecting you, but I realized I was only protecting myself."

Kaelyn watched as Arrow took several steps closer. "Protecting yourself from what?"

Arrow took another step closer. "First, I thought I was your weakness. That as long as we were together, people could use me to get to you. Then, I realized that was just part of it. I've never been in love before, and I was scared. Scared of a bunch of things I can't see coming and scared that I'd do it wrong, that I'd end up without you in the end, and I didn't know how to handle that. I panicked and retreated to what I knew. It was stupid, and I'm sorry."

Kaelyn moved to touch her but stopped herself. "You love me?"

Arrow took Kaelyn's hand in her own. "I love you. I loved you when I left, and I love you now. Being away from you has been the hardest time in my life."

Kaelyn didn't let her finish whatever she was about to say. She put her arms around her neck and pulled her into a kiss. When their mouths touched, Kaelyn knew Arrow was telling the truth. The passion that had always been there when they kissed still overwhelmed her, but there was more now. There was a tenderness, a feeling of home.

CHAPTER FORTY-THREE

The Hand of God is demanding that we release Nora MacLeod into their custody." Kaelyn flopped down on the sofa.

Arrow kissed the top of her head and handed her a glass of the wine. "Of course they are. You're not going to, right?"

Kaelyn leaned into Arrow and put her head on her shoulder. "Absolutely not. You don't release rabid animals."

Arrow stroked Kaelyn's arm and smiled when it caused her to shiver. "We need to pull the remaining Hand of God forces into the light. The longer they stay hidden, the angrier they become. Fear and anger are deadly combinations. Do you know their most current location?"

Kaelyn sipped her wine and almost spit it out. "This is terrible."

Arrow laughed. "They haven't perfected the grapes yet."

Kaelyn set her glass down. "They have several locations. They might be getting stronger. We don't have any intel to prove that yet, but that's what all the great military minds seem to think."

"We could set a trap." Arrow spoke into the side of Kaelyn's head.

Kaelyn turned to look at her. "Who's we?"

"Me and a couple of other key people. Nora is familiar with me, and it's not like I don't have the training for this."

"You want me to approve sending you out into the field, with Nora MacLeod, to deal with the Hand of God and all the weapons they managed to smuggle out?" Kaelyn wrapped her arm around Arrow's middle, pulling her closer.

"It is what I do, Kaelyn." Arrow made sure there was no bite in her answer.

Kaelyn sighed. "I just got you back two months ago."

Arrow tilted Kaelyn's face up to her and kissed her. "I can do this. With Phoenix Two leading the military now, I know we can do this."

Kaelyn rolled her eyes. "You sure do have a thing for Phoenixes."

Arrow laughed and kissed her again. "There's only you. It will always be you."

Arrow watched as Kaelyn pulled herself on top of her, straddling her waist. "I hate that I can't say no to you."

Arrow slid her hands up the side of Kaelyn's ribs. "Then we can start tomorrow."

Kaelyn pulled off her shirt. "Yes, but tonight, you're mine."

"Tonight and ten thousand more," Arrow said as she kissed her.

"You have yourself a deal, Lieutenant Colonel."

With Kaelyn here, like this, tomorrow seemed like a lifetime away. Arrow knew the future was breathing down their necks. There were still people to catch, institutions to rebuild, people to train, and an entire generation of people to assimilate. Nora MacLeod wasn't going to give up her family's legacy without a fight, and she had an army willing to do her bidding. It might be a lot smaller than the one she'd had before, but it was enough to cause real problems.

But right now, at least the next few hours, touching, feeling, and falling into Kaelyn was all she cared about. Arrow had learned that life could change instantly, with no warning, and without permission. She needed to take the time gifted to her without question. She wanted to appreciate all the stolen moments that were afforded to her and string them together to create a lifetime of happiness. Regardless of the dark and painful spaces between, she wanted to use those glimmers to lead her like a beacon to the next stolen moment. She wanted to keep as many as she could find and tuck them close to her heart, treasures to nourish her soul when she felt like she couldn't push herself any further. This would be what she would fight for; this was what she would live for.

Love would always bring her home.

About the Author

Jackie D was born and raised in the San Francisco, East Bay area of California. She now resides in central Pennsylvania with her wife, their son, and their many furry companions. She earned a bachelor's degree in recreation administration and a dual master's degree in management and public administration. She is a Navy veteran and served in Operation Iraqi Freedom as a flight deck director onboard the USS *Abraham Lincoln.*

She spends her free time with her wife, friends, family, and their incredibly needy dogs. She enjoys playing golf but is resigned to the fact she would equally enjoy any sport where drinking beer is encouraged during gameplay. Her first book, *Infiltration*, was a finalist for a Lambda Literary Award. Her fourth book, *Lucy's Chance*, won a Goldie in 2018.

Books Available from Bold Strokes Books

All of Me by Emily Smith. When chief surgical resident Galen Burgess meets her new intern, Rowan Duncan, she may finally discover that doing what you've always done will only give you what you've always had. (978-1-163555-321-5)

As the Crow Flies by Karen F. Williams. Romance seems to be blooming all around, but problems arise when a restless ghost emerges from the ether to roam the dark corners of this haunting tale. (978-1-163555-285-0)

Both Ways by Ileandra Young. SPEAR agent Danika Karson races to protect the city from a supernatural threat and must rely on the woman she's trained to despise: Rayne, an achingly beautiful vampire. (978-1-163555-298-0)

Calendar Girl by Georgia Beers. Forced to work together, Addison Fairchild and Kate Cooper discover that opposites really do attract. (978-1-163555-333-8)

Lovebirds by Lisa Moreau. Two women from different worlds collide in a small California mountain town, each with a mission that doesn't include falling in love. (978-1-163555-213-3)

Media Darling by Fiona Riley. Can Hollywood bad girl Emerson and reluctant celebrity gossip reporter Hayley work together to make each other's dreams come true? Or will Emerson's secrets ruin not one career, but two? (978-1-163555-278-2)

Stroke of Fate by Renee Roman. Can Sean Moore live up to her reputation and save Jade Rivers from the stalker determined to end Jade's career and, ultimately, her life? (978-1-163555-162-4)

The Rise of the Resistance by Jackie D. The soul of America has been lost for almost a century. A few people may be the difference between a phoenix rising to save the masses or permanent destruction. (978-1-163555-259-1)

The Sex Therapist Next Door by Meghan O'Brien. At the intersection of sex and intimacy, anything is possible. Even love. (978-1-163555-296-6)

Unexpected Lightning by Cass Sellars. Lightning strikes once more when Sydney and Parker fight a dangerous stranger who threatens the peace they both desperately want. (978-1-163555-276-8)

Unforgettable by Elle Spencer. When one night changes a lifetime… Two romance novellas from best-selling author Elle Spencer. (978-1-63555-429-8)

Against All Odds by Kris Bryant, Maggie Cummings, M. Ullrich. Peyton and Tory escaped death once, but will they survive when Bradley's determined to make his kill rate one hundred percent? (978-1-163555-193-8)

Autumn's Light by Aurora Rey. Casual hookups aren't supposed to include romantic dinners and meeting the family. Can Mat Pero see beyond the heartbreak that led her to keep her worlds so separate, and will Graham Connor be waiting if she does? (978-1-163555-272-0)

Breaking the Rules by Larkin Rose. When Virginia and Carmen are thrown together by an embarrassing mistake they find out their stubborn determination isn't so heroic after all. (978-1-163555-261-4)

Broad Awakening by Mickey Brent. In the sequel to *Underwater Vibes*, Hélène and Sylvie find ruts in their road to eternal bliss. (978-1-163555-270-6)

Broken Vows by MJ Williamz. Sister Mary Margaret must reconcile her divided heart or risk losing a love that just might be heaven sent. (978-1-163555-022-1)

Flesh and Gold by Ann Aptaker. Havana, 1952, where art thief and smuggler Cantor Gold dodges gangland bullets and mobsters' schemes while she searches Havana's steamy Red Light district for her kidnapped love. (978-1-163555-153-2)

Isle of Broken Years by Jane Fletcher. Spanish noblewoman Catalina de Valasco is in peril, even before the pirates holding her for ransom sail into seas destined to become known as the Bermuda Triangle. (978-1-163555-175-4)

Love Like This by Melissa Brayden. Hadley Cooper and Spencer Adair set out to take the fashion world by storm. If only they knew their hearts were about to be taken. (978-1-163555-018-4)

Secrets On the Clock by Nicole Disney. Jenna and Danielle love their jobs helping endangered children, but that might not be enough to stop them from breaking the rules by falling in love. (978-1-163555-292-8)

Unexpected Partners by Michelle Larkin. Dr. Chloe Maddox tries desperately to deny her attraction for Detective Dana Blake as they flee from a serial killer who's hunting them both. (978-1-163555-203-4)

A Fighting Chance by T. L. Hayes. Will Lou be able to come to terms with her past to give love a fighting chance? (978-1-163555-257-7)

Chosen by Brey Willows. When the choice is adapt or die, can love save us all? (978-1-163555-110-5)

Death Checks In by David S. Pederson. Despite Heath's promises to Alan to not get involved, Heath can't resist investigating a shopkeeper's murder in Chicago, which dashes their plans for a romantic weekend getaway. (978-1-163555-329-1)

Gnarled Hollow by Charlotte Greene. After they are invited to study a secluded nineteenth-century estate, a former English professor and a group of historians discover that they will have to fight against the unknown if they have any hope of staying alive. (978-1-163555-235-5)

Jacob's Grace by C.P. Rowlands. Captain Tag Becket wants to keep her head down and her past behind her, but her feelings for AJ's second-in-command, Grace Fields, makes keeping secrets next to impossible. (978-1-163555-187-7)

On the Fly by PJ Trebelhorn. Hockey player Courtney Abbott is content with her solitary life until visiting concert violinist Lana Caruso makes her second-guess everything she always thought she wanted. (978-1-163555-255-3)

Passionate Rivals by Radclyffe. Professional rivalry and long-simmering passions create a combustible combination when Emmett McCabe and Sydney Stevens are forced to work together, especially when past attractions won't stay buried. (978-1-163555-231-7)

Proxima Five by Missouri Vaun. When geologist Leah Warren crash-lands on a preindustrial planet and is claimed by its tyrant, Tiago, will clan warrior Keegan's love for Leah give her the strength to defeat him? (978-1-163555-122-8)

Racing Hearts by Dena Blake. When you cross a hot-tempered race car mechanic with a reckless cop, the result can only be spontaneous combustion. (978-1-163555-251-5)

Shadowboxer by Jessica L. Webb. Jordan McAddie is prepared to keep her street kids safe from a dangerous underground protest group, but she isn't prepared for her first love to walk back into her life. (978-1-163555-267-6)

The Tattered Lands by Barbara Ann Wright. As Vandra and Lilani strive to make peace, they slowly fall in love. With mistrust and murder surrounding them, only their faith in each other can keep their plan to save the world from falling apart. (978-1-163555-108-2)

Captive by Donna K. Ford. To escape a human trafficking ring, Greyson Cooper and Olivia Danner become players in a game of deceit and violence. Will their love stand a chance? (978-1-63555-215-7)

Crossing the Line by CF Frizzell. The Mob discovers a nemesis within its ranks, and in the ultimate retaliation, draws Stick McLaughlin from anonymity by threatening everything she holds dear. (978-1-63555-161-7)

Love's Verdict by Carsen Taite. Attorneys Landon Holt and Carly Pachett want the exact same thing: the only open partnership spot at their prestigious criminal defense firm. But will they compromise their careers for love? (978-1-63555-042-9)

Precipice of Doubt by Mardi Alexander & Laurie Eichler. Can Cole Jameson resist her attraction to her boss, veterinarian Jodi Bowman, or will she risk a workplace romance and her heart? (978-1-63555-128-0)

Savage Horizons by CJ Birch. Captain Jordan Kellow's feelings for Lt. Ali Ash have her past and future colliding, setting in motion a series of events that strands her crew in an unknown galaxy thousands of light years from home. (978-1-63555-250-8)

Secrets of the Last Castle by A. Rose Mathieu. When Elizabeth Campbell represents a young man accused of murdering an elderly woman, her investigation leads to an abandoned plantation that reveals many dark Southern secrets. (978-1-63555-240-9)

Take Your Time by VK Powell. A neurotic parrot brings police officer Grace Booker and temporary veterinarian Dr. Dani Wingate together in the tiny town of Pine Cone, but their unexpected attraction keeps the sparks flying. (978-1-63555-130-3)

The Last Seduction by Ronica Black. When you allow true love to elude you once and you desperately regret it, are you brave enough to grab it when it comes around again? (978-1-63555-211-9)

The Shape of You by Georgia Beers. Rebecca McCall doesn't play it safe, but when sexy Spencer Thompson joins her workout class, their non-stop sparring forces her to face her ultimate challenge—a chance at love. (978-1-63555-217-1)

Exposed by MJ Williamz. The closet is no place to live if you want to find true love. (978-1-62639-989-1)

Force of Fire: Toujours a Vous by Ali Vali. Immortals Kendal and Piper welcome their new child and celebrate the defeat of an old enemy, but another ancient evil is about to awaken deep in the jungles of Costa Rica. (978-1-63555-047-4)

Holding Their Place by Kelly A. Wacker. Together Dr. Helen Connery and ambulance driver Julia March, discover that goodness, love, and passion can be found in the most unlikely and even dangerous places during WWI. (978-1-63555-338-3)

Landing Zone by Erin Dutton. Can a career veteran finally discover a love stronger than even her pride? (978-1-63555-199-0)

Love at Last Call by M. Ullrich. Is balancing business, friendship, and love more than any willing woman can handle? (978-1-63555-197-6)

Pleasure Cruise by Yolanda Wallace. Spencer Collins and Amy Donovan have few things in common, but a Caribbean cruise offers both women an unexpected chance to face one of their greatest fears: falling in love. (978-1-63555-219-5)

Running Off Radar by MB Austin. Maji's plans to win Rose back are interrupted when work intrudes and duty calls her to help a SEAL team stop a Russian mobster from harvesting gold from the bottom of Sitka Sound. (978-1-63555-152-5)

Shadow of the Phoenix by Rebecca Harwell. In the final battle for the fate of Storm's Quarry, even Nadya's and Shay's powers may not be enough. (978-1-63555-181-5)

Take a Chance by D. Jackson Leigh. There's hardly a woman within fifty miles of Pine Cone that veterinarian Trip Beaumont can't charm, except for the irritating new cop, Jamie Grant, who keeps leaving parking tickets on her truck. (978-1-63555-118-1)

The Outcasts by Alexa Black. Spacebus driver Sue Jones is running from her past. When she crash-lands on a faraway world, the Outcast Kara might be her chance for redemption. (978-1-63555-242-3)

Lightning Source UK Ltd.
Milton Keynes UK
UKHW010928060223
416537UK00002B/684

9 781635 552591